...ted at Eton and McGill University,
...isher for thirty years including editorial
director of Weidenfeld & Nicolson and a partner in O'Mara
Books. He has published a series of ten detective novels set in the
1930s featuring Lord Edward Corinth and Verity Browne. He is
married and lives in London and Wiltshire.

Praise for David Roberts

'Intricate and enthralling'
Michael Dobbs

'Lovers of golden-age crime fiction need mourn no longer.
Roberts takes us back to the world of the aristocratic sleuth'
Natasha Cooper

'Roberts pays meticulous attention to period detail and the
result is a really well-crafted and charming mystery story'
Daily Mail

Also by David Roberts

Lord Edward Corinth & Verity Browne Series

SOMETHING
WICKED

A murder mystery featuring
Lord Edward Corinth & Verity Browne

DAVID ROBERTS

CONSTABLE • LONDON

CONSTABLE

First published in Great Britain in 2007 by Constable,
an imprint of Constable & Robinson Ltd

This paperback edition published in 2008 by Robinson,
an imprint of Constable & Robinson Ltd

Reissued in 2017 by Constable

1 3 5 7 9 10 8 6 4 2

A CIP catalogue record for this book
is available from the British Library.

ISBN 978-1-4721-2815-7

Printed and bound by CPI Group (UK) Ltd, Croydon, CR0 4YY

Papers used by Constable are from well-managed forests
and other responsible sources

Constable
An imprint of
Little, Brown Book Group
Carmelite House
50 Victoria Embankment
London EC4Y 0DZ

An Hachette UK Company
www.hachette.co.uk

www.littlebrown.co.uk

For Violetta and Fernando

I am most grateful to Kelly Russell, Wendy Bann and all at The River and Rowing Museum at Henley for helping me research the 1938 Henley Royal Regatta. I am also grateful to James Crowden CVO and to Christopher Dodd whose book *Henley Royal Regatta* is rightly regarded as definitive. Thank you to Henley Royal Regatta Headquarters, in particular Gino Caiafa and Paddy for showing me Temple Island. Many thanks also to Rebecca Caroe who took me to the 2006 Regatta and explained its rites and rituals.

I am also grateful to Mark Ryan who took me up in his Tiger Moth and Tim Bruce-Dick whose grandfather was Secretary of Phyllis Court in the 1930s. Thank you also to Gregory Bowden, Nick Mann and Olivia and Katharine Williams.

With so much help, I have no excuse for getting things wrong.

By the pricking of my thumbs,
Something wicked this way comes.

Shakespeare, *Macbeth*

As flies to wanton boys, are we to the gods;
They kill us for their sport.

Shakespeare, *King Lear*

June and July 1938

Prologue

James Herold looked out of the drawing-room window towards his beloved apiary. He was too lame, too weak, too feeble to look after the bees himself. Since his first heart attack he had found even walking difficult. His lungs seemed made of metal, each little breath an effort of will. And this for a man who, in his twenties, had run a mile in four and a half minutes and had climbed the Matterhorn. This was a living death.

But who was that out near the hives? Watkins? No, he had gone into town to get the mower mended. He called to his wife, his voice thin and reedy, but remembered she had gone shopping. And his nurse – where was she? Of course, it was her day off. He struggled out of his armchair, reached for his stick and stumbled out into the hall. He had trouble with the side door. It was stuck and he tugged on it petulantly. It sprung open, almost knocking him backwards. A sense of urgency, almost panic, seized him. The sunlight blinded him but he forced himself on. He had the idea that he was late for an appointment. There was a meeting he had half-forgotten but which it was absolutely necessary he attend.

He stopped, leaning on his stick, panting heavily. He wiped the sweat off his brow and wished that he had put on his old straw hat to cover his naked head. He shaded his eyes with his hand. Was it Watkins? He did not think it could be. This man seemed taller and surely broader in the chest. Watkins was a weedy fellow whom he had always despised but had to put up with. Good with the bees – he must be fair – but not strong. Whoever it was in Watkins' smock beckoned to him across the iridescent grass. He thought for a moment he almost recognized the man but he could not be sure. He wore gloves thick as a wicket-keeper's. His legs were encased in heavy wellington boots. His head was covered by a wide-brimmed hat from which hung a veil. Herold passed his hand over his hairless skull. A drone began in his head like insects nesting. Was it *his* hat the man was wearing?

He shuffled across the lawn, so closely cut but a jungle to a man in his condition. Then his heart began to race. He saw the man go over to one of the hives and begin to shake it. It was a heavy wooden structure but it began to move on its brick base and he could hear, quite distinctly, the bees buzzing, angry at being disturbed. Herold gestured to the man to stop. What he was doing was madness – vandalism. He wanted to shout to him to desist but he could not find the breath. He tried to walk faster and his shuffle became almost a trot. He was now less than a hundred yards away. What was the man doing? He would have the hive over if he wasn't careful. Why, there it went! Now the man had moved to another hive and was wrenching that over too.

Suddenly the hum became a roar and a dark cloud of bees poured out of the despoiled hives looking for their enemy. The man in the bee-keeper's costume began to walk purposively towards him. It was only then that Herold realized the danger he was in. He turned and tried to run but missed his footing and his stick spun away from between his legs. He lay on the ground like an insect helpless on its back and looked up. The man lifted his veil and Herold recognized his nemesis. He saw in the face of the god his own death and knew that this was murder. The bees covered every inch of his flesh. They masked his eyes and left their hooked stings in his eyelids. He put his hands to his face to try to scrape them off but he was too weak. The bees coiled about his head like writhing snakes to make a ludicrous wig. He understood that they had been sent to take him with them into that other world beyond anger and pain. And he was not ungrateful. The venom from a thousand stings stopped his heart and ended his suffering. He had, after all, made his meeting and found that his appointment had been with death.

1

'Wider . . . open wider. I can't get at it if you won't open wide.'

Lord Edward Corinth was Mr Silver's last patient. He had told the receptionist she could go early so they were alone in the surgery. The drill buzzed like an angry wasp as the dentist probed the cavity. Edward's knuckles whitened as he clenched the arms of the chair. He had faced danger in his time – even dodged a bullet or two – but this was worse, much worse. He had had a horror of the dentist's chair ever since his tenth birthday when his mother had promised him a treat. He had set out joyfully, his hand in hers, on a long-anticipated visit to the circus. They did go to the circus but, traitorous woman, not before he had been unsuspectingly taken to a room in Wigmore Street, placed in a black chair and attacked by a man in a white gown. Never again did he trust his mother. He had forgiven her – of course he had – but from that day forward he was suspicious of any promise of future delight. There was always going to be a catch. There would always be a worm in the bud.

Take the news that Verity Browne, his fiancée – how he loved to use that word – was returning to London. He had heard from his friend Lord Weaver, the proprietor of the *New Gazette* and the employer of the woman who had so recently and unexpectedly promised to be his wife, that she was coming home after only a few weeks in Prague as the paper's correspondent in that troubled city. His heart had leapt with delight but his joy was quickly soiled by suspicion.

'Why, Joe? What's the matter?'

'She hasn't wired you? Probably didn't want you to fuss. The fact is she collapsed at some official dinner. The doctor thinks she has an ulcer but there's just a chance it might be . . . you know, TB.'

Tuberculosis! The word fell on his ears like earth on a coffin.

'TB! Oh, my God! I told her she couldn't go on living such a rackety life and not get ill. When she came back from Vienna she was exhausted. She could hardly eat anything. I *told* her she should see a doctor but she said she was just tired.'

He blamed himself bitterly for not having frog-marched her into his doctor's surgery and insisted that she have a thorough check-up, but Verity was not easy to compel. Now he thought about it, he realized she must have suspected she was not well before she went to Prague but had refused to admit it.

When he collected her at Croydon Airport, his attempts to disguise his anxiety had been unsuccessful. Her skin was an unhealthy grey and her eyes were dull. She had insisted on walking to the customs hall but, when they reached the Lagonda, she had given up any pretence that she was all right and sat slumped beside him, uncharacteristically silent, her eyes closed. He had put her to bed in her flat in Cranmer Court and summoned his doctor. Verity had never consulted a doctor – never needed to – and had no name to suggest. Dr Clement had taken one look at her and called an ambulance. She was now in the Middlesex Hospital undergoing tests. If she was seriously ill she *must* let him take care of her, he thought grimly and hated himself for thinking it.

When Mr Silver had finished and removed the cotton wool from his mouth, Edward said, 'I had forgotten how much I hated that.' He rinsed his mouth, feeling the new filling with his tongue. 'Am I making a fuss or do you find most of your patients hate putting themselves at your mercy? It's something about lying so helpless in your chair and having to watch as you fit a new head to the drill. I know, rationally, that you are going to take away the pain in my tooth but every nerve in my body is telling me to make a run for it.'

Mr Silver did not seem to hear him and Edward saw that he was preoccupied. Instead of reassuring him that he was no more of a coward than other men, he said, 'You remember I told you I wanted to talk to you about something . . . to consult you?'

'Of course, fire away.' Edward hoped that this wasn't going to be embarrassing. Was he having trouble with his wife? No, he remembered Silk had no wife. His business then . . .?

'I don't really know how to say this. It seems so absurd.'

'Get it off your chest, man,' Edward urged him. He wanted to go to the hospital – sit beside Verity and feed her grapes. She hated hospitals and was a bad patient. She would need a lot of support in the coming weeks.

'Well, the fact of the matter is . . .' Mr Silver hesitated. 'You know about murder, don't you? I mean, you can recognize it?'

'What an odd question, Silver. I think I'd know if someone's been murdered or not. It's very rare, you know – murder.' Edward suddenly felt uneasy and stopped thinking about Verity. 'Who's been murdered?'

'No one – or rather no one seems to think it might be murder.'

'Silver – you're not making any sense. You think there's been a murder but nobody else thinks so? Is that it?'

'Three murders.'

'Three!' Edward was disbelieving.

'Three of my patients. No, don't look at me like that. I didn't kill them. James Herold was killed by his bees. Hermione Totteridge was poisoned by the spray she was using to kill her greenfly and Sir Ernest drank flies and died.'

'There was an old lady who swallowed a fly. Do you think she'll die?' The rhyme came unbidden to Edward and he stifled the urge to laugh. 'Three deaths connected with insects? Is that it?'

'Well, quite. It sounds absurd, I know, and of course the police refuse to make the connection.'

Edward very much wanted to get away but he had known Eric Silver for almost twenty years and felt he owed it to him to hear him out. 'You say they were all patients of yours?'

'Yes, though I had not seen Herold for five years.'

'Herold? The mountaineer?'

'That's right. He was always so sure he would die on a mountainside. That's what he wanted, so when he was diagnosed with heart disease . . .'

'I remember reading his obituary. There was something odd about his heart attack, wasn't there?'

'He was stung to death.'

'So that's what you meant when you said he was killed by his bees! It's coming back to me. I read a report in the *New Gazette*. He could hardly walk but had somehow got among his hives and the bees swarmed.' Edward shuddered. 'They said, with his weak heart, he would have died almost instantaneously.' He had a thought. 'You don't suppose it was suicide? I mean, he might have wanted to end his life and thought this was a way of doing it relatively painlessly. If I had been as active as he was, I wouldn't want to drag out a miserable existence imprisoned in my armchair.'

He spoke with conviction. He had occasionally wondered what he would do if he were crippled in some way or caught some awful disease. He thought once again of Verity and the urge to go to her was almost overwhelming.

'That's what the coroner believed,' Mr Silver said, 'but to spare the widow he was able to say it was an accident.'

'There was no note or anything?'

'No suicide note but there was an unexplained piece of paper stuffed in his trouser pocket.'

'Was there something written on it?'

'Buzz buzz.'

'Buzz buzz? That's all?'

'Yes.'

'In his handwriting?'

'It was in capital letters but his wife was almost certain it wasn't his writing. It's difficult to tell with block capitals. It was his pen, though. A Parker he always used. It was beside his body when he was found.'

'How do you know all this?'

'I went to the inquest. He was an old friend.'

'Where did he live?'

'Just outside Henley . . . on the river.'

'And the other two deaths?'

'I don't know so much about them. Hermione Totteridge was a well-known botanist . . .'

'I see. You think it odd she died of . . .?'

'She was apparently experimenting with a new insecticide.'

'And Sir Ernest . . .?'

'Sir Ernest Lowther. I had seen him only a month before he died. He was in fine fettle. He'd had trouble with his blood pressure but he was certainly not contemplating suicide.'

'General Sir Ernest Lowther. The name's familiar. He won a VC during the war – a hero of sorts. Was that the man?'

'Yes, a gallant soldier. I was proud to know him.'

'And how did he die?'

'He liked his wine. He was a widower – lived alone. When his housekeeper came to clear up after dinner she found him on the floor. It looked as though he had tried to get out of his chair but had been felled by a heart attack. He had the wine bottle in his hand as though he was looking at it.'

'Another heart attack! What was it – the wine?'

'Clos des Mouches. We had actually talked about it when he last came to see me. It's a Beaune from Joseph Drouhin. He recommended it – said '33 and '35 had been vintage years.'

'*Mouches* – flies! So you think all three deaths involve insects? Did they test the wine to see if it had been poisoned?'

'Not as far as I know. There was nothing in the paper about it being a suspicious death. It sounds crazy but here's another thing. All three lived near Henley.'

'Let me get this straight – Herold was the first to die?'

'No, Miss Totteridge was the first. Then, a week or so later, General Lowther . . .'

'Followed by James Herold.'

'That's right, but all three within two months. I have written down the details for you.'

Edward looked down the sheet of paper the dentist gave him. It was neat, succinct and to the point. 'Curiouser and curiouser!' he murmured. 'Did Lowther and Hermione Totteridge also have notes in their pockets from our murderer?'

'I don't know. I couldn't think who to ask. Then, when you telephoned for an appointment, I remembered hearing that you had investigated poor General Craig's murder a few years back so I thought I'd consult you.'

'It's all so far-fetched!' Verity was trying to sound

interested but she was so tired it was hard to concentrate. She was by herself in a light, airy room overlooking Cleveland Street. As a good Communist, she had tried to insist on a public ward but the doctor would not hear of it. 'Until we know what the matter is we must keep you in isolation. Wouldn't do to infect the other patients, would it, Miss Browne?'

Edward knew that, in normal circumstances, the doctor's tone of voice would have grated on her but she had no fight left in her and merely nodded her head meekly.

'I'm sorry, V. I ought not to bore you. I'll leave you to get some sleep.'

'No please, stay with me for a bit.' She clutched his hand. 'My stock has definitely gone up having you visit me. Even the doctors treat me with respect and one of the nurses was swooning over you.'

'What rot!' It had genuinely never occurred to him that he was becoming quite famous. His photograph appeared in the illustrated papers on a regular basis and his reputation for solving crimes was gradually becoming known to a wider public however much he tried to keep a low profile. People he had never met asked him to pontificate on murder investigations he knew nothing about. The *Daily Mail* had actually asked him to be their crime correspondent, an offer he had indignantly refused. Verity had laughed when he told her and said it was a compliment.

Of course, it was also becoming common knowledge that he and Verity were more than just friends. The engagement was still supposed to be a secret – even his family had not been told officially, though it would be no surprise to Edward's brother and sister-in-law when it was announced. He had noticed a photographer outside the hospital – a film star was recovering in the Middlesex after a suicide attempt – but the man had recognized him and taken his photograph.

He was resigned to reading in the newspapers coy speculation on why he was so often at the bedside of the celebrated foreign correspondent, Miss Verity Browne.

'I'm so sorry to be such a wet blanket,' she was saying. 'I was hoping that next time I was in London we could play at being a courting couple. You could take me to gay parties and show me off to your relatives and we could tell all our friends.'

'I don't go to parties and you already know all my relatives,' he smiled. 'I'm still waiting to be introduced to yours, by the way.'

'My father? I do want you to meet him. He's supposed to be back in England in a couple of weeks.'

'Does he know about your . . .?'

'My illness? I got his chambers to telegraph him – he's in Buenos Aires of all places – but they haven't heard anything yet.'

'When will you get the results of the tests?'

'Soon. Tomorrow, probably. It's so stupid. I don't know why I collapsed like that. I just feel so tired. A week or two of rest . . .'

'I've been thinking about that . . .'

'Mersham?'

'Not there. I know Connie would love to have you,' he added hastily, 'but the castle's still crawling with children.' These were Jewish refugees from Nazi Germany. Mersham Castle had become one of the main 'clearing houses', as one official had named them, where the children were looked after until families could be found to take them.

Verity had winced to hear him say firmly that Connie would be so delighted to have her. The Duke, she knew, would not be so pleased. He had made it clear to her that he thought she was not good enough for his younger brother. 'No, it wouldn't be fair on them,' she said quickly. 'They've got enough on their plate already and since it was my idea to bring the children to Mersham . . .'

'Gerald loves it. He told me the other day he feels so much happier now that he's doing something to help and the sound of children's voices in those big empty rooms . . . well, he said it lifted his spirits no end. Those were his exact words.'

'Still, if I have what the doctors think I have, I'm infectious . . .'

'I've got a better idea. A friend of mine, Leonard Bladon – we were up at Trinity together – he's a doctor . . . has a sort of clinic, I suppose you'd call it, but it's more of a hotel – a place to recuperate for people who aren't ill enough to be in hospital but who still need a bit of looking after. I thought it might fit the bill.'

'And you can do a bit of sleuthing when you're not ministering to me,' Verity said with a little smile which made his heart turn over.

'Something like that,' he agreed.

'Edward, you're so sweet, but what if . . . what if I don't get better? What if the doctors find something . . . something bad? I'm scared.' Her voice was so low he had to bend his head to hear her. 'You know what I'm like. I don't mind rushing about a battlefield. A bit of danger makes me feel alive but to be ill . . . to lie in bed and know . . . or, worse still, *not* know.'

'V, darling . . .' Edward fought to find the right words. He knew that she badly needed reassurance but not empty platitudes. 'We'll know the worst soon enough. You're a fighter and if . . . if the doctors say it's serious, then we'll fight it together. You've got lots of work to do so we can't have you lying in bed for too long.' He hastened to distract her. 'Tell me about what you were up to in Czechoslovakia. I haven't had a chance to ask what with all this . . .' he tailed off.

14

Verity smiled wryly and squeezed his hand. 'Not much to report, really. Like this – a waiting game. The Czechs mobilized their armed forces when it looked as though Germany was going to invade, as you know, but then nothing happened. The Germans didn't invade. It seems Hitler's pursuing a more subtle approach than merely marching across the border as he did in Austria – at least for the moment. I guess he's testing the reaction of France and Britain to a gradual takeover. If, as seems likely, our government makes no protest, they'll take over the whole country piecemeal. German civilians are pouring into the Sudetenland and, as they take jobs and businesses, refugees – not only Jews but Czech patriots of all kinds – leave for Prague. The city's full to the brim of the dispossessed sitting in cafés making one small cup of coffee last a whole afternoon.'

Edward nodded his head. 'I suspect the great British public isn't interested in Czechoslovakia. They'd not support the government if they promised to go to the aid of the Czechs.'

'And the British press won't kick up a fuss about what Hitler is doing in Europe. We're so bloody cosy behind our moat. The editor spikes most of my reports and Joe Weaver lets him. But I just know it's all going to blow up while I'm tied to this bloody bed.'

It was rare to hear Verity swear and it signalled how depressed she was. Before he left the hospital – promising to return early the next day – Edward found the doctor who had examined her. He was a brusque young man – busy, efficient and not unsympathetic but he refused to allay any of his fears.

'Come back tomorrow, Lord Edward. We'll have the results of the tests and the X-rays before midday. Then we can decide what to do. One thing I can tell you – it will take a while before Miss Browne recovers her strength. I know mentally she's not one to give up the struggle but physically she's at the end of her tether. She's going to need a lot of looking after.'

'Answer that, will you, Fenton?'

Edward was stropping his razor – a ritual he enjoyed. He found it made him relax. He owned a safety razor, of course, but the whole business of soaping his face with the shaving brush and the feel of the cold blade against his skin was how he preferred to greet the day. He did not like being interrupted and so it was with irritation that he had heard the insistent ring of the telephone and with surprise bordering on indignation that he now heard Fenton at the bathroom door.

'It's Chief Inspector Pride, my lord. I told him you were engaged but he insists on talking to you. He says it's urgent.'

Edward reluctantly wiped the soap off his face with a towel and pulled on a dressing-gown. He had to admit he was curious. He knew Pride of old but had not seen or talked to him for at least eighteen months. What had suddenly made him telephone at – he glanced at his watch – eight fifteen, before the day could properly be said to have started?

He grabbed the receiver. 'Pride? Is that you?' He had a sudden thought that he might want to talk to him about Verity. She was so often at odds with authority but he quickly remembered that, whatever problems she had to face, the police would not be one of them.

'Sorry to bother you so early, my lord, but I wonder if you could come up to Devonshire Place, number sixty-two?'

'That's Eric Silver, my dentist's address. What on earth are you doing there, Chief Inspector?'

'It says in the appointment book that you saw him at five yesterday evening.'

'That's correct. I was his last appointment.'

'His receptionist tells me that he usually had a five-thirty but he'd cancelled that appointment and sent her home early.'

'That's right. He wanted to consult me about something. Why, what's the matter? Is Silver all right?'

'I'm afraid not, my lord. He's been murdered.'

'Murdered!'

'Yes, the receptionist – Miss Wilton – came in twenty minutes ago and found him in his chair. Someone had used his drill to make a hole in his head. And a very messy business he made of it.'

Edward almost dropped the receiver. 'That's horrible, disgusting. Who on earth would do such a thing? I say, Chief Inspector, you don't think I had anything to do with this, do you?'

'I do, I'm afraid. I found a piece of paper – a page torn out of the appointment book as a matter of fact. On it were written in block capitals the words *Aquila non captat muscas*. If I am not mistaken, my lord, that is the legend to be found on the Mersham family arms.'

'How did you know?'

'I remembered it from my visit to Mersham Castle.' Three years before, Pride had investigated the murder of General Craig at the Duke of Mersham's dinner table.

'That's very impressive, Chief Inspector. What a memory you have. But, do you think . . .?'

'I think, Lord Edward, that this whole business concerns you. Someone has just sent you a peculiarly unpleasant message.'

Edward finished shaving, cutting himself in the process, dressed hurriedly and downed a cup of black coffee, all the time going over in his mind Eric Silver's suspicion that the deaths of three of his patients were somehow connected. He had been inclined to dismiss these fears as fanciful. On balance, he thought it was mere coincidence that three elderly people had died doing what they most enjoyed – Herold playing with his bees, Hermione Totteridge in her garden and General Lowther drinking himself into oblivion. However, Silver's murder and the unequivocal challenge his killer had left him quite altered the situation. The murderer was not interested in concealing his crimes. On the contrary, he was arrogant enough to throw the gauntlet down for Edward to pick up.

By the time the cab had dropped him in Devonshire Place, he had determined to avenge his friend's brutal murder. It was by no stretch of the imagination his fault that Silver had been killed but it was clear that the murderer had somehow discovered that the dentist was expounding his theories to him and retribution had been swift and savage. But why had the murderer not killed Silver *before* he had spoken to him? Perhaps he had just happened to recognize Edward entering the surgery and it had aroused his suspicions. Perhaps he had actually overheard the conversation. How else could he know what Silver would say? Edward shivered as if someone was walking over his grave, as his old nanny used to say. He had heard nothing and nobody in the surgery apart from the dentist but then he was hardly listening for anyone and his ears were still ringing from the noise of that dreadful drill.

The photographs had been taken by the time he arrived and the surgery dusted for fingerprints but the corpse, mercifully covered by a sheet, was still in the dentist's chair.

'It's not a pretty sight,' Pride warned before nodding to one of his men to lift the sheet. Edward took one look and turned away in horror. For a moment he thought he might vomit but he regained control of himself and looked again. The drill had been thrust into Silver's ear and, through that, into his brain. Blood and gore covered the wound but the drill itself was still attached to the electrical wire that drove it.

Pride signalled for the sheet to be replaced and ushered Edward out of the room. 'I'm sorry you had to see that but I thought you might notice something.'

'Forgive me, Chief Inspector, but I must have some air. Such a gruesome . . . the murderer must be mad . . . a sadist.' The two men went out into the street and walked up and down until Edward began to feel better, but the horror of what he had just seen still made him want to retch. 'Thank you. I'm sorry about that,' he said at last. 'I thought nothing could shock me but that . . . He was killed in his chair?'

'Yes. I have to say it's the most macabre murder I have ever investigated. Vindictive is the word which comes to mind.'

'Indeed. Who else saw Silver yesterday, apart from me?'

'He had four appointments in the morning and two in the afternoon before you. We'll talk to them all, of course, but Miss Wilton says they are all regulars.'

'She must be terribly shocked. Who's looking after her?'

'Her mother. One of my men has taken her back to Cricklewood. The doctor gave her a sedative but she was, as you would expect, in deep shock.'

'She had worked for Silver for some time, I think.' Edward was trying to get his brain to work.

'About three years, I understand.'

'As far as I know, Silver had no relatives. He wasn't married and I remember him telling me his parents were dead.'

'Was he . . .' Pride hesitated, 'a homosexual?'

'I don't know. It never occurred to me.' Edward was shocked by the question but knew it had to be asked. 'Not as far as I know,' he said as firmly as possible. 'May I see the piece of paper left with the body?'

They walked back into the building and took the ancient-looking lift up to the second floor. As the lift doors clanged open, Edward saw two policemen struggling down the stairs with a stretcher on which lay the shrouded body of his erstwhile dentist.

'I really can't get over this, Chief Inspector. You see someone full of life one moment and the next he's struck down by a madman.'

Pride passed a sheet of paper to him. Seeing Edward hesitate, he said, 'Go ahead. There are no fingerprints on it. No bloodstains . . . nothing at all. The killer used the pen on the receptionist's desk. Either he was wearing gloves or he wiped everything clean afterwards . . . My guess is that he was wearing gloves and perhaps a white coat. Miss Wilton seems to think there's one missing. There must have been a lot of blood. Now, if we could find those . . . '

Edward examined the paper and the writing on it with care.

'It must have been written by someone who knows you reasonably well – well enough to know your family's coat of arms and to have recognized you going into the surgery,' Pride commented.

'And he's well educated,' Edward remarked, 'or the Latin wouldn't have meant anything to him.'

'*Aquila* – the eagle – *non captat muscas*. The eagle won't catch flies. Am I right?'

'Quite right, Chief Inspector.'

'Can you guess at its significance or is it just that the murderer wants you to know that he knows who you are?'

Edward chewed his lip. 'You'll probably laugh me out of court, Pride, but there does seem to be an entomological significance. First, though, I've got to tell you what Mr Silver wanted to consult me about.'

'I wish you would,' Pride said drily. 'After all, that must explain why the man was killed.'

When Edward had finished, Pride smiled thinly. 'So you think our murderer is a bug hunter?'

'Well, Herold was killed by his bees, Hermione Totteridge died from the poison she was using to kill her greenfly and the General drank a wine called Mouches – flies.'

Pride scratched his head. 'I've never heard the like. Until we have talked to the local police we can't know whether the theory stands up but if it turns out to be true . . . Perhaps Silver was misinformed and General Lowther died drinking something else. What about his own murder? There were no bugs involved as far as I can see – apart from your Latin motto.'

Edward sucked his lip and hesitated. 'I expect the murderer was forced into this killing and hadn't the time to plan something clever but . . .'

'But?'

'It's probably just my odd way of looking at things but do you remember the Victorian explorer, John Hanning Speke?' Pride shook his head. 'He went to Africa with Richard Burton and was the first European to see Lake Victoria. No, I'm sorry, Chief Inspector, I'm being ridiculous.'

'Go on. I've come to respect your hunches, Lord Edward.'

'Well, I don't know whether it's true or just a myth but, as you can imagine, those early explorers in Africa were plagued by bugs and beetles of every kind.

Anyway, as I remember the story, Speke woke up in his tent one morning on the shores of Lake Tanganyika to find a beetle wriggling about in his ear. He poked it with his finger and shook his head but nothing seemed to dislodge it. The feeling of the beetle squirming and buzzing in his head was driving him mad so in the end he picked up a compass from the map he was making and thrust the point into his ear.'

Pride winced. 'And did it . . .?'

'It killed the bug and deafened him.'

'You spent some time in Africa, didn't you, Lord Edward?'

'Yes, Kenya mostly. Paradise – at least for us Europeans . . . Can you imagine one wonderful day after another . . . The Rift Valley bathed in a golden glow from sunrise to sunset. Only the insects to worry you, particularly the mosquitoes . . . ' He stopped and considered. 'I see what you're getting at, Chief Inspector, but if we're talking geography, I think it's much more significant that all three of Silver's patients died in the Henley area.'

'It could be,' Pride admitted grudgingly. 'So the murderer was punishing Mr Silver for having told you what he suspected.' He frowned. 'But why not kill him *before* he had a chance of telling you anything?'

'Why didn't he murder me, for that matter? Perhaps he thought he could take Silver by surprise but the two of us would have been too much for him. So he decided to deal with me at a later date.'

'He'll know you'll be on your guard.'

'Yes,' Edward said meditatively. 'He's very sure of himself.'

'The question is how did he know you were coming to the surgery and that Mr Silver had cancelled his last appointment so that he had time to talk to you, or was it just a coincidence that he saw you in Devonshire Place?'

'I don't know but it should be possible to find out who saw the appointment book. Who were the – how many did you say? – the six who had appointments with Silver yesterday? Could Miss Wilton have mentioned to someone that I was coming in? Was a stranger seen in the building? Who else has offices here?'

Pride could see that Edward was becoming agitated. 'Calm yourself, Lord Edward. We've not always seen eye to eye but you know me to be thorough. We'll investigate everyone who might have been near the surgery yesterday.'

'I'm sorry, Chief Inspector, but I counted Eric Silver as a friend.'

'The savagery of his murder is something else, eh, Lord Edward? The others – if they turn out to have been murders – were macabre but not nearly so brutal.'

'And this one took place in London not Henley and the victim wasn't elderly like the other three.'

'But what puzzles me is why make it so obvious that Mr Silver was murdered because he had seen you? If he hadn't left that message, I would not necessarily have linked it with you. I mean, I would have talked to you because you were in all probability the last person – bar the murderer – to see Silver alive, but this does make it personal.'

Edward tried to grin. 'Yes, I'm rather disappointed that you haven't yet asked me to account for my movements yesterday. You must have considered that I might have killed Mr Silver and left the note as a distraction. I would then have gone home and asked my valet Fenton to launder my bloody clothes. '

Pride laughed – a tight little bark. 'All true, Lord Edward, but, putting that aside for the moment, from what I know of you I find it quite impossible to cast you in the role of sadistic murderer.'

'Thank you for that, Chief Inspector. Another thing – if the poor man was conscious, he would have screamed. Did no one hear him?'

'That I will be trying to establish. At the moment, it is not at all clear what time the murder was committed. However, I have already ascertained that the building was empty last night except for a caretaker who lives in the basement and heard nothing. In any case, the murderer had stuffed Silver's mouth with cotton wool.'

Edward shuddered. 'Oh, my God! The man who did this must be found, Pride, before he kills again.'

'I agree,' the Chief Inspector said soberly. 'And it's you I'm worried about. I have no doubt that, by leaving your family motto at the scene of the crime, he was warning you that you would be next. Lock all the doors and don't take risks.'

'Thank you for those comforting words,' Edward replied grimly. 'I had already worked that out for myself.' He managed a smile. 'I prefer to look at it rather differently. The murderer has thrown down the gauntlet. He's challenging me to find him before he finds me. I must tell you that it's a challenge I intend to take up.'

2

'Please sit down, Lord Edward.' The sharply dressed young doctor indicated the chair beside Verity's bed. 'Miss Browne has specifically asked that you be here even though you are not a relative.'

He looked severe as though he scented immorality. Edward suspected that the doctor was rather enjoying himself though he probably didn't realize it. He had important news to convey and Verity Browne and Lord Edward Corinth were moderately famous. Not as well known as the film star who had swallowed a bottle of barbiturates after finding her husband in bed with her co-star who just happened to be a man, but certainly of some social significance. He had mentioned to his wife that Miss Browne was under his care and that Lord Edward – who was rumoured to be her lover – was a constant visitor and she had been impressed. What was more, Lord Edward's doctor, a man of the highest repute in Harley Street, was also present. It could do him no harm if he got a good report from Dr Clement.

'We are engaged to be married,' Edward said firmly, 'but at present we wish to keep it a secret.'

Verity glanced up at him but said nothing.

The young doctor coughed. 'Of course. I quite understand. I didn't mean to suggest . . .'

'Tell them what you have just told me, will you, Tomlinson,' Dr Clement said brusquely. He was getting a bit fed up with this know-it-all young man. He had the reputation of being very clever in his field but Clement's impression was that he was altogether too pleased with himself.

Tomlinson straightened his shoulders. 'The bad news is, Miss Browne, that the X-rays show quite clearly a shadow on your right lung.'

'And that means I have . . .?'

'Pulmonary tuberculosis,' Tomlinson finished her sentence and hurried on. 'The good news, however, is that it is by no means a severe case. The lesion is small and should heal given rest, fresh air and a healthy diet.'

'So I'm not going to die?' Verity said, trying to smile.

'We are all going to die,' Tomlinson replied pompously, 'but no, you should recover your health if you follow the regime I shall prescribe.'

'How did she pick up TB?' Edward asked. 'I thought – to be brutal – it was a slum disease.'

'From what you have told me, Miss Browne, of your time in Spain reporting the civil war, I have no doubt that you were exposed to disease on a daily basis.'

'It's true,' Verity said weakly. 'Many of the comrades fighting for the Republic were from the poorest backgrounds who for months on end were living in squalid conditions on a starvation diet. I used to smoke at least a packet of cigarettes a day because someone told me it would stop me catching anything.'

'I'm afraid they were wrong,' Clement said severely. 'That's just a myth. Wouldn't you agree, Tomlinson?'

Tomlinson stroked his chin but refused to agree. 'Maybe, but we know so little about what causes tuberculosis. Miss Browne, were your own living conditions in Spain very bad?'

'Not really. For the most part we journalists lived in comfortable hotels.'

'Hardly comfortable!' Edward protested.

Verity wrinkled her nose. 'I have to admit that one of the worst things about war is not so much the bullets as the smell. Spanish latrines are the sort you have to squat over and, what's more, they all seem made of smooth stone – very slippery – and, of course, they were always blocked. I used to ask myself, how can we defend democracy against Fascism in such sordid conditions?'

There was a stunned silence. The men had never heard a well-brought-up woman discuss defecation so frankly and they felt profoundly uncomfortable. Finally, Tomlinson said, as though Verity had not spoken, 'Well, somewhere along the line you came into contact with someone with infectious TB. Whoever it was coughed and disseminated small droplets containing the tubercle bacilli which you inhaled.'

'And it took this long to show itself?' Edward was indignant, as if he suspected that Verity had been played some underhand trick.

'It can take a year or perhaps never. It is possible to have a mild infection and never be aware of it.'

'You mean you can have the bacillus, or whatever it is, without any symptoms?' Edward asked in disbelief.

'Yes. In this case, however, Miss Browne suffered an acute episode of right pleuritic chest pain, fever and dyspnoea.'

'Dyspnoea?' Edward queried.

'Difficulty in breathing,' Clement explained.

'And there is no medicine she can take?' Edward appealed to his friend.

'A course of colloidal silver and a few months in a Swiss sanatorium should do the trick. Mountain air . . .'

Verity and Edward looked at one another in dismay.

'Months in a Swiss sanatorium!' Verity was shocked into raising herself in her bed as if intending to walk out in protest.

'Rest, fresh air and a healthy diet,' Tomlinson repeated.

'If you don't follow my advice, I can't be held responsible for the consequences.'

'Tomlinson's right,' Clement said gravely. 'You have to rest and put on weight. I know that for someone like you that's not easy advice to follow but it is essential. We don't want to lose you.'

'After three months I will do more X-rays,' Tomlinson added, 'and then we'll see.'

'What will we see?' Verity grumbled.

'We'll see if the lesion has healed or if . . .'

'If I am going to die,' Verity finished off his sentence for him.

After they had left Verity, Edward joined Dr Clement in Tomlinson's office. 'Man to man, Edward,' Clement said, looking shifty, 'there's something I've got to say to you. You say that you and Miss Browne are engaged to be married?'

'That's correct,' Edward agreed.

'Well – and Tomlinson will back me up on this – pulmonary TB is very infectious. You must not get too close to her. You must not breathe her breath. You must not kiss her. Her sputum is chock-full of bacilli and . . .' he coughed nervously and Tomlinson stared at his feet, 'forgive me for saying this but on no account must you sleep with her if you don't want to come down with TB yourself. You understand me?'

Edward's first instinct was to be angry but what was the point? It was the duty of these two doctors to tell him the facts and they had discharged their duty.

'I understand,' he said with as much dignity as he could muster.

'Now, as you know, Miss Browne cannot remain in this hospital. She presents a risk to other patients and staff. Until arrangements are made to take her to a sanatorium . . .'

'I've thought of that,' Edward interrupted. 'I have a friend – someone I was up at Cambridge with as a matter of fact – who runs a sanatorium near Henley. A Dr Bladon. Do you know him?'

Clement's face cleared. 'Indeed, I do – a very good man. I was going to suggest his clinic to you myself. Don't look so gloomy, Edward. The chances are she will make a full recovery. She's not spitting blood . . .' Edward went pale. 'I'm sorry, but I know you don't want me to hide things from you. As I say, as long as she gets no worse and is properly looked after, she will recover.'

Tomlinson made a moue of dissent. 'Henley, you say? She ought to be in a Swiss sanatorium in the Alps or at least by the seaside.'

'I think she would die of boredom,' Edward broke in crudely. 'She must be near her friends, her work . . .'

Edward appealed silently to Clement. He coughed. 'Tomlinson's right, of course, but I take your point, Edward. If her morale plummets then it may affect her physical health. Let's give this a go . . . Bladon's place, I mean. Then, if after three months her condition worsens . . .'

'So be it, Clement, but don't say I didn't warn you,' Tomlinson said, pursing his lips in disapproval.

Pride's mention of Africa had given Edward an idea. When he got back to Albany, he went to his desk and retrieved a letter he had received a couple of weeks earlier from an old school friend inviting him to come and stay at the house he had just inherited in Henley of all places. He had been meaning to refuse but now he was glad he hadn't. He lit a cigarette and read the letter again carefully. It might serve his purpose, he thought, but it was almost too convenient.

Harry Makin was back in England after years in Africa. In Nairobi, he had been something of a legend. One of the Muthaiga set, very good-looking, a first-class shot and a notorious heart-breaker. Always short of money, Harry survived by sponging off his women and taking parties of gun-crazy British and American tourists into the bush to blaze away at the wildlife. As Old Etonians, it was natural that they had chummed up when Edward had first gone to Kenya. Makin had shown him the ropes and they had shot game together until Edward began to tire of so much carnage.

Even at Eton Harry had been restless, adventurous, even foolhardy – a reckless gambler with a bottle of champagne always at his elbow to which the housemaster, who was much taken by Harry's charm, turned a blind eye. Altogether a dangerous role model, he had led Edward into numerous scrapes, one of which had got him – in Eton jargon – 'whacked by the head man', caned by the headmaster, which had not gone down well with Edward's father. In the end, Harry had been sacked for a relatively trivial offence – though perhaps banishment had been the outcome he sought – when his pet owl had mistaken his tutor's hairpiece for a mouse and removed it in front of the whole form. Edward had not seen Harry again until he had bumped into him at Muthaiga Club on his first day in Nairobi.

For a time they were inseparable – as they had been at school – but Edward had gradually begun to see his friend for what he really was. Behind his charm, he was quite ruthless and yet, paradoxically, totally without ambition. There was nothing he really wanted to do. He delighted in stringing along several women at the same time – caring for none of them – and his parties were altogether too wild for Edward. Gambling, cocaine, *dagga* and morphine washed down with champagne and easy, meaningless sex was not Edward's recipe for a good time. He thought his friend was driven by self-hatred and, unwisely, told him so. Harry called him a prude and a bore, after which they saw very little of each other. Of course, Edward continued to hear the gossip – how Harry had dropped in on a girlfriend in his Tiger Moth with a gift of cheetah pelts and then, taking to the air again, had gone straight on to see some other girl with an even more exotic gift.

It was in the air that both Harry and Edward found they were happiest. What could be more exciting than to fly at a hundred miles an hour over land marked on the map as 'unsurveyed'? And to see not just one beast through the telescopic sights of a rifle but vast herds ranging over the land unchecked and untroubled by man – that was indeed something!

What at the time had seemed to be the final break came as a result of a car accident – quite a common event on Kenya's unmade-up roads which, in the rainy season, could at a moment's notice turn from desert track to foaming torrent. It was after dark and Edward was on his way back to Nairobi from a friend's farm at Naivasha when he had seen a car coming down the potholed road towards him at high speed. It was obvious that the driver was under the influence of drink or drugs as the vehicle was swaying from one side of the road to the other, always on the point of going off the track altogether. The lights of Edward's car must have disoriented the driver because, with a screech of brakes, the oncoming vehicle careered off into the undergrowth. Edward could hear the screams of the passengers and then a loud bang as the car hit a rock or a tree. Edward pulled off the road and, cursing, went to see what he could do to help. He had a lantern and was relieved to see that the other car had remained upright. As his eyes adjusted to the dark, he thought the accident did not seem serious. Two girls were struggling out of the back seat and the driver, who Edward saw was Harry, appeared unhurt. He was leaning over a girl in the passenger seat who was slumped forward.

Edward knew her too. She was the wife of Lord Redfern – one of the leading figures in the colony.

'You stupid bugger!' Harry said as he looked up and saw Edward. 'What in the hell did you think you were doing?'

Edward opened his mouth to protest but Harry had already turned back to the girl. 'I say, can you feel a pulse?'

Edward put a hand to her neck but it was quite obvious she was dead. Her neck had been snapped like a twig by the impact.

It was a nasty business. The girl ought not to have been with Harry and there were plenty of witnesses to the fact that he had been drinking at the club before, on a whim, they all piled into the car 'to go and see animals' as the barman put it. Lord Delamere – the virtual king of the colony, a gnome-like figure with a protruding nose and small, piggy eyes – was not amused and his displeasure was one of the factors that made Edward decide to leave Kenya. Harry, however, had stayed on and had apparently succeeded in riding out the storm.

Now he was back in England and had invited Edward to stay at the barn of a place he had inherited from a distant cousin, along with a title. Edward had been doubtful about renewing the friendship but the fact remained that Harry – now Lord Lestern – lived just outside Henley which would be convenient for seeing Verity and as a base for 'sleuthing' as she had called it.

After a moment's thought, he took out a sheet of writing paper before deciding it would be easier to explain the situation by telephone and ask his friend's permission to use his house as a hotel from which to visit Verity. He could hardly keep disappearing to Bladon's sanatorium without explaining where he was going so it was best to be quite open about why he wanted to come and stay.

'By all means use the old place as a hotel,' Harry had replied. 'To tell the truth, it's all been rather too quiet for my taste. People are such snobs. I tried to join Phyllis Court – know what I mean? The country club – but they took one look at me and froze me out. "Long waiting list", "Try again in a couple of years" – that sort of thing. Maybe you can help me find a sponsor. I'm damned if they're going to get away with saying Harry Makin ain't good enough to join their rotten little club. I told them: I'm an Old Etonian and I've got a title and if I was good enough for Muthaiga, I ought to be good enough for a few hoity-toity stockbrokers.' The snub had clearly hit a raw nerve. 'The thing is I've been so long in Africa that I don't know a lot of people in the old country so to have an old chum to stay would cheer me up. It'll provide me with an excuse to give a few dinner parties, meet the neighbours – ingratiate myself with the local worthies. You won't mind, will you?'

Edward groaned inwardly but all he could say was that he would enjoy meeting Harry's neighbours. He comforted himself with the thought that he might pick up some gossip about the three 'local worthies' who had met such peculiar deaths.

Tomlinson wanted Verity to stay in hospital for two or three more days so he could complete his tests and, as Edward had some business to clear up in London, he arranged with Harry that he would drive down at the weekend, settle Verity in at Dr Bladon's and then come on to Turton House. He told himself he would stay with Harry for a day or two and see how it went. He could always make some excuse to return to London if it didn't work out.

Whether it was *knowing* what ailed her, Edward's support and encouragement or her instinctive determination not to be defeated by the 'bloody thing', as she called it, but Verity very quickly recovered her spirits. In a couple of days, she was out of bed and pacing around her room like a caged animal saying she was better and wanted to go back to work. Tomlinson lectured her but he was already beginning to think that Dr Bladon might find it hard to keep her on the 'straight and narrow' as he called the regime he had prescribed.

Superficially, Verity had indeed recovered quickly. She started smoking again and boredom made her irritable and ungrateful. When Edward arrived to take her to Henley, she refused and insisted on going to the *New Gazette* to see Lord Weaver. Striding out of the hospital, she promptly collapsed before reaching Charlotte Street. Passers-by ran to her aid and helped Edward half-carry her back to the Middlesex where Matron – the only person in the hospital of whom Verity was genuinely afraid – greeted her with a frown of concern and annoyance. The experience shook her and she was compelled to accept how low were her reserves of strength. She was put to bed and the move to Dr Bladon's sanatorium was delayed for twenty-four hours.

On the drive down to Henley in Edward's Lagonda – Verity had indignantly refused to travel in an ambulance – Edward tried to interest her in the investigation into the savage killing of his dentist. He had asked Tomlinson if he could discuss it with her and the doctor had conceded that anything which took her mind off her condition and gave her something to think about was probably to the good.

'And Pride is happy for you to look into the deaths of Mr Silver's patients – the three he believed had been murdered?' she inquired after hearing him out.

'Yes. He thinks it might be easier for me – on an informal basis – to talk through the circumstances surrounding the deaths with Inspector Treacher, the local man, than for him to get involved. Pride doesn't want to look as though he is casting doubt on Treacher's investigative skills.'

'It's not like Pride to be worried about upsetting people,' Verity commented acidly. When they had come up against Pride before, he had shown near contempt for Edward as a bumbling amateur and undisguised suspicion of Verity as a Communist and a woman in a man's world.

'He seems to have mellowed. He knows us better and, in any case, I suspect my old friend Major Ferguson may have had a word with him.'

'The man from Special Branch?'

'Yes, I know you don't like him . . .'

'I don't know him and I don't want to,' Verity broke in. 'But I do know Special Branch has waged a war against the Party for as long as I can remember when it would have been much better employed investigating Mosley's thugs.'

'That's unfair, V! He has taken strong measures against British Fascists and infiltrated the BUF so successfully that he knows what Mosley is planning almost before he does himself.'

'Well,' Verity grunted, 'I'll take your word for it but *my* old friend, Claud Cockburn, who was with me in Spain and writes for the *Daily Worker*, begs to differ. He was saying to me not so long ago that Special Branch reads all his letters and, he believes, listens in to his telephone calls.'

Edward wanted to say that, in his view, such precautions were entirely justified but thought he had better keep the comment to himself. Cockburn was an amusing but unscrupulous journalist and a strong supporter of the Communist Party. Verity had once managed to drag him to hear the man speak at a public meeting in Wandsworth Town Hall and Edward had been shocked by his cynicism. According to Cockburn, all journalism was propaganda and there was no such thing as objective truth. Facts were just part of a pattern to be made into a story, as a novelist would. It was – he had to admit – an accusation he had made from time to time about Verity's dispatches from Spain but he knew she was too honest ever consciously to select her facts in order to make the case for the Republican cause. It was just that, for her, her view of events *was* the true story.

'And what's more he says Mosley is being funded directly from Germany. He has evidence but of course the police won't act.'

'I don't believe that. Mosley wouldn't be so stupid.'

'He's stupid and arrogant,' Verity riposted angrily. Then she laughed but without much humour. 'But why should I expect you to believe me?'

'V!' Edward protested. 'I believe you but I don't necessarily believe Cockburn. Or rather he'll give us the facts he wants us to have – arrange them for a particular purpose. Isn't that what he says he does?'

Thinking about it later, Edward had to admit that in a murder investigation that was just what *did* happen more often than not. The available facts were arranged into a pattern that made sense to the detective, but that was not always the same as arriving at the truth. What he had not confessed to Verity was that Ferguson had asked him to do a little job for him. It was hardly more than acting as an escort, but he knew she would not approve if he told her and, in any case, he had made Ferguson a promise that she should hear nothing about it.

Edward had met Major Ferguson a year or two back and now found himself – informally and unpaid – a member of Special Branch, the small section of the police force charged with protecting the state against political extremists and ill-intentioned foreign nationals. It was all rather nebulous but Ferguson's remit had taken on greater urgency with the increasing likelihood of war. He had had to increase his staff and that occasionally meant using odd characters like Edward whom, in normal times, he would have neither wanted nor needed to use. Edward had the advantage of being able to go where an ordinary policeman could not without causing comment and had shown he could be sensitive and flexible in his approach to problems with a political edge to them. On the other hand, he was difficult to control and not subject to discipline.

Edward had gone to see Ferguson, at the latter's request, in his office over a shabby public house near Trafalgar Square after spending the afternoon with Verity in hospital. When not actually in his presence, he always found it difficult to summon up a clear image of Ferguson. It was as though he made a great effort to be forgettable. He was a small man with thick-lensed glasses which failed to hide the scar above his right eye. He wore a military moustache as most men did who had been in the war. He would immediately be labelled by a casual observer as one of the thousands of ex-army officers who jealously guarded the rank of major or colonel, despite having been relieved of the authority that went with it. However, Edward knew Ferguson should not be underestimated. He had the tenacity of a bulldog and the sharp brain of a man who spent his life weighing up the danger posed by extremists at both ends of the political spectrum.

'I wondered if you would be prepared to undertake a simple but delicate task for me, Lord Edward,' he said, motioning him to take the hard chair in front of his desk from which Edward could just see part of Nelson's cocked hat. 'We have been warned that we are to be visited by one of the leaders of the German opposition to Hitler.' He saw Edward's look of surprise. 'Oh yes, there is an opposition but we don't know what it amounts to – probably not very much. He'll spend about forty-eight hours in this country and has asked to meet Vansittart and Mr Churchill and maybe – if Vansittart advises it – Lord Halifax. Of course, the Foreign Secretary will not see him in any official capacity but if he can be smuggled in the back door, so to speak . . .'

'Who is this man?'

'Ewald von Kleist-Schmenzin. He owns a large estate in Pomerania. He's a conservative Christian and is almost certainly on a fool's errand.'

'But why me? Why not get one of your men to escort him around? I'm not a professional bodyguard.'

'I appreciate that but this is very sensitive. He needs someone to tell him what to do and say if the newspapers get wind of his being here or anyone else for that matter. And you know Vansittart and Churchill and von Trott . . .'

'Von Trott? Is he one of them?'

Adam von Trott was the young German aristocrat with whom Verity had believed herself to be in love the previous summer. He had been kidnapped in Vienna on Himmler's orders and the next time Verity had heard from him he had been studying philosophy in the East. In other words, he was too well known and from too distinguished a family to be shut away in a prison camp so he had been sent to the other side of the world out of harm's way.

'Yes, he's involved with Kleist-Schmenzin but how I'm not sure. I thought you would like to have news of him,' Ferguson said disingenuously, knowing perfectly well that von Trott was – or at least had been – a rival for Verity's heart.

'Well, I'll do it but on condition that Miss Browne hears nothing about it.'

'Of course. I was going to say the same thing! By the way, I was sorry to hear of her illness. How is she?'

The days were long gone when Edward would have been surprised by how much of his private life was known to Ferguson or to the even more shadowy figure of Guy Liddell, the head of MI5, but it still annoyed him. He bit back a sarcastic remark. 'She's got TB. Not too bad, the doctor says, but she needs at least three months' rest and recuperation. I don't want her worried.'

'Of course not,' Ferguson repeated.

'Is Kleist-Schmenzin the first contact we have had with those who oppose Hitler?'

'Pretty well. A man called Carl Goerdeler, a former mayor of Leipzig, travelled to Paris in March but the French didn't know what to make of him. They saw him as a traitor to his country and more or less refused to deal with him.'

'But are we supposed to see him as a patriot?'

'You can make up your own mind,' Ferguson said shortly. 'We've got to look at anything which might destabilize Hitler.'

'When's he due?'

'In ten days. I'll give you details when I know them.'

***

To Edward's relief, Dr Bladon and Verity took to each other at first sight. Bladon was Edward's age, good-looking with a twisted smile which made him appear younger than his thirty-eight years. His hair, though prematurely grey, was thick and wavy, his eyes black and large. It suddenly crossed Edward's mind that Verity, in her weakened condition and bored by having nothing to get her adrenalin pumping, might fall for him but he suppressed the thought.

Very ill patients had their own rooms but those, like Verity, who were not too badly affected were encouraged to share rooms. She was put in with two girls younger than herself who had obviously been briefed as to who she was and that she might be difficult. In fact, Verity was at her most gracious. Jill Torrance was a student nurse who had worked at the Middlesex for a time and knew Dr Tomlinson. The other girl, Mary Black, was the daughter of a backbench Conservative MP – rather spoilt-looking, Edward thought, but pretty in a conventional way. They were both dressed because it was Bladon's policy to keep all but the very ill patients up and about, taking as much fresh air as possible in the clinic's extensive gardens.

Right up until the moment Edward got up to go, Verity was her normal self but, as she went to the front door with him, she suddenly fell weeping into his arms.

'I'm never going to leave this place, am I?' she sobbed. 'Oh, Edward, we'll never get married. I'll never have children. I'll just waste away here until I become a skeleton like the boy we saw in the garden.'

'Hey, chin up,' Edward said, taken aback by the power of her sobs. 'You'll be out of here in three months and back at your post by the new year. In any case, you don't want children.'

'No, I know, but I just feel I'm going to disappear – vanish off the face of the earth – and leave nothing behind. I'll be forgotten and you'll marry someone else . . .'

'V! Where does all this self-pity come from?' he said gently, holding her in his arms. 'It's not like you to give way. I know you hate being ill. So do I. I'd be much less brave than you. You'd tell me to buck up. You're not dying and you won't be forgotten.' He released her but still kept hold of her hands. 'I'll be here tomorrow about ten. All your friends will visit you. You won't have time to be bored let alone forgotten.'

He kissed her forehead but, when she lifted her face for him to kiss her, he hesitated.

'Why won't you kiss me?' she demanded.

'I . . . the doctors say I mustn't . . . not till they give you the all clear.'

Verity looked puzzled and then it dawned on her. 'They think I'll infect you?'

'Well, I . . . It's possible, yes.'

'Please go now,' she said, pulling away from him. 'I'll see you tomorrow. No!' She backed away as he tried to embrace her once more. 'I've just got to get used to being a pariah.'

It was with a heavy heart that Edward got into the Lagonda and drove the three or four miles to Turton House. Harry welcomed him warmly, led him into the drawing-room and thrust a large whisky and soda into his hand.

'You look as though you need this,' he said.

'You're right, I do. It's not much fun watching the girl you love laid low with what could be a fatal disease.'

'It's not as bad as that, surely? I mean I know it's TB but nowadays . . .'

'There's still no cure for the bloody thing,' Edward replied, unconsciously using Verity's phrase for it. 'They prescribe colloidal silver but God knows if it does any good. It all depends on the body and Verity has lived such a rackety life, not eating properly, not sleeping enough, living off her nerves – well, she's not nearly as strong as she thinks she is.'

'Poor Edward,' Harry said. 'And you're going to marry this girl?'

'God willing, yes. As soon as she's better . . .'

'You're cut up, I can see. I'm so pleased I'm able to help. I've not met Dr Bladon – in fact, as I told you, I haven't met anyone much since I got back from Africa.'

Edward eyed his host and noted the thinning hair and the thickening waist. He was still handsome but not quite the heart-throb he had once been. Heavy drinking had left its mark – burst blood vessels and a high colour. He hoped he had worn better.

'You've got no woman, then?' Edward felt permitted to ask the question since Harry had been so direct with him.

'No. To be frank with you, these English women seem rather milk and water compared to the ones in Happy Valley.'

'I'm not sure that's true. No one could call Verity milk and water. Tell me, Harry, when I got your letter I was puzzled. You always said England was too small for you. Shouldn't you be exploring the Mountains of the Moon rather than being holed up here?'

'Yes, you're right. I've only been in England for a few months and I confess I'm bored. I think I'll have one summer here and then sell up and go back to Africa. Get myself eaten by a lion or something. Mind you, since the slump, it's not been the same in Kenya. The glory days are over. There's no money to be made out of agriculture – flax, coffee and all the rest of it aren't worth the effort. You remember Algy Robertson? When the crops failed three years on the trot – it was locusts the last time – he shot himself.'

'No! I'm so sorry, but surely there's still money to be made out of the visitors? Don't you still take tourists out on safari?' Edward heard himself sounding almost contemptuous but Harry didn't seem to mind.

'I've more or less given that up. To tell the truth, I got a bad mauling some months back. All my own fault. I was sleeping off too good a lunch and woke to find this mangy old lion breathing down my neck. In fact, it was his stinking breath which woke me up. Talk about a hangover, that old beast needed his teeth seeing to, that's for sure.'

'You didn't have your gun?'

'No, idiot that I was.'

'So what did you do?'

'We looked each other in the eye for a rather long minute, then I got up and made a run for it shouting for help. Fortunately, I was only just outside the camp or I wouldn't be around to tell you the story. Jake Gore – do you remember him or was he after your time . . .?'

'After my time.'

'Well, he heard me shouting and came with his gun and shot him dead. Though not before . . .' Harry rolled up his sleeve and Edward saw the scars of three long claw marks running from elbow to wrist. 'I was lucky not to lose my arm. I suppose that was the moment I began to wonder if I wasn't a bit too old for the game.'

His rakish grin – the same one with which he had described every prank at school – sent Edward back to the days when they had been as David and Jonathan. He found himself smiling in response.

'Then you heard you had inherited a title?'

'Yes, it means nothing really but I was curious to see the place I'd been lumbered with, so here I am.'

He gestured with his good arm. Edward idly picked up a book from a pile lying on the table beside Harry's armchair.

'Walt Whitman? I didn't know you liked poetry?'

'I've rather taken to it. The old man seems to express my philosophy of life as well as anyone. "Afoot and light-hearted I take to the open road, Healthy, free, the world before me, The long brown path before me leading wherever I choose."'

Edward saw that the other books by the armchair were also poetry and plays – Ben Jonson, John Webster, Shakespeare. He was impressed. 'It's a long time since I read Whitman. I can see why he appeals to you.'

'It's a funny thing. I wasn't much of a reader at school but there's so damn little to do in Kenya that I began to find – after you left – I was eating up books – poetry in particular. Less hard work than women . . .' he laughed, sounding rather shy, 'and in many ways more satisfying.'

The coolness which had been between them seemed to vanish, re-establishing the intimacy they had shared at school. Edward had no wish to spoil the atmosphere but felt he had to ask. 'Lady Redfern – did that . . .?'

'I had a sticky few weeks but, in the end, they couldn't pin anything on me. It was just an accident. You scurried off as quick as your feet would take you.'

'I made a statement to the police,' Edward said defensively.

'I don't blame you for getting out of it, old man.'

'I didn't "get out of it". It was nothing to do with me. It was your accident – not mine.'

Harry visibly restrained himself, shrugging his shoulders. 'No hard feelings, old boy. Just one of those things, eh? Anyway, it's good to have you here. I'm going to put together a bit of a party for the regatta. You don't mind, do you?'

'Not at all. I'm hoping Verity may be fit enough to enjoy a little gentle boating. It's still a week or two off, isn't it?'

'Yes. It begins on the twenty-ninth and ends on the second of July. You rowed at Eton, didn't you?'

'Not seriously. I was a dry-bob. I rowed a bit at Cambridge but I've always been more of a cricket man. I remember you rowed.'

'Yes. It's one of the attractions of this place – being able to get on the river. In fact, I've been asked to make up an Old Etonian four during the regatta but I don't think I'll risk it. My puff isn't what it used to be. Getting old, I suppose.' He changed the subject. 'Your young woman – how is she getting on with Bladon? By the way, isn't he a Cambridge man?'

Edward winced at the thought of how Verity would hate this description. 'That's right. He was up at Trinity with me.'

'Is he a good doctor? I don't hold with them myself. Kill as soon as cure, I've always said.'

'I think so. He's very clever and strong enough to stop Verity exhausting herself. She hates not doing anything. That's why I'm so keen to get her working on this business of my dentist.'

'Oh yes, you mentioned it on the telephone. It sounds most macabre but can't the police deal with it? Why are you getting involved?'

'I've drifted into doing a bit of sleuthing,' Edward said, rather embarrassed. Here was one person who had not read about anything he had done and he should have been glad of it. Instead, he thought he ought to explain himself a little.

'You remember when poor Molly was murdered?' Molly Harkness was a woman they had both known in Nairobi. 'Well, I managed to help . . . you know, get to the bottom of the affair.'

'Oh, I say! You're not a private eye, are you? I thought they were only in America.'

'Don't rib me, Harry. I'm not in the mood,' Edward responded, irritably. 'I'm not a private detective. I mean I don't do it for money but I have solved one or two problems that the police . . .'

'You *are* a private eye! Of course, I'm sure you are very good at it. Now, you must let me help you. It sounds like good clean fun.'

'Not for Eric Silver, it wasn't,' Edward said roughly. 'I'll tell you all about it later. In the meantime, would it be possible for me to have a wash before dinner?'

'I'm so sorry!' Harry said quickly, getting up from his chair 'I didn't mean to josh you. Come, I'll show you your room. Your man arrived a couple of hours ago.

Everything should be ready for you. Take a bath. There's plenty of hot water. I thought we'd dine at eight – just the two of us. Don't dress. I wear an old smoking jacket when I'm alone, like I did in the bush.'

'That suits me.'

'Funny about the dentist though.'

'Funny?'

'Well, old man, you remember what Emerson said about being dead?'

'You read Ralph Waldo Emerson?' Edward was amused. 'What did Emerson have to say about death and dentists?'

'He said that when you're dead, "at least you're done with the dentist." Of course, in this case, it's death which did for the dentist.'

The smile faded from Edward's lips. He was no longer amused.

3

Turton House was a big, ramshackle place of no particular architectural period or interest but with a splendid view of the river, and before dinner Edward strolled down to the river bank to think about Verity. He always loved gardens like this where the lawns sloped gently down to the water. It was soothing to his troubled spirit and, in the gathering dusk, the river looked serene and infinitely gentle although he knew that even the Thames could be dangerous if taken for granted. He peered into a large boathouse containing several small craft including rowing boats and two fast-looking 'riggers' which reminded him of his school-days. A young man wearing grey flannels, vest and cap sculled by, his long, elegant strokes hardly ruffling the water. He thought it would do Verity good – weather permitting – to lie in a punt and watch athletic young men row up and down.

It wasn't quite as it had been before the war when Henley Royal Regatta was one of the great social events of the season but it was still an important date in the sporting and social calendar. As he had reminded his host, Edward had been a dry-bob at school but, although cricket was his game, he had rowed a bit and had many friends at school and university who virtually lived on the river. He had been to the regatta once before as a guest of his friend Tommie Fox – an accomplished sportsman who had rowed for Eton and Cambridge and won a blue for boxing – who was now a hard-working, underpaid vicar in North London.

He had an idea that, if she were well enough, Verity might find the jollities diverting. A great deal of beer, champagne and Pimm's was drunk during Henley week and it would have been a good moment to introduce her to the world at large as his future wife. Nothing had yet been said between them about delaying the official announcement of their engagement but Edward was aware that, until Verity felt she had beaten her illness, she would not want to think about marriage.

He sighed deeply. What would he not give to have her on his arm as they paraded among men wearing striped blazers and straw boaters or coloured caps, and women in frocks more suited to an Edwardian garden party than a sporting event.

Lost in thought, he did not hear his host crossing the grass with a gin and tonic in each hand.

'Still your tipple?' Harry asked. 'The gnats are beginning to bite,' he added amiably, slapping his cheek.

'Sorry, yes, it's still my tipple. It's good to be here, Harry. You're sure you don't mind me using you as an hotel? I'll have to go to London on business at some point but it's wonderful not to have to drive up and down the Great West Road every day to see Verity.'

'You really love her?' Harry sounded amused and faintly envious.

'Yes, I do. Did you ever love any of your girls?'

'That one who died – I loved her.'

'But she was . . .'

'I know, another man's wife. Still, we loved each other in our own way. I suppose it wouldn't have lasted but . . . well, you never know and now I never will.'

'You really loved her?' Edward asked in amazement.

'Don't sound so surprised, old man. I am capable of love – at least I thought so then. I had the feeling that if only we had managed by some miracle to get away from that place – the Club, the bores, the stupid empty days of idleness – she might have made something out of me.'

'It's not too late. I always admired your gifts. You could charm the birds off the branches.'

Harry grimaced. 'Charm! Things came too easily for me. God, I was bored! So bored.'

'And will you be bored here?'

'Probably,' Harry said with his crooked grin. 'Unless I can make it more interesting.'

Edward was conscious of an unease stealing over him. This tranquil place soothed him but Harry . . . It would be just like him to make life interesting by killing a few bores and leaving a cheap challenge on the corpses to tease the police. Ah! What was he thinking? Whatever else he might be, his friend was not a murderer. Although he possessed the necessary ruthless streak – Edward knew that for a fact.

'Did you know any of the people I mentioned?' he asked abruptly.

'The murder victims?' Harry looked at him with grim enjoyment. 'You think I might have killed those two old boys and that old woman? No, I didn't know them so why would I kill them?'

'I didn't say I thought you might have killed anyone . . .'

'Oh, I've killed people before now. You remember my "boy" – Gustav, I called him, though I think his name was Koondo? I killed him. I came back unexpectedly from safari and found him smoking one of my best cigars and drinking my brandy.'

'And you killed him?' Edward was shocked.

'I threw him down the steps and he broke his neck.

Oh, and one of the Germans . . . one of those fat, porcine ones. He found me with his wife. We were up country and no one knew. I shot him and fed him to the lions. Said it was a terrible accident.'

'But surely there were witnesses . . . his wife?'

'She was glad to be rid of him. Fat bastard liked to tie her to a tree and beat her. No witnesses, just our secret.'

'Are you serious, Harry?'

'Of course I'm bloody serious. By the way, I lied to you. I did know one of the people you were talking about.'

'One of the murder victims?'

'The mountaineer – what was his name?'

'James Herold.'

'That's the chap. He came on safari with me once and I climbed in the Drakensberg with him. Good man, I thought. Sorry to hear he had that illness. Glad to be released from it, I expect. I know I would be.'

Edward shivered and Harry said, 'It's turning a bit chilly. In any case, it's time for dinner. Let's go back to the house.'

'Tell me you were joking,' Edward said as they turned to go inside.

'About killing? I wasn't joking. Why should you be shocked? We can all kill if we need to – kill or be killed,' he amended. 'That's why I'll have to go back to that great dark continent as Conrad calls it. Have you ever read *Lord Jim*? No? You ought to. He tells the truth about the journey we all have to make.' He put his arm round Edward's shoulders. 'Hey, don't look so glum. I'd like to meet that woman of yours. From what I hear, she's my kind of girl.'

Over dinner – an excellent sole followed by cheese and an admirable vintage port – they jawed about Africa: blue velvet nights on the veldt tracking impala, kongoni antelope or the musky scent of waterbuck through grass which flayed their ankles drawing blood through the toughest trousers. They recalled a night of high drama under a smoky-red moon when they had been faced with a pride of six lions attracted by the scent of the gazelle chops they were roasting over the campfire. Or had it been the Mozart? Harry took his gramophone on safari with him and, predictably perhaps, *Don Giovanni* was his favourite.

They laughed over the memory of a hippo which had almost done for Edward beside a crocodile-infested river and remembered the delectable taste of tinned peaches after a long day tracking leopard. Edward relived a magical flight in Harry's Tiger Moth. Creeping across the vast African sky, they had seen far beneath them over a thousand elephant covering the Mara like a grey blanket. Later they had cracked open a bottle of warm champagne and toasted their youth and the great adventure that was Africa.

Good though it was to share such memories, Edward was all the time aware that he was breaking bread with a murderer. On his own admission, Harry had killed an African servant and a German who had caught him tupping his wife. Could he kill again? *Had* he killed again?

'Do you remember the day Jami came to you?' Edward asked dreamily, recalling Harry's Somali servant.

'As noble a savage as I ever hope to meet,' Harry said.

'Memory plays such tricks. Why should I remember Jami when I haven't thought of him for goodness knows how many years?'

The conversation turned to motor cars and Edward asked his friend what he was driving now. 'You've not still got the Bugatti, I suppose? You remember when we raced from Nairobi to Nakuru and the Bugatti beat my

Hudson by twenty minutes? Of course, now I would never drive anything but my Lagonda. I was saying to Verity . . .'

'I don't drive now, old boy. Not in England, anyway.'

'But you were mad about . . .'

'You're really going to marry her?' Harry interrupted, as if he could hardly believe anyone would voluntarily surrender their freedom for the bonds of matrimony.

'As I told you earlier, we're engaged but it's not official,' Edward replied stiffly.

'Your secret's safe with me,' Harry said, a touch ironically. 'After all, I don't know anyone. So why does it have to be such a big secret?'

'It's hard to explain. She's an independent spirit and it took a good deal of effort on my part to persuade her to accept me. She thinks marriage might interfere with her career.'

'"'Tis just like a summer birdcage in a garden: the birds that are without despair to get in, and the birds that are within despair and are in a consumption for fear that they shall never get out."'

Edward didn't like the reference to consumption but was impressed. 'Who wrote that?'

'John Webster in *The White Devil*. I've rather taken to reading Revenge Tragedies. They are so expressive. "We are merely the stars' tennis balls, struck and bandied which way please them." Rather good, eh? Tennis balls!' Harry laughed.

'Webster's too violent for me,' Edward responded.

'Did you say she's a journalist?'

'A foreign correspondent. She was in Prague when she fell ill.'

'Of course, I read her reports from Spain. But forgive me, Edward – why choose someone who does not want to marry you when there are so many women who would give everything to . . .? Stop me, if I'm being impertinent.'

'It's just one of those things.' Edward waved a hand. 'You don't choose who to love. She never bores me for one thing,' he added and then gave up trying to explain. 'Wait till you meet her, then you'll understand. But come to that, why aren't you married?' He hesitated, wondering if he was probing too deeply. 'You said you loved Lady Redfern – Christobel!' The name suddenly came to him. 'But after . . .'

'There was a girl – she was in the car when the crash happened, as a matter of fact. She was very good to me but it didn't work out.' Harry got up and walked towards the French windows which opened out on to the lawn.

'I ought not to have asked.'

'No, I'll tell you all about it sometime but here's Ransome. I expect he wants to clear the table.' The butler said nothing but raised an eyebrow questioningly at his employer. 'Let's take the port and the cigars into the library. Shelves of books. I've begun to sort through them. Then I find something like *Leaves of Grass*, settle down to read and that's the day gone.'

They didn't go to bed until late but Edward slept well and at nine the following morning he strolled round to the police station. Henley was a pretty enough town of some six thousand inhabitants – hardly more than an oversized village – with a medieval church complete with fifteenth-century tower and an even earlier chantry house, a charming theatre and a suitably picturesque bridge – dated 1786 – over the river. There were pleasant pubs and tea-shops for the tourists who flocked to the town – not just during the regatta but throughout the summer – and the Brakspear brewery supplied good ale to the Red Lion and the Angel on the Bridge. Near the bridge, on the Berkshire bank, was the headquarters of Leander, the premier rowing club in the country. On the other bank was Phyllis Court, the fashionable country club.

Henley, Edward supposed, was a sleepy place and he imagined there was very little crime for the local police to investigate. He took it for granted that in Inspector Treacher he would find what his American friends called a hayseed, sucking on the end of a straw. In fact, when he pushed through the swing doors of the small police station and was shown into a sparsely furnished office, the man who got up to shake his hand was small, bright-eyed, yellow-haired, about thirty years of age with a pleasant smile parenthesized by bushy side-burns. He had the look of an agricultural sales representative or a dealer in cars or horses. He was shrewd, quite confident of his own authority and ready to meet this aristocrat in his perfectly cut suit with an open mind. Chief Inspector Pride had warned him not to underestimate Lord Edward Corinth and he had no intention of doing so.

When each man had finished eyeing up the other, the Inspector offered tea and Edward accepted. Nothing was said until a young woman had brought in not just a cup of tea but a teapot and milk jug with ginger biscuits on a separate plate.

'You do yourself well, Inspector,' Edward smiled.

'I think better with a cup of tea in my hand,' he said, offering Edward the sugar bowl. 'I gather you have some doubts about the deaths of three of our local worthies,' he added without further ado.

Edward, appreciating his directness, nodded his head. 'Chief Inspector Pride will have mentioned to you that they were all patients of Eric Silver, my dentist. Silver told me that he suspected all three deaths were not the accidents they were taken to be at the time but murder. I was inclined to think there was nothing in it but, after I left him, Mr Silver was himself murdered.'

'Definitely murdered?'

'In the most barbaric and sadistic manner. His drill was used to penetrate his ear . . . quite disgusting. I can hardly bear to think about it. Chief Inspector Pride is investigating the killing and I have every confidence in his thoroughness and professionalism. I have known him for several years. He investigated the death of General Craig who was poisoned at my brother's dinner table,' he added, in case Treacher thought he was presuming to judge where he ought not to.

'Pride said there was an entomological connection between the deaths.'

'Yes, Inspector,' and Edward proceeded to outline it.

'*Mouches* – flies!' Treacher chuckled. 'I grant you that completely passed me by.'

'Flies, yes, although I believe that in the area in which the wine is made *mouches* also means bees.'

'Bees . . . flies . . . fascinating!' The Inspector sounded unconvinced.

'As I said, in the cold light of day it all seems rather tenuous but I wondered if – purely to satisfy my own curiosity – you would permit me to look at your case notes or, if that is not possible, to talk to those who discovered the bodies.' He saw the look in Treacher's face and hurried on. 'I just want to see if there was anyone or anything they had in common – someone they all knew, for instance. You weren't looking for a connection – there was no reason why you should – but Silver gives us that initial link.'

Treacher hesitated. 'It's most irregular, Lord Edward, but as a favour to Chief Inspector Pride for whom, like you, I have considerable respect, I will permit it though, as you will understand, this has to be on the basis of absolute confidence. If the press were to get hold of it . . .'

'I promise, Inspector. As it happens, I have a valid reason for being down here. I am staying with an old friend, Lord Lestern. And furthermore . . .' he felt a cad for using Verity but thought she would understand, 'my fiancée is recuperating from a bout of TB at Leonard Bladon's sanatorium. Do you know it?'

'Yes, I've met Dr Bladon. A very pleasant gentleman. I am sorry to hear about Miss Browne.' Edward was startled. 'Chief Inspector Pride apprised me of the situation,' Treacher explained, sounding momentarily embarrassed.

'There was another thing I wanted to ask you, Inspector. As you know, when Mr Herold was found by his wife she also found a sheet of paper on his body on which someone – presumably the murderer – had written "buzz, buzz" – possibly a taunting reference to the way he died. When Mr Silver was found there was a similar taunt that seemed to refer directly to me.'

'Yes, so Chief Inspector Pride informed me. It's the motto on your family's coat of arms, I understand.'

'Which can be roughly translated as "eagles don't catch flies". Was there anything similar found on the bodies of Miss Totteridge or General Lowther?'

'I've been thinking about that,' Treacher said, stroking his chin. 'As it happens, a piece of paper was found on Miss Totteridge. I'm afraid I took no notice of it at the time. It was a quotation from Shakespeare, so my wife told me when I mentioned it to her – from a sonnet, I think she said, "So shall thou feed on Death".'

'". . . that feeds on men, and Death once dead, there's no more dying then,"' Edward murmured. 'You found just those first six words – not the rest of it?'

'No, just that first bit on a page torn out of her horticultural diary. She kept a day-by-day record of what she did in the garden – what she planted, what died, what needed attention . . . I'm a bit of a gardener myself and

I found it very interesting. There's no doubt she had a remarkable knowledge . . .'

'So how did she manage to poison herself?'

'You'll see from my notes. She was testing out a new insecticide for a chemical company.'

'A new insecticide? What kind exactly?'

'It's called DDT. Here . . .' He riffled through his notebook. 'Dichlorodiphenyltrichloroethane – a proper mouthful and I don't know how to pronounce it. Anyway, it's going to be the new wonder drug, apparently. It'll kill everything from malaria-carrying mosquitoes to greenfly.'

'And human beings.'

'Only if they drink it in their tea.'

'In their tea?'

'Yes, we found traces in the bottom of her cup.'

Edward carefully replaced his cup in the saucer. 'Didn't that make you think it could be murder?'

'I discounted the idea. Who would want to kill the old lady? I assumed she'd just made a mistake and dropped some in her tea.'

'But you found the paper with the quotation about feeding on death?'

'Not until after the inquest, I'm afraid.' Treacher looked uncomfortable. 'Miss Totteridge's sister, Mrs Booth, was clearing out the house. It's going to be sold which is a shame as her garden is so well known. Anyway, she was sorting out Miss Totteridge's clothes for a jumble sale. She decided to burn her gardening clothes which were too dirty to be of use to anyone. That's when she found the piece of paper in a pocket.'

'In a pocket of . . .?'

'The boiler suit she always wore to garden in.'

Edward bit back a question as to why Miss Totteridge's clothes had not been thoroughly searched when her body was found. He did not want to antagonize Treacher if he could help it. 'What about the General? Was any note found on his body?'

'Not to my knowledge,' the Inspector said, sounding distinctly unhappy. 'No, that's not quite correct now I come to think of it. I believe the housekeeper did show me something. I'm afraid I . . .'

Edward did his best to save Treacher's blushes by not appearing to attach much importance to his oversight. Instead, he said lightly, 'Would you mind if I nosed around, Inspector, and talked to his housekeeper? I'm sure you did a very thorough job but now this connection has turned up . . .'

'By all means, Lord Edward, if you think you might find something I missed.'

Hearing the tone of his voice, Edward decided not to ask any more questions for the moment. He knew only too well that if Treacher felt he was out to make him look a fool or, worse still, incompetent, he would do everything he could to prevent him finding out anything.

'I am most grateful, Inspector,' was all he said.

When had finished telling Verity about his interview with Inspector Treacher and what he had discovered from a preliminary examination of his case notes, he saw that she was eyeing him speculatively.

'What is it, V? Why are you looking at me like that?'

'I was just thinking what a bore it must be for you to have to waste time with me when you could be investigating. I know I'd hate it.'

'It's not as bad as all that,' he joked. 'In the first place, I love you and would rather be here than anywhere else and, in the second place, I find it clears my brain to tell you everything. Anyway, you're my partner in sleuthing – you always have been and always will be.'

'Good answer. I can't fault it but still . . .'

'I know you're bored and . . .'

'The truth is I'm more angry than bored. There's so much I want to do . . . to report. Oh God, I'm sorry. I mustn't be pathetic. I've no reason to be sorry for myself beyond the obvious one.'

'You're not lonely, are you?'

'No! The girls I share with are nice. Jill's a bit of a goose but Mary Black's intelligent. I can talk to her about politics and the international situation though she's a great supporter of Chamberlain so we argue like anything. Lots of people have promised to come and see me. Adrian and Charlotte are coming later this week as a matter of fact. You know Charlotte's new novel is a bestseller?'

'I didn't. What's it called? I've forgotten.'

'*Secret Relations*. She said she'll bring me a copy. We missed the launch party, don't you remember? I thought about sending for Basil but apparently Bladon won't have dogs here so that's no good.'

She looked so gloomy for a moment that Edward longed to take her in his arms but he didn't want to make her cry. Instead he said, 'I'm afraid you'll have to make do with me for the moment.'

Over the next few days, Edward went through Inspector Treacher's case notes and, when not doing that, he sat beside Verity willing her to get better. Harry was a perfect host, allowing him to treat Turton House as an hotel and come and go as he pleased. Edward observed Verity closely and was encouraged to see how quickly she regained some colour in her cheeks. The dark shadows round her eyes began to fade and the sharp bones in her face softened. To him, she looked more beautiful than ever, her eyes so huge and black against the pallor of her skin, but it was a beauty which frightened him. And she was gentler – less ready to snap at him. She had always seemed so strong – indomitable was the word that came to mind whenever he thought of her – that finding her biddable, even resigned, made him uneasy. Bladon encouraged him to 'take Verity out of herself' as he put it. Edward had the impression that he too was worried that she might lose the will to fight her disease.

At first, when he discussed the investigation with her – if that was what it amounted to – he could see that it was an effort for her to concentrate but gradually she became interested. The sun shone and the temperature crept up into the high seventies. On the fourth day of her stay he asked Bladon if he could take her out in the car for an hour or two.

'She'll tire easily,' he warned. 'She needs rest above everything but that doesn't mean a little fresh air wouldn't do her good. Take her out by all means. Just be careful and don't overdo it.'

Tenderly, Edward put Verity in the car and wrapped a thick plaid travelling rug round her knees. She made some small protest about 'not being at death's door quite yet' but let him have his way which was in itself a sign of how weak she was. Driving slowly, he took the back lanes to Phyllis Court. He had telephoned the secretary, Mr Bruce-Dick, to ask if he and Verity could become temporary members for the summer. Edward thought he should make it clear why Verity was in Henley and explained that she was recuperating in Bladon's sanatorium after having been diagnosed with TB. Bruce-Dick listened to him in silence and Edward felt called upon to add that she would not expect to use any of the club facilities except to sit in the garden. She would not swim, have massages or in any way spread infection to members or staff.

Bruce-Dick hummed and hawed, understandably hesitant about allowing Verity to contaminate the club, but in the end agreed that Edward could become a temporary member and Verity, as his guest, could use the deck-chairs and even the tennis courts, should she be strong enough to play, but nothing more. To eat in the restaurant might, he thought, be a step too far.

'You understand my position, Lord Edward? I don't want to sound unsympathetic but it would not be fair on members and might damage the reputation of the club if . . .'

'I quite understand,' Edward said soothingly, 'and I am most grateful. I promise Miss Browne will keep away from your members and their guests.'

It was after eleven when he parked the Lagonda in front of the clubhouse and, arm in arm, they strolled over to the tennis courts where several figures in white were slamming balls back and forth. He tucked her into a deck-chair and draped the rug over her despite her protests that she was quite hot enough already. Edward then left her to beard Bruce-Dick.

That proved not to be as difficult an interview as he had feared. Although Bruce-Dick was elderly, he was no fool and studied Edward with interest. Since he had spoken to him on the telephone, he had made a few enquiries and was impressed by what he had heard. It helped that he had been in the same regiment as Edward's brother Frank who had been killed in the first few days of the war in France.

'He was a splendid chap. Terrible tragedy that he was the first of our young men to go. And you, Lord Edward – I heard a rumour that you were working for the FO and detecting crimes . . .' He became almost roguish. 'The Duke – does he . . .?' Seeing Edward's face, he quickly changed the subject. 'Miss Browne is, I believe, a famous foreign correspondent. My dear wife was quite overcome when I told her you were visiting us. She would be delighted if you . . . if both of you . . .' he added bravely, 'would care to dine with us one night.'

Edward, rather sourly, was reminded of something Verity had once quoted at him. She had been reading *The Ordeal of Richard Feverel* and Meredith, who was obsessed with the nature of snobbery, had noted – rather acutely, Edward considered – that 'the national love of a lord is less subservience than a form of self-love; putting a gold-lace hat on one's image, as it were, to bow to it.' He thought this was a case in point. Had he but known it, Emily Bruce-Dick had gone quite pink when she suggested to her husband that he might proffer the invitation.

'That is very kind of her,' Edward said, with as sincere a smile as he could muster, 'but Miss Browne is recuperating – as I mentioned – from a slight bout of TB and is not allowed out of the sanatorium for more than an hour or two at a time.' He noticed that Bruce-Dick was trying not to look relieved. 'But I, on the other hand, would be delighted to come.'

Bruce-Dick beamed with pleasure. Phyllis Court was not short of aristocrats among its members but Lord Edward was someone rather special – not just the son of a duke but famous in his own right – and Bruce-Dick had visions of appearing in the illustrated papers arm in arm with his new friend.

The formalities over, Edward returned to find one of the tennis players sitting beside Verity and engaging her in conversation. Fearing that it might be too much for her, he hurried to her side. He was relieved to find her animated and enjoying the attention of the attractive young woman who rose to her feet when she saw him. She held out her hand.

'Kay Stammers,' she said, without waiting for Verity to introduce her. 'You're Lord Edward Corinth, aren't you? We met briefly at Brooklands. You won't remember.'

'Of course I remember, Miss Stammers. I am so pleased to meet you again and have an opportunity to wish you luck at Wimbledon.'

Kay Stammers had beaten Helen Wills Moody when she was only seventeen and won the Wimbledon women's doubles with Freda James in 1935 and 1936. She had won the French Open and was confidently expected to win the women's singles at Wimbledon. She was also an accomplished aviatrix who had learnt to fly at the London Aeroplane Club.

'I am so thrilled to meet Miss Browne. I have just been telling her that, as soon as she is feeling stronger, she must let me take her up in my plane. Don't look like that, Lord Edward. She would be perfectly safe and has just been telling me the doctors have prescribed fresh air.'

There was something so frank and engaging about Kay Stammers that Edward felt himself relax. She was the sort of woman Verity liked – afraid of nothing and no one. She might be just the person to give her a new interest in life and stop her feeling as though her world had collapsed as a result of her illness.

Edward found that it was not altogether true that Harry knew none of his neighbours. Returning to Turton House that evening, hoping to slip upstairs and have a bath before dinner without having to chat to his host, he was collared halfway up the stairs and introduced to a couple he disliked at first sight – Jack and Una Amery. He knew perfectly well who they were. Jack was the younger son of Leo Amery – a Conservative backbench MP and a strong opponent of the Prime Minister's policy of appeasing Hitler instead of standing up to him. Edward had met him once with Winston Churchill but his son was of quite another complexion – unstable, a constant worry to his father, anti-Semitic and a strong supporter of General Franco.

Jack had married an 'actress' – a prostitute in all but name – and it was his whim not to allow her to tell people that they were man and wife. She supposed it was because he was ashamed of her. Only a woman as submissive as Una could have tolerated living with him. His sexual tastes were fetishistic and perverse and he liked to treat her as his slave and humiliate her. Edward had also heard that the man was a gambler and a cheat – a few years back he had been arrested in Paris on a Greek warrant for the fraudulent purchase of diamonds in Athens. The English papers had been full of it and Leo Amery had had to bail him out at some considerable cost.

Edward tried to look enthusiastic as they shook hands but visibly failed.

'You didn't meet each other in Tanganyika?' Harry asked, sounding surprised. 'Great times, eh, Jack? No one to tell us what to do and what not to do!'

'What were you doing there?' Edward asked Jack Amery, attempting to be polite.

'Making a film – *Jungle Skies*.'

'Was it ever shown? I don't remember . . .'

'No, the bastards wouldn't pay the money they owed me so it was never finished.' Jack turned back to Harry. 'I say, Henley's the bloody limit! We stopped to buy some stuff for Una. I parked my car quite legally and then I'm fined fifty pounds – I mean fifty pounds! – and threatened with prison. I ask you!'

'Fifty pounds!' Edward exclaimed.

'Don't take any notice of him,' Una interjected. 'He's had over a hundred fines for motoring offences, haven't you, darling? And it's never his fault.'

'Well, it isn't – not this time at any rate. Look, what I wanted to say is there's a new club opened in Maidenhead . . .' He stopped abruptly to address Una. 'Teddy Bear, go and get the car, will you? I've just got something to say to Harry.'

Taking the hint gratefully, Edward followed Una out to the car. 'Why does he call you Teddy Bear?'

'Oh, he's obsessed with them. His favourite teddy goes everywhere with us. He's in the car now.' She giggled nervously. 'He's quite mad, you know.'

'Really?'

'Yes, really. He thinks everyone's out to get him. I mean, when we get home, he'll make me get out of the car first and check there's no one hiding in the bushes waiting to jump on him.' She opened the glove box. 'See?'

It contained a revolver. She snapped it shut as Amery came out of the front door with Harry. 'Don't say I told you!' she whispered urgently.

After the car had sped off showering gravel behind it, Harry said, 'Well, what did you think? Una's a nice little thing, isn't she? Wears too much make-up of course, but she's terribly loyal.'

'Where do they live?'

'A place called Ditton Lodge in Maidenhead. They don't own it. Jack has no money. They rent it off some damned insurance broker who's always giving them grief.'

Edward's immediate reaction was one of sympathy for the landlord.

'What does he do? Is he a film producer?'

'Nothing, really. I mean, he's tried his hand at practically everything you can think of but it never lasts. He's opened an off-licence – a wine shop – in Maidenhead but I think he must be its best customer.'

'It must be hard for his father.'

'Not easy,' Harry agreed. 'He's really taken with the Fascists. His great friend is Jacques Doriot. Have you heard of him?'

'I don't think so. Unless you mean the French politician . . .?'

'That's the one. He was a Communist. Then, a couple of years back he saw the light and founded the Fascist *Parti Populaire Français*. They're a bit too violent for me – like most converts they go to the other extreme but they have the measure of the Communists. Oh, I forgot, sorry. Isn't your girl a Communist?'

'Yes,' Edward said shortly, 'and I remember she told me once that Jack Amery had been gun-running for the rebels in Spain.'

'Yes, he's one of Franco's most fervent followers. He joined the Spanish Foreign Legion and I think he became a Spanish citizen – to avoid his creditors mainly. But you can ask him tonight.'

'Tonight?'

'Jack wants us to join him at this new place in Maidenhead – what was it called? I remember, the Hungaria. I bet it's awful but at least he's never dull.'

'Oh, I don't know. I was thinking of having an early night.'

'Not a bit of it. You must come. You can ask him about Herold.'

'Herold? Why? Were they friends?'

'Great chums in the old days. The one thing Jack can do is climb mountains. It satisfies his restless streak and it's dangerous. He and Herold climbed in the Alps several years running.'

4

Verity knew she must be getting better because she felt so cross. Here she was stuck in some kind of prison while outside everything that was important to her continued as if she didn't exist. Lord Weaver had sent flowers with a note in his own hand wishing her a speedy recovery but she was ungrateful enough to think it might as well have been a wreath. As far as the *New Gazette* was concerned, she was history. Someone else was reporting from Prague – quite competently, she was forced to admit. There had been nothing from the editor. That was no surprise as he disliked her and resented her influence with his proprietor. But – more hurtfully – none of her colleagues on the paper had thought to visit her. She was enough of a realist to know that out of sight meant out of mind, but still . . .

It was therefore with delight that she welcomed Adrian and Charlotte Hassel. Adrian was a painter whose work she did not particularly like but who was her oldest male friend. Charlotte was a novelist 'on the fringes of the Bloomsbury set', as she had once put it. She went to parties at which Virginia Woolf appeared although she would only talk to her own little coterie. Charlotte – a kind person – put this reserve down to shyness rather than intellectual snobbery. Mrs Woolf hated being lionized or asked to sign books. Public speaking was torture to her but, since the huge success of *Orlando* which had been published ten years earlier, she had been famous whether she liked it or not.

'So, Verity, imagine my surprise when she came over at the opening of Duncan Grant's exhibition' – Grant was a painter friend of Adrian's – 'and told me how much she had liked my new book. I was completely bowled over.'

'What else did she say?'

'Nothing really. Well, actually I mentioned you. I hope you don't mind. It appears she reads your stuff and seemed genuinely upset to hear you were ill. She said she'd send you some books.'

'That was kind of her.'

'She said she and Leonard wanted to invite us to stay with them in Sussex. I'm sure she didn't really mean it but it was so exciting. I almost burst, didn't I, Adrian?'

'You did, my darling, but you shouldn't have been so surprised. *Secret Relations* has had some wonderful reviews and the publisher says it's going to be selected by the Book of the Month people as one of their top choices.'

'That's wonderful! I'm so thrilled, Charlotte. As Adrian says, it's no surprise but it is good to see you getting the recognition you deserve.'

'And the money!' Adrian added enthusiastically. 'I've told her, Verity, that I'm going to live the life of the gigolo and enjoy it.'

'Come on! Your last exhibition was a success.'

'It was all right,' Adrian agreed, modestly. 'Anyway, enough about us – what about you? You look frightfully pale. When are they going to let you out of here?'

'You're supposed to say I'm looking so much better,' Verity reprimanded him with mock severity. 'The stupid thing is that I feel perfectly all right most of the time but as soon as I try and do anything – I mean *anything* – like walk more than a hundred yards, I go all weak at the knees. It's as though someone has filleted out my spine. Too maddening.' She coughed and added, 'And I cough too much. Not very nice, I'm afraid!' She tried to sound cheerful and failed miserably.

'And Edward?' Charlotte inquired.

'He's been wonderful. You know he's staying down here with an "old school friend"?' She said 'old school friend' with irony because it was her contention that England was run by people who had gone to school together – Eton mainly but also two or three lesser establishments – and then Oxford or Cambridge, and that 'democracy' was a meaningless word to them.

'So what's he doing when he's not sitting by your bed holding your hand?'

'Shut up, Adrian,' Verity said, a little colour seeping into her cheeks. 'He's sleuthing again, if you must know. You haven't heard about his dentist?'

'His dentist? No,' Charlotte echoed. 'Tell all.'

Verity relayed everything Edward had told her, knowing he would have no objection to her confiding in their friends.

'That's terrible, isn't it, Adrian?' Charlotte said when she had finished. 'I knew Hermione Totteridge. She was a great friend of one of my aunts.'

'You never mentioned her name to me,' Adrian said.

'Oh, I must have. At one time, I thought of her as an honorary aunt but somehow – I don't know why – we rather lost touch. I haven't seen her for years and I had no idea she had died. I suppose there must have been obituaries but I never saw any. I feel very bad. I stayed with her once or twice when I was a child.' She put her hand over her eyes as she thought back. 'And Edward thinks she might have been murdered? Why, that's awful! Is there any way I could help, I wonder? I remember her sister lived in Norfolk. I must write to her. Aunt Hermie, as I used to call her, was an absolute dear and she got me really interested in gardening. In fact,' she looked shyly at Adrian, 'it's one of the things I thought I might do with the money from the book. I get so fed up only having a pocket-handkerchief-sized piece of grass in London, I thought we might buy a little cottage in the country where I could write and you could have a studio – and with a garden – a big garden . . .'

'Golly!' Adrian exclaimed. 'She's never said anything about having a garden to me before, Verity, but of course I don't mind. It's your money, darling, and you must spend it how you like.'

'I expect she wanted to wait until there was a witness before springing it on you so you couldn't be really angry,' Verity said astutely. 'I'm so sorry, Charlotte, to have given you such a shock. Of course, I had no idea . . .'

'How could you have known? It's just rather beastly.'

'And you can come and recuperate at the cottage.'

'Oh, Adrian, I do hope I'm better long before then,' Verity said, her face falling.

Adrian realized he had made a mistake and quickly corrected himself. 'Of course you'll be better before we've done anything about the cottage, but we could all take a place somewhere in the country quite soon. You could watch the grass grow and I could bustle around with trowels and trugs.'

'So, have you decided when the wedding's going to be?' Charlotte asked brightly, trying to change the conversation to a safer topic but managing to stumble on an even more sensitive area.

'Oh that,' Verity replied dismissively. 'We haven't even discussed it. I've got to get better first. I can't marry anyone when I'm like this. You know he's not even allowed to kiss me? I'm pure poison.'

'Don't talk such nonsense!' Charlotte said sharply. 'You're not marrying just anyone. It's Edward we're talking about and he's not going to be fussed by having to push you up the aisle in a wheelchair.'

'There's not going to be an aisle.'

'Well, whatever they have in Chelsea Town Hall. Verity, I've known you long enough to speak my mind. You've messed that poor man around long enough. It's time you stopped finding excuses not to . . . not to go through with it.'

Verity looked mutinous. 'I'm not making excuses. I'm ill. I wish I wasn't. As soon as I'm better, I'll get on with my life.'

Charlotte felt she had gone as far as she dared so she merely said, 'That's all right then.'

After an uneasy pause, she found that she was still thinking about Hermione Totteridge.

'I kept meaning to get in touch with her – Hermione, I mean. I didn't see much of her after I left school. We exchanged cards at Christmas, though she wasn't really a Christmas sort of person. I remember being rather shocked when she said it was sentimental gobblede-gook. I went to a lecture she gave on orchids at the RHS in Vincent Square once . . . but that was years ago.'

'You said you knew her sister . . .? Edward might find it helpful to have an entrée.'

'I suppose I must have met her a couple of times – three at the most. I can't believe it! Who would want to murder Aunt Hermie? Everyone loved her.'

'Well, maybe not everyone,' Verity suggested.

'You mean she might have been killed by a rival orchid grower? That's ridiculous.'

'It's not ridiculous. Her sister found that note about feeding on death in the pocket of her boiler suit, and is it likely – if she was experimenting with a dangerous new chemical – that she would drop it in her tea?'

'What do you know about the sister, Charlotte?' Adrian asked.

'Hermione had two sisters. Daphne, who I never met, married a soldier – cavalry, I think – and went to India. She was killed in a car crash, I seem to remember.'

'In India?'

'No, in England. She was the youngest. The other one, Violet, married a country doctor and lived in Norfolk – Burnham Market. Or at least she used to. I haven't thought of her for ages, I'm afraid. Oh God! Poor Aunt Hermie. I just can't get over it. I feel so sad and so guilty.'

Edward rubbed his head. A night at the Hungaria in Maidenhead with Harry and the Amerys had given him nothing but a headache. Jack had got drunk – first melancholy drunk and then violent drunk – which had embarrassed him but not Harry or Una. He rather thought she might have slept with Harry. They were certainly intimate enough but then, he thought uncharitably, she probably slept with anyone in trousers. She was like a stray dog desperate for affection.

He tried to concentrate on the exercise book – one of a small pile beside him on the desk. He found Inspector Treacher's case notes on his investigation into the three deaths notable only for being sketchy and unilluminating. Treacher might well be a good policeman when it came to investigating the activities of local villains but he seemed singularly ill equipped to decide whether a murder had been committed. It was just understandable that he should have concluded that Hermione Totteridge's death was accidental. Who, as he had said, would kill a harmless old lady held in respect and some affection locally? She was a character, an eccentric, and her reputation as a gardener was something of which the whole town could be proud.

General Lowther's death was surely much less easy to dismiss as an act of God. There had been a post-mortem by the local doctor who had been happy to conclude that he had died of heart failure. Edward was shocked to find that the remains of the wine in the glass and in the bottle had not been analysed. Assumptions had been made and the coroner had failed to ask the right questions. The only thing that might still make it possible to discover if he had been poisoned was that the body had been buried rather than cremated. Even so, every day that passed would make it more difficult to find traces of poison in the body should Edward ever turn up enough evidence of foul play to justify an exhumation.

As for Herold, the Inspector had obviously concluded that his wife had helped him commit suicide but had decided – presumably for her sake – to call it an accident.

The one thing he did not want to do was alarm Treacher. No one likes to be shown up as incompetent and Edward decided he must do what he could to guide the Inspector towards discovering his failings, which would allow him to correct them without being made to eat humble pie. Once Treacher began to think of him as an enemy, there would be no more cooperation and his own investigation would be made much more difficult. So, when he called in at the police station to return the case notes, he made no criticism but merely asked if the Inspector would have any objection to him talking to the General's housekeeper and Miss Totteridge's sister.

Treacher hesitated but was unable to think of any reason why Edward could not interview whomever he wanted. There was a niggling doubt at the back of his mind that perhaps he had been a little too ready to accept the result of the post-mortem on General

Lowther. Old Dr Compton was getting lazy – he was shortly to retire – but at the time there had seemed no justification for bringing in someone else to examine the body. Why should it not have been a heart attack? However, if Lord Edward Corinth turned up something that threw doubt on it . . . but then how could he? He had interviewed the General's housekeeper, Mrs Venables, at length and had been satisfied that no one had tampered with the wine. There was no reason to think that she would change her story. She had been with the General since the end of the war and was beyond suspicion. There was a parlour maid, he recalled, a silly girl who was so timid he could hardly get her to tell him her name. It was inconceivable that she could have been up to anything.

Treacher scratched his head. Something told him that he had to get a grip on the new investigation and take what credit he could for anything this nosy trouble-maker turned up. Lord Edward seemed friendly enough but there was something faintly arrogant in the way his cool grey eyes surveyed him. Assessing the risks in a matter of seconds, he concluded that, on balance, it would wiser to accommodate the interfering young aristocrat, who knew too many powerful people for comfort, than stand in his way. In any event, if Lord Edward wished to speak to the General's housekeeper, he had no legal way of stopping the man. Much better that he should be seen to have nothing to hide – which was, of course, the case.

'She lives with her sister in a little village called Frieth between here and Marlow,' he informed Edward. 'I seem to remember she doesn't have a telephone but I don't suppose she goes anywhere. The bus service isn't good.'

'Where would she do her shopping?'

'The village shop, I suppose. But if I were you, I

would just turn up. I'll give you a letter of authority but I doubt you'll need one.'

In truth, he could hardly see Mrs Venables being brave enough to ask Lord Edward Corinth what right he had to question her about her late employer with or without a letter from him.

'That would be very good of you, Inspector,' Edward said smoothly. 'You seem to have interviewed her very thoroughly so I doubt I shall get anything else from her. But, you never know, something may have occurred to her since the inquest. Is she married, by the way?'

'She and her sister are both spinsters but, as you know, a housekeeper takes authority from being addressed as Mrs.'

'Indeed. Ah well! I'd like to see a bit of the country-side and the Lagonda needs a run so I might trot along this afternoon. No point in putting it off if I'm going to try my hand, eh, Inspector?'

Edward very often found that if he made himself out to be a bit of an ass he was able to put 'authority' at ease, but the Inspector was not deceived. Lord Edward Corinth was nobody's fool and Treacher knew it.

Before he set out, Edward visited Verity and told her what he was doing. He was pleased to see she was genuinely interested in his 'digging around', as she called it. Charlotte Hassel turning out to be almost a relation of Hermione Totteridge had made it all much more personal and Verity enjoyed having something to contribute to the investigation.

'So that's where you should go next,' she said when she had finished telling him. 'Get Charlotte to come with you to see the sister. That way you'll be welcomed as a friend, not a nosy parker.'

He looked at her with affection. 'I wish it were you who could be with me.'

'It will be soon. I'm feeling so much better. Now, don't worry about me. My new friend, Kay Stammers, is coming to take me to watch her play tennis at Phyllis Court.'

'That's good but promise me you won't get too tired. You are looking better but . . .'

'I can see I'm going to get fed up with people saying that to me! I know it'll take time before I get my strength back. I'll be careful, I promise you. Go now!'

'I wish I could kiss you.'

'Me too! You'll just have to make do with a peck on the cheek. I don't expect you'll catch anything from that.'

It was another glorious June day and, with its hood down, the Lagonda was as good a place to enjoy it as anywhere. The narrow lanes did not allow for speeding but Edward was in no hurry. He felt king of the road like Toad of Toad Hall – a production of which he had noted was being presented during the regatta by the Henley Players at the picturesque little Kenton Theatre in New Street.

Skirting the duck pond, he drove up the hill into Frieth, past the pub and stopped outside the church. A man was clipping the hedge and turned to view the Lagonda with something approaching awe. It took a minute or two for Edward to make himself understood but he was at last directed, in a broad Buckinghamshire accent, back down the main street to a little cottage covered in roses and protected from the road by a flint stone wall. He decided to leave the car by the church because the road was narrow and it was easier to walk, but he also felt he might look as though he was swanking to arrive in such an automobile.

He opened the little gate in the wall and walked down a path made almost impassable by the lavender bushes which invaded it. He knocked on the simple wooden door and it was opened by a lady resembling Mrs Tiggywinkle. She was hunched, bright-eyed and wore a woollen shawl over a smock of some kind.

'Mrs Venables?' he inquired.

'I am Miss Venables. Is it my sister you wish to talk to?'

'I believe so. Was she housekeeper to General Lowther?'

Miss Venables looked at him distrustfully. 'Why do you want to know? Are you a policeman? You don't look like a policeman.'

'No, I am not a policeman but Inspector Treacher suggested that I talk to your sister. I am making a few inquiries into the General's death.' She still looked suspicious – understandably enough – so he fished out the Inspector's letter.

'I haven't got my glasses,' Miss Venables said severely. Then turning, but still clinging to the door handle, she called, 'Margery! There's a man here wants to talk to you about the General.'

A somewhat younger version of Miss Venables appeared. 'Yes, Jane? Who is it?'

Edward explained himself and was at last ushered into the front parlour where he perched on an uncomfortable chair not designed for the male of the species and tried to be charming. He put in five minutes' hard work before he made much headway but he did get the impression that Mrs Venables had not thought much of Inspector Treacher.

'And that old fool, Dr Compton,' she said scornfully. 'I really believe he had been at the morphine.'

'Margery!' her sister said, shocked, 'You ought not to say such things.'

'Perhaps not but it is still a fact, Lord Edward, that the man is incompetent.'

'You thought there was something suspicious about the General's heart attack?'

'I did. There was nothing wrong with his heart. He was as fit as a fiddle.'

'He liked his drink?' Edward ventured.

'He liked his wine but he was no alcoholic – if that's what you are insinuating, young man.'

Edward, rather flattered at being called young, decided he liked this forthright woman. 'No, I meant was there anything about the body which surprised you?'

Mrs Venables hesitated. 'I don't rightly know. I was so shocked to find the General dead like that, I wasn't thinking clearly. I do remember that when I looked at his face there was the faint smell of almonds. I thought it was queer because I knew the General didn't like nuts and there were certainly none in the dining-room.'

Edward sighed. Lowther must have taken cyanide. It ought to have been obvious to the doctor – a slight burning of the lips, mouth and throat – but old Dr Compton had been a fool. The murderer had been fortunate. Mrs Venables was studying him and he realized she had guessed that she had unwittingly given him vital information. 'You knew the General better than anyone – did he have relatives? Did anyone come to see him in the weeks before he died?'

'Two questions – which shall I answer first? No, he had no relatives. His wife died many years ago during the war, before I knew him. She may have had a sister or a brother. In fact, I rather think she did but the General didn't keep up with them. Now I think about it I believe he once told me he had a nephew in Australia or Africa. I can't remember which.'

'No one came to see him . . . no one you hadn't seen before?'

'The vicar – he came every now and again.'

'When was the last time?'

'Just before Christmas. I remember because they discussed whether Miss Truscott's baby could be Baby Jesus in the Nativity play which the village school mistress puts on every year. The vicar said you couldn't have a baby born out of wedlock playing Jesus and the General said – rather to my surprise, I must say – that babies were innocent and, as he recalled, Christ himself was conceived by an unmarried woman.'

'So the vicar sometimes visited him? Who else?'

'You don't think the vicar murdered him, do you?'

'Of course not!' Edward said hurriedly. 'I just meant that the General did have visitors. He wasn't a complete recluse.'

'No, as well as the vicar he saw the doctor and the schoolmistress, Miss Tiverton. He liked her.' She shrugged her shoulders and pursed her lips as if there was something more to be said but this wasn't quite the moment to say it.

Edward made a mental note to talk to Miss Tiverton in due course.

'Did he go to London?'

'Yes. He did go up for the day once a month,' she said grudgingly, 'to see his wine merchant and his stock-broker and occasionally his dentist. He had trouble with his teeth. I'm not sure who else he saw. It wasn't for me to inquire.'

'And when was the last time he went to London?'

'About a month before he died.'

'Was that when he came back with the wine?' Edward was taking a wild leap into the dark and it didn't surprise him when she said no. Then she added, rather pityingly, 'He couldn't manage crates of wine on the train. They arrived a few days later, by carrier.'

'I don't suppose you know where he bought his wine, do you?'

'Justerini and Brooks in St James's Street.' She was obviously impressed and Edward was too.

'Well, he couldn't have bought it from a more respectable firm. By the way, you didn't by any chance find a piece of paper on the body, a note of some kind?'

'What sort of paper?'

'Something odd, something you didn't expect to find.'

'You remember, Margery,' Miss Venables said, jogging her sister's mind. 'You found that verse.'

'Of course! I had forgotten all about it.'

'Do you still have it?' Edward tried to sound matter-of-fact.

'I do, as it happens. I kept it. Was that wrong of me? It seemed . . . it seemed so appropriate somehow.'

'Where did you find it exactly?'

'In the breast pocket of his dinner-jacket. He never used to dress for dinner,' she added apologetically. 'He used to say, who was there to dress for and he felt more comfortable in his old . . . well, I suppose it was more what you call a smoking jacket. Very grubby but he wouldn't hear of it being cleaned. He said he liked the smell of it. I ask you!'

'May I see the piece of paper?'

'Yes. Now where did I put it?'

'It's on the table by your knitting,' Miss Venables reminded her sister.

'Of course! I'm getting so forgetful.' She disappeared and returned with a scrap of ruled paper. 'I thought it was odd at the time but the Inspector didn't seem interested. It's written on a piece of paper torn out of the General's wine book. He kept a careful record of everything. When he had bought it, when he had drunk it, whether he liked it or not. He called it his Bible.'

'I'd like to see it.'

'I think it's still in the house.'

'By the way, this may sound impertinent but do you know who inherited the General's estate?'

'I heard that he had left most of it to Miss Tiverton,' she said with another shrug of her shoulders.

Yes, Edward thought to himself, it was what she had wanted to be asked. Mrs Venables had expected her employer to leave his estate to her.

'I'm surprised he did not think to leave you anything for all your years of service,' he said mildly.

'That's exactly what I said.' Miss Venables nodded her head energetically.

Her sister said nothing, which was eloquence enough.

Edward examined the scrap of paper. 'And is this the General's handwriting?'

'Oh no,' she said with quiet certainty. 'I would know his hand anywhere and this isn't his.'

Edward looked at the paper and read: 'As flies to wanton boys they kill us for their sport.'

When he had finished reading the old housekeeper said, 'It's not Kipling. He loved Kipling.'

'No,' Edward agreed, 'it's not Kipling. It's from *King Lear*.'

'Shakespeare! It doesn't mention wine,' Mrs Venables said, sounding puzzled.

'But it mentions flies,' Edward said, grimly, 'and "flies" were what he was drinking when he died.'

'Bingo!' Edward said, placing the scrap of paper on Inspector Treacher's desk with, perhaps, tactless excitement. 'I think this proves that the General was murdered. We must ask Chief Inspector Pride to get his people to examine all three notes and see if they can confirm they were all written by the same person.'

81

Treacher rubbed his chin thoughtfully. It went against the grain but he had to admit that he ought to have made more of this note. When Mrs Venables had mentioned it to him, he had glanced at it dismissively and thrown it to one side. Now he knew he had been wrong and he was a big enough man to admit it.

'I congratulate you, Lord Edward. I seem not to have been thorough enough. You have got more from Mrs Venables than I expected. In the light of the other murders – if that's what we must now call them – we can see some sort of pattern emerging.'

'Yes, but what puzzles me is that General Lowther's wine was delivered by Justerini and Brooks – a highly respected wine merchant. We must find out what carrier they used but we should assume it wasn't interfered with until it reached the General's house.'

'And Mrs Venables said there had been no visitors to the house in the weeks before he died – no strangers, anyway,' the policeman went on. 'And since the note was found in the pocket of the General's smoking jacket, it must have been someone who knew him intimately.'

'Perhaps . . .'

'Could it have been Mrs Venables?' the Inspector suggested without much confidence. 'She might have discovered he hadn't left her any money.'

'I don't see it. She could not know that he had left it all to Miss Tiverton. Anyway, she had worked for him for so long, why wait until that day to kill him?'

'Perhaps she had suddenly discovered the General had made a new will. Maybe she had witnessed it.'

'Yes, that's a possibility, I suppose, though a witness would not have seen what was in the will.'

'But if you witness a will, you can't be a beneficiary,' the Inspector persisted. 'If she had been asked by him to witness what she thought was his will, she might have deduced that she would not inherit.'

Edward wasn't convinced but if Treacher wanted to follow up his hunch that was up to him. 'Well, Inspector, I'll leave that for you to follow up. I'll talk to Miss Tiverton and see what she's got to say.'

'Miss Tiverton – yes, I remember interviewing her all right. The village schoolmistress! She taught me nothing. Oh dear, Lord Edward, you are making me feel foolish.'

'Not at all, Inspector. I'm coming at it from a different angle, that's all. I'm starting with a presumption that the deaths were murders. You did not. There is another possibility as to how the Shakespeare quotation got into his pocket. Perhaps, when he went to London that last time, he met someone who gave it to him.'

'Someone gave it to him . . .' mused the Inspector, 'and he kept it because it meant something to him. He didn't necessarily see it as a threatening message . . .'

'It's a possibility – that's all we can say until we find out more.'

'I'll put together a complete list of everyone who could have been in or near the house in the weeks before the General died,' the Inspector offered. He looked at Edward anxiously. 'I suppose we ought to exhume his body to see if there is any trace of poison.'

'I'm afraid so, Inspector.' Edward was tempted to say something consoling along the lines of 'you shouldn't blame yourself', but decided it would sound patronizing. Anyway, damn it, it had been an inadequate investigation and the Inspector needed to face up to it.

'I should also officially reopen the investigation into Hermione Totteridge's death,' the Inspector added gloomily.

'I fear so. Might I suggest . . . a friend of mine, Charlotte Hassel, knew Miss Totteridge – she was a sort of honorary aunt to her when she was a child. She has offered to introduce me to her sister, Violet Booth. I gather she lives in Norfolk. I'd like to talk to her before there's any suggestion that the coroner's verdict might have to be challenged. Would that be all right with you?'

Treacher nodded his head. 'I'd be grateful for any help you can give me, Lord Edward. The fact is that I feel rather out of my depth. There seems to be a murderer on the loose in and around Henley and I have to confess that I've never had to investigate a murder in all my years in the force. Perhaps I should call in Scotland Yard. Chief Inspector Pride would, I don't doubt . . .'

'Yes,' Edward said hurriedly, 'we *will* need to brief him after I have seen Mrs Booth because I am quite sure his investigation into Eric Silver's death is linked to these murders. The quotations found on all four bodies can by no stretch of the imagination be coincidental.'

'If we assume that they were all left by the same person, do they tell us anything about our murderer?' Treacher asked, almost meekly.

'Apart from my family motto which was left on Silver's body, they're all quotations from Shakespeare. The General's is from *King Lear*, as I'm sure you know . . .' The Inspector nodded unconvincingly. 'Herold's is from *Hamlet* and the offering left on Hermione Totteridge is from Sonnet 146 – a particularly gloomy poem. Shakespeare urges us not to worry about earthly wealth when death is so close but, instead, concentrate on building up spiritual riches.'

'Can't argue with that, I suppose,' Treacher said morosely. 'But what message is the murderer sending us or are they just – how would you describe them? – taunts?'

'Hard to tell but, if they do mean anything, I would suggest that the General was being accused of killing someone quite wantonly – as flies are killed for sport by

84

little boys. Presumably, in the army, he must have been responsible for a number of deaths and that's something we need to look into. Miss Totteridge was told she was feeding on death and the only way to stop her was by killing her. There's no more death then, as the sonnet says.'

'Someone objected to her spraying poison on living things?' Treacher suggested.

Edward shrugged his shoulders. 'Possibly.'

'And Herold's "buzz, buzz",' Treacher continued, 'could mean, as I understand it, that someone thought he talked a lot of nonsense, like Hamlet thought Polonius talked nonsense. Could that be a reference to his political views? I gather he admired Sir Oswald Mosley.'

'A good thought, Inspector. Of course, it might just refer to his bees.'

Treacher sighed. 'And I thought they said dead men tell no tales! I'll borrow my wife's *Complete Works of Shakespeare* when I get home and think about it.'

'Do that, Inspector!' Edward said encouragingly.

Treacher shook his head sadly. 'I never had any doubt about Herold's death. We all took it for granted – even his widow – that he had more or less committed suicide by disturbing his bees and getting stung to death. He had been a prisoner of his bad heart for so long and, after the life he had lived, it seemed obvious that he couldn't stand it any more.'

'But – reading your notes – you don't appear to have asked how, in his condition, Herold managed to knock over several heavy hives. And, in any case, he died some fifty yards from the nearest one – or so I gather from your description of the scene.'

Treacher looked uneasy. 'If you want to know the truth, Lord Edward, I suspected his wife had helped him commit suicide and – perhaps wrongly – no, quite wrongly, I decided to let sleeping dogs lie. I thought there was no point in stirring things up.'

'Like the bees had been stirred up?'

The Inspector ignored his flippancy. 'What would it have meant if we had got Mrs Herold to confess that she had pushed over the hives? She would have gone to prison for a long time for helping her husband out of his misery. It just didn't seem right. It's not as though she's going to kill anyone else – if she did do it.'

'Yes, but what about the piece of paper on his body? Surely, that must have made you think someone else was involved? I mean, Mrs Herold found it. She would hardly have written it and then "found it" unless she were mad.'

'She's certainly not mad,' Treacher said unhappily. 'She's a good-looking woman with a clear idea of how she wants to live her life.'

'Why do you say that?'

'I had the impression she might have had a lover,' Treacher said, sounding almost ashamed.

'And you didn't investigate who he might have been?' Edward was genuinely aghast.

'I . . . I . . . I thought whoever helped Herold die had done him a favour. I was wrong. I know that now. I suppose I knew it at the time but I . . .' He fell silent.

Edward sighed. 'Well, with your permission . . .' he tried not to sound sarcastic, 'I'll go and talk to Mrs Herold and "stir things up". After all, her husband may have wanted to give up this mortal coil but, if the same person who helped him die also helped Hermione Totteridge and General Lowther to their deaths, then we have a multiple killer on our hands.' And I may be next on his list, he thought but did not say.

Treacher pulled himself together with an effort. 'The man who killed these people is intelligent and well read.'

'Reasonably well read,' Edward corrected him. 'All you'd need is a book of quotations. The quotations from Shakespeare – except perhaps the sonnet – are very well known, bordering on the obvious.'

Treacher nodded his head, trying not to feel that his education had been lacking something. 'I suppose we can assume the murderer is a man?'

'I think so, Inspector. I can't believe a woman would be strong enough to kill Eric Silver.'

'Nor sadistic enough.'

'Women can be sadistic but I agree that it's much less likely a woman would do something so horrible. Of course, the other three deaths might have been the work of a woman. They say poison is a woman's weapon but my instinct says a man did all this. He's a cold-blooded killer who carefully planned what he thinks are perfect murders. Forgive me for saying this – I don't mean to sound arrogant – but I can't help feeling the killer was annoyed that the . . .' he tried to think of a tactful way of putting it, 'the initial investigations dismissed the deaths as accidents. He killed Mr Silver and left me a note telling me to take up the investigation.'

'If you are right, then your life is in danger.'

'I am aware of it, Inspector. And what is more, I believe the murderer will make himself known to me.'

'How do you mean?'

'I think he will want to watch me at work. He'll want to tease me and I am hoping that, in doing so, he will give himself away.'

5

Leonard Bladon had been warned that he faced a challenge when he took Verity into his clinic. To put it crudely, most of his patients were too ill to do more than lie on their beds or, when the weather was as warm as it was now, relax on the long chairs in the garden soaking up the sunshine. Verity was unable to stay still for more than a few minutes at a time. The sight of patients iller than she made her depressed and angry. She would not be one of those etiolated wrecks – that she swore. She read quite a lot. Mrs Woolf had delivered on her promise and sent her a pile of books. She and her husband, Leonard, ran the Hogarth Press which published books about social issues as well as poetry and fiction. Verity was particularly interested in one book they had published the year before called *The Roots of War* in which some of the great and the good explained how Britain had come to this pass and berated the Prime Minister for his policy of appeasing Hitler. Verity thought wryly that their complaints came rather late in the day.

Her friends visited her but she suspected – probably unfairly – that they must resent having to travel out of London to see her and that she was being a bore. She hated to be in anyone's debt but, paradoxically, would have been downcast if her friends had not made the effort to visit her. When they arrived they made a point of kissing her on the cheek to show they weren't afraid of 'catching anything nasty'. They talked too loudly and told her she looked well and forecast brightly that she would be 'out of here in a week or two'. In short, they tried too hard. Their conversation sounded rehearsed and, since she herself hated hospitals, Verity knew, or thought she knew, precisely what they were thinking and feeling. She was grateful that they had come but glad when they went – all except Edward who provided her with a lifeline to the normal world from which she had had to withdraw.

She was more at her ease with her room-mates who, being in the same predicament, could not pity her. They complained about the food together and fantasized about Dr Bladon's love life like silly schoolgirls. There was something about being in this sort of place – so like a boarding school – which infantilized them. Everything was done for you and your only responsibility was to rest and get well. Jill Torrance, the student nurse, seemed very much in awe of her room-mates. 'Oh dear! I feel so ignorant beside you two,' she giggled nervously. Shyly, she asked about Verity's travels and listened open-mouthed to her stories – only slightly embellished – of ducking bullets and seeing men killed all around her. Verity lectured Mary Black on the evils of the class system and the social inequalities which left children to grow up stunted and sickly in loathsome slums while people like themselves lounged about in country houses waited on hand and foot. She expatiated on the failures of Chamberlain's government to stand up to Hitler and was surprised and perplexed when Mary forcefully disagreed with her.

After one such debate, Mary told her tartly that she would shortly have the opportunity of telling her father what she thought of his party's foreign policy as he was coming down to see her on Saturday. He was a widower, Verity knew. Mary's mother had died two years ago. 'I'm glad she never had to see me like this,' she had said when Verity had commiserated with her.

When the day of Mr Black's visit came, Verity rather annoyed herself by finding that she was taking unusual care with her appearance. Why should she want to impress her friend's father? He was just one of those largely silent, and no doubt ignorant, backbench Conservative MPs who were wheeled into the lobby to vote for the government whenever Mr Chamberlain decreed. It was another in a string of perfect English summer days with the temperature in the seventies. How long this 'heat wave', as the papers were calling it, would last no one could say but Dr Bladon urged all his patients to make the most of it. He strongly believed in the healing powers of the sun's rays and it was certainly true that Verity was regaining her strength and putting on weight.

They were waiting in the garden for Mr Black to arrive when the conversation turned to death. One of the patients had succumbed to his illness – quite unexpectedly – earlier in the week and everyone had been made uncomfortably aware of their own mortality.

'I've never seen a dead body, you know,' Jill said mournfully. 'I don't think I can call myself a nurse until I've looked death in the face, do you?'

'Oh, I don't know,' Verity replied airily. 'Death isn't so very awful. I'm not afraid of it.' She stuck out her chin. She *was* afraid of dying wretchedly of a disease she had never given a thought to before it was diagnosed but she wasn't going to admit it in front of Mary and Jill. 'Messy sometimes, or stupid . . . but then so is life.'

'Stupid? I want to die beautifully – like Violetta, La Dame aux Camélias.' Jill acted out a theatrical swoon.

'Yes, stupid,' Verity insisted. 'People don't look beautiful or dignified in death – or not the ones I remember seeing. Their jaws hang open and the skin looks . . . looks like . . .' she searched for the right words, 'white or yellow rubber. No, that's not right, more like that awful Formica in the passage.'

Mary Black said, 'I saw a dead body once – in Africa, when I was little. He was a black man so perhaps it doesn't count.'

'What on earth do you mean?' Verity said angrily. 'Why shouldn't it count? What does it matter what colour we are?'

Mary looked puzzled. 'Of course it matters. You wouldn't marry a . . .'

'I would if I was in love. Some of the Algerians I saw in Spain were magnificent savages . . .' She stopped, wondering if this was the right way to talk of the men who had fought against the Republic with such courage and cruelty. 'Well, anyway, they were mostly on the other side so I didn't get to meet many of them.' She added after a pause, 'I didn't know you had been in Africa, Mary?'

'No reason why you should. I was born in Kenya but my mother died when I was ten and my father brought me back to England to be educated.'

'So who was the black man you saw dead? Do tell!' Jill insisted.

Mary's face clouded. 'It wasn't very nice but that's the way it was then. I didn't understand it – I was only a child. They said it was a hunt but I realize now that it was more of a lynching. It was beastly and I've never managed to forget it though I've tried. He can't have been more than eighteen or nineteen though he seemed grown-up to me then. He'd been accused of . . . I don't know – not raping but "interfering", I think they called it, with a white girl about the age I was then – or maybe a year or two older. I've no idea if it were true or not but the white boys hunted him down. He ran for our house because I think my father had a reputation for being just. I remember hearing him banging on the front door. I'll never forget the sound. Unfortunately, my father wasn't at home and our houseboy wouldn't open the door. There was only me and my mother in the house so I expect he made the right decision.'

'So what happened?' Verity demanded.

'They cornered him as he tried to get into the house. Four of them grabbed him and took him on to our front lawn and beat him to death with sjamboks.'

There was a horrified pause and then Jill asked, 'What's a sjambok?'

'It's a kind of whip they use on the cattle, made of rhinoceros hide.'

'They whipped him to death?' Jill whispered.

'And you saw it?' Verity asked disbelievingly.

'My bedroom overlooked the front porch. I saw *everything*.'

There was something almost voyeuristic about the story which made Verity uncomfortable. It was horrible enough but it seemed to her that Mary had enjoyed telling it, or at least seeing the effect it had on her audience.

At that moment they heard the solid clunk of an expensive car door closing and Dr Bladon appeared with Mr Black – a good-looking man in his early sixties who wore an air of authority like a familiar cloak he put over his shoulders whenever he went out. He walked with the swagger of a man of the world that made even Bladon appear smaller and less significant.

He kissed his daughter on the cheek and Bladon introduced him to Verity and Jill.

'Miss Browne, I am delighted to meet you,' he said in a gruff but rather attractive growl as he shook her hand. 'I have heard so much about you. The *New Gazette* is a much duller read without your dispatches from the front.'

Verity desperately wanted to dislike this man who represented so much she abhorred in English political life but found herself, to her annoyance, enjoying his flattery. She tried to remind herself that this was the way the upper classes always disarmed their enemies – by taking them to their bosom. Look at Ramsay MacDonald, the first Labour Prime Minister. Duchesses had him fawning on them before he had been in office a week, and the Irish patriot, Michael Collins, was made to look a fool in exactly the same way. He had come to London in 1920 hating all things British and ended up the lapdog of the ruling class and the lover of the wife of one of them. She told herself she must be resolute in defence of her principles. Her friend David Griffiths-Jones, a senior member of the Communist Party, had told her she could mix with the aristocracy as much as she liked as long as she remembered they were the enemy. And Mr Black wasn't even an aristocrat!

'Mary, dear,' her father continued, 'I thought we might go on the river as it's so clement. Would your friends like to come with us? That would be all right, wouldn't it, Bladon?'

'So long as you aren't too long. In fact, I think the fresh air would do them good.'

Jill refused as she was feeling too weak but Verity – happy to have a distraction – accepted the invitation. Mr Black's chauffeur touched his hat and opened the door of the Bentley. As they slid silently away, Verity felt a surge of gratitude to this man whatever his politics. Mary and she were lepers, rightly shunned as carriers of disease and possibly death. To come across someone who seemed unafraid of being tainted was a shot in the arm for her self-confidence. She felt that she might, after all, one day rejoin the human race.

It seemed Mr Black had been so confident of his invitation being accepted that he had already organized a motor launch to take them upriver. When Verity jokingly said something to this effect, he informed her that he owned it. 'I use it a good deal in the summer, particularly when coaching my son Guy,' he explained. 'He's a mad keen rower, as I was in my day.'

The *Henley Hornet* was a substantial craft with a small enclosed cabin and a more powerful engine than most of its kind. The chauffeur, after helping them aboard, passed to his master a picnic basket, several rugs and a cold box which rattled pleasantly as it was set down beside Mary. He then saluted respectfully and withdrew.

'Would you ladies like to go below and rest or do you prefer it here on deck?' Mr Black asked. He indicated several comfortable-looking basket chairs. They both said they wanted to stay on deck and watch the watery world go by.

He cast off and expertly steered the *Hornet* into midstream. Verity lay back on the cushioned chair to soak up the sun and relax.

'This is so kind of you,' she murmured but Mr Black, intent on avoiding the many small craft wandering this way and that, ignoring the rule of the river to keep to the right, did not hear her. Verity's eyes closed and she slept. It annoyed her that, though she did not sleep much at night, during the day and particularly if she were relaxed, she would drop off to sleep at odd moments. Dr Bladon said it was all part of the healing process, and perhaps it was, but she never liked to be caught napping.

She woke up with a start, unsure if she had slept for a few seconds or an hour. Mary was awake, trailing her hand in the water. Her father was still at the wheel, looking rather grim-faced for a pleasure outing. Perhaps, she thought, he was worrying about his daughter's health.

'Where are we going?' she asked idly, sitting up straight.

'Maidenhead. Not far now. It's the house of a friend of mine. He's invited us to have our picnic in his garden.'

Verity did not reply but her peace of mind was disturbed by a feeling of unease. What was she doing on this rich man's boat? Why had Mr Black invited her? He must know she was his natural enemy. Was it pure kindness or was there something behind it? But why should there be? She was being absurd. What possible interest could he have in her?

A few minutes later, he waved to a man on the river bank and expertly brought the boat alongside a low brick wall into which steps had been cut. After he had helped the two girls out of the boat, he introduced them. 'Jack, this is my daughter Mary.'

'Mary! Of course I remember you. We met in London last year. I was so sorry to hear you had been ill, but you're looking well.'

'Thank you, Mr Amery. I am feeling better but I'm still rather weak. I hope you will forgive us if we don't rush around too much.'

'Of course, my dear, and this is . . .?' He put out his hand.

'This is the celebrated Verity Browne. She shares a room at Bladon's place with Mary. Do you know each other?'

Amery withdrew his hand and looked first at Mr Black and then at Verity, as though wanting to know what joke was being played on him. Whether Black was being mischievous or whether he really didn't know that Jack Amery was a fervid supporter of Franco and the rebels in Spain while she was a noisy supporter of the Republic, Verity could not say, but here she was, a guest of one of the men she and her friends most excoriated. She was taken by surprise and had no idea how to react. One thing was certain, she was not going to shake his hand.

'Verity Browne!' She saw that Amery was as taken aback as she was and acquitted him of being complicit in Black's little joke, if that was what it was. She was sure he had had no idea of her identity until he heard her name. He pulled himself together, saying 'I fear, old chap, that you have dropped a bit of a clanger. Miss Browne and I do not see eye to eye on Spain, and on much else, I suspect.'

'Oh, but that's rubbish, Jack. I insist on you knowing Miss Browne. She won't bite.'

Amery seemed less than sure about this and, to Verity's relief, said, 'I say, if the ladies will forgive us, I'd like to have a word with you in the house.'

'Is Una at home?' Black inquired.

'No, I'm afraid not,' he replied shortly.

'Mary, lay out the picnic, will you? We won't be long.'

Verity's heart was beating fast. How could she break bread with this Fascist arms dealer? She could wear a mask of courtesy when talking to people whose views she violently disagreed with but this man was disgusting. She forced herself to admit that Amery probably thought the same of her. She wondered if he would make some excuse not to return to share their picnic. The trouble was she could not escape. She had no money with her even if she had had the strength to walk somewhere to summon a taxi. She looked at the river but, perversely, it was suddenly empty. But what a wild idea even to think of hailing a passing launch to take her back to the clinic, as though she was in Piccadilly Circus hailing a taxi. No, she must wait and hope that Amery would do the decent thing.

'Mary, is your father an old friend of Mr Amery's?'

'I have never heard him say so. Take the strawberries, will you? His father is a great friend.'

'Leo Amery – the MP?'

Oddly enough, Edward had been talking to her about him the previous day and had mentioned his meeting with Jack at Turton House. He had been far from sure about Leo Amery. He said Churchill had called him the 'straightest man in public life' and congratulated him on a speech he had made in the House of Commons at the time of the Abyssinian crisis castigating the Prime Minister for his pusillanimous stand against Mussolini's naked greed. The Italian dictator had been able to seize Ethiopia for his shoddy new empire without serious opposition. On the other hand, two or three years earlier Amery had returned from a visit to Hitler calling him 'a bigger man' than he had expected and talking of 'the fundamental similarity of many of our views'.

Jack was a constant source of embarrassment to his father and Edward had said that he admired Amery for his loyalty to his boy whatever scrapes he got into. He had gone on to ponder how it was that so many good men in public life – even Winston Churchill and Stanley Baldwin – had unsatisfactory sons who caused their fathers much heartache. Perhaps, Verity had suggested, it was impossible to be devoted to politics and still make time for family life. Edward had wondered if she was alluding to her own reluctance to marry and have children.

To Verity's immense relief, Mr Black came back on his own, carrying a Gladstone bag which he tossed in the launch before joining them on the grass.

'I do apologize, Miss Browne. I had forgotten until Jack reminded me that you and he are on different sides when it comes to the war in Spain. He thought it better not to accept my invitation to share our picnic. It's a sad thing that events in foreign countries can cause such wide divisions in our society.'

'We have to stand up for what we think is right,' was all Verity would say, not wishing to be rude, preferring to sound self-righteous.

He seemed rather to enjoy arguing with her and they batted between each other their views on all the main issues of the day, almost always disagreeing but neither of them becoming angry. Mary, too, quietly made her opinions known and sharply rebuked her father when he started praising Sir Oswald Mosley and the British Union of Fascists.

By three o'clock, seeing that Mary and Verity were tiring, Mr Black gathered up the detritus from the picnic and flung it into the boat. He helped them aboard and took them back to Henley. Nothing much was said on the return journey and, once again, Verity fell asleep in her comfortable chair. She awoke as the *Hornet* bumped against her mooring to find that the chauffeur was preparing to help them disembark. The Gladstone bag was gone – no doubt already in the car – and Verity wondered idly what Jack Amery had given her host. It must have been something bulky but she had not thought it polite to ask.

Back at the clinic, she thanked Mr Black for a delightful day out.

'I hope I didn't tire you.'

'I am tired,' she admitted, 'but nicely tired. I am sure the sunshine and the river did me good. It was very kind of you to invite me. I hope I didn't intrude.'

'Not at all. When you are better, you must let me give you lunch at the House. I really think I might convert you.'

Verity smiled weakly. 'I am afraid that would be too hard a job, Mr Black, even for you . . .'

'Please call me Roderick.'

'Well, I was just going to say . . .' she could not bring herself to use his Christian name so she called him nothing, 'that, though we profoundly disagree on so many things, I very much enjoyed debating them with you. I feel so isolated here and it always helps to think things through if one can discuss them with someone who doesn't agree with you.' Changing the subject, she asked, 'I wonder where Jill is?'

At that moment, Dr Bladon entered the room without knocking. 'Not too exhausted, I trust? I'm afraid I have some bad news about Jill. She was taken ill while you were out and has had to go into hospital. I hope she will be back with us soon.'

Though he spoke confidently enough, Verity got the feeling that he did not believe it and her spirits, which had been lifted by the day on the river, fell into her boots. Selfishly, perhaps, her immediate thought was, 'Is that what will happen to me? Will I be rushed into hospital at death's door?'

No, she decided. That would *not* be her fate. She would get better. She had so much to do and the world was so interesting. She would fight not to lose it.

6

Mrs Booth, Hermione Totteridge's sister, lived in Burnham Market in a pleasant house called Boltons which was – as her husband later told him – of some historical interest: Horatia, Nelson's daughter, had been married from there. The church was just a few hundred yards away and Edward strolled across the street. The church door was unlocked and he entered the cool interior. He picked up a booklet which gave him some information about its history. The fourteenth-century tower with its battlemented parapet was its chief glory but was spoiled by two huge brick buttresses added in the 1740s when it was feared that the tower was about to collapse. A well-meaning Victorian architect had destroyed much of the original medieval interior although the seventeenth-century bells remained. Edward could well imagine the daughter of England's greatest hero entering married life down St Mary's long aisle.

In the churchyard he leant against one of the tombs and lit a cigarette. These Norfolk churches were surely one of England's chief glories but he wondered how long they could survive as the population dwindled. Year after year more and more people left the land, their arduous labour no longer required when the ploughing and reaping could be done so much more cheaply and quickly by modern behemoths. The

Blythe family monument, for instance, against which he was resting, was unlikely to remain the repository of twentieth-century Blythe bones for very much longer as they lived and died in cities far from the origin of their tribe.

Yet he would not say, glibly, that this was England 'going to the dogs' – as he knew his father would have termed it – because in previous centuries the agricultural labourer had lived a short and wretched life racked by rheumatism from damp and cold, the East Anglian wind cutting him to the bone for most of the year. Life was short when poverty, ignorance and inbreeding took their toll. The cottages he saw – so picturesque in the sunshine and now being renovated and suburbanized – had been, until the end of the Great War, insanitary sties, hardly fit for animals. He chuckled as he realized that his way of thinking could be put down entirely to Verity's lectures on the evils of capitalism. She always claimed that, although the city slums were a disgrace to a prosperous and so-called civilized society, rural poverty was in many ways more deeply ingrained and ruined more lives.

Just as he was about to throw away his cigarette and leave, he was hailed by a good-looking, cheerful fellow wearing a dog-collar whom he took to be the rector.

'Admiring our fine church?'

'Indeed, though I was also wondering how it could be maintained when congregations are declining and the cost of replacing the roof is now beyond the purse of most of us. But it is a magnificent church,' Edward added hastily, fearing he had sounded sententious. 'No doubt God or the government will provide.'

'We must hope so. By the way, my name is Joyce – John Joyce.'

'Edward Corinth,' he responded, shaking hands.

'I encourage myself,' Joyce went on, 'by remembering

that during the Black Death most of the population was wiped out and there were four inductions. In other words, the shepherd died with his flock but somehow some survived and even prospered. That tomb you were leaning on is a case in point. It belongs, as you probably observed, to a local family, the Blythes, who have been buried here generation after generation. You will find similar tombs for the Hammonds, the Ives, the Spencers and many others. And inside the church there is a brass on the north wall portraying a lady with three of her children. The inscription tells us that it was dedicated to John Huntley and bears the date 1523.'

'Yes, and, to judge from the number of gravestones set up just after the war, the 1918 flu epidemic took almost as great a toll as the Black Death.'

'Indeed, indeed!' sighed the rector.

'Our history – the history of the English people – is recorded in these churches, Rector, and that's one of the reasons why they should be preserved and nurtured.'

The rector looked surprised at the stranger's eloquence and Edward, realizing that he might have sounded pretentious, hurried on. 'But tell me, are the current owners of Boltons churchgoers?'

'They are, I am glad to say. Why, do you know our good doctor?'

'I am about to call on Dr Booth,' Edward replied, evasively. 'He's been here a long time?'

'Yes, indeed. All his life. When we talk about "the doctor" round here, we mean Booth.'

When the rector had said his farewells, Edward strolled around the churchyard. He noticed several gravestones bearing the name Booth, one dating back to 1680. As he scraped off the lichen to read the inscription, he wondered why the Booths appeared to have no family tomb. Perhaps they had simply not been rich enough.

Dr Booth proved to be a mild-mannered man in, Edward judged, his late sixties. His interest in local history and Nelson in particular was obviously important to him but he was careful not to bore his visitor.

'I suppose it's living in this house and being so near to the sea,' he said apologetically, 'but the older I get, the more I enjoy researching the history of this place – Boltons in particular. You see, my family has lived in the house for almost three centuries. That is really rather remarkable, is it not?'

'It is. I met the rector in the churchyard and he told me how well respected you are here. He said that when people talk about "getting in the doctor" they mean you.'

'That is very kind of him to say so. It's true that I have given my life to looking after the sick here but that is nothing to what Burnham Market has given me. To put it simply, it is my world and if, God forbid, we go to war again, I shall "do my bit", as we used to say in the last conflagration, for England, and by England I'm afraid I shall mean this little piece of it.'

'Were you in the army in the war? I was just too young, thank the Lord.'

'And I was too old to go to the front but we had our bad times here – the Spanish flu in 1918 and 1919 . . .' He shook his head. 'We were burying people who had succumbed to it as late as 1920. We came to the conclusion it was brought to Burnham Market by soldiers returning home after the war.'

'I noticed that when I was strolling round the church-yard,' Edward said. 'Talking of which, I saw a gravestone for a young man called Peter Lamming. I knew a Peter Lamming when I was in Kenya. I wonder if it could possibly be the same one.'

'I imagine it was, Lord Edward. How very strange! He was a nephew by marriage of my dear wife. He was married to Daphne's daughter, Isabella. He died of . . .' He hesitated. 'He died four years ago and was buried there.'

'So the stone is not above a grave? That's most unusual, surely?'

'Alas! It is above a grave but not his.' Dr Booth spread his hands in a graphic expression of despair. 'Isabella came back to live with us after Peter died. She insisted on erecting a memorial to him – somewhere for her to lay flowers and remember him. The rector was most understanding.'

'So Daphne was your wife's sister?'

'Did I not say so? Yes, there were three sisters. Daphne was the oldest, then Hermione and then Violet, my wife. Daphne and her husband – he was in the army in India – died in a car crash when Isabella was five and we brought her up. We loved her as though she was our own child. She was a great joy to us as . . .' He hesitated but obviously decided that he had gone too far to stop. 'You see, we found – Violet and I – that we could have no children of our own.'

'But you said Peter's tombstone is a grave?' Edward wrinkled his brow.

'You may well look puzzled, Lord Edward.' He sighed heavily. 'Izzy, as we called her, died just a year ago and we buried her where she would have wanted. We are waiting to have her name engraved below Peter's on the stone.'

'She died of . . .? Forgive me! I do not wish to intrude on your grief.'

'No, that's all right, Lord Edward. The truth is that it's a relief to talk about it. Violet won't. In fact, she cannot even bring herself to commission the lettering on the stone. It's as though Izzy cannot really be dead until her name appears below Peter's.'

Edward nodded his head sympathetically. 'Was it . . . an accident?'

'She became ill and I'm afraid I did not take it seriously enough. Her appendix ruptured and she died before I could get her to hospital.'

'I'm so sorry. What a tragedy! I remember Peter well. He was a very nice boy. You are sure I haven't upset you? It must be very painful for you . . .'

'No, no, Lord Edward. As I told you, I don't mind talking about it. I find it eases my heart but please don't mention anything of what I have told you to Violet unless she raises it herself.'

'I won't, of course.'

'Death may have no dominion over the departed, as the Prayer Book tells us, but sometimes it seems to have over the living. I gather from Charlotte's letter that you want to talk to my wife about poor Hermione. Another tragedy! Such a dreadful business. Violet was very distressed.'

'Were they close?'

'Not close exactly but they got on well enough. They had a shared interest.'

'Gardening?'

'Yes. Although, as Violet is the first to admit, she was never in Hermione's class. Anyway, I'll take you to her. I have my rounds to do. I expect you will be gone before I'm through so I'll say goodbye. What a coincidence you having met Peter in Kenya and knowing little Lottie so well – though I suppose she isn't so little now. I'm afraid we haven't seen her for a long time.'

They walked across the lawn towards a kneeling figure. 'Violet, my dear, here is Lord Edward Corinth.' Dr Booth put out his hand and Edward took it. For a moment, he thought he saw a warning of some kind in his eyes but decided it must have been his imagination. The doctor smiled. 'I'll leave you two to chat. Goodbye again, Lord Edward. I am so pleased to have met you.'

As she struggled to her feet – she had been on her knees weeding the border – Edward saw that Violet Booth was a handsome, stocky woman who in her youth might have been beautiful. She had strong bones and a firm chin. He thought she would not be someone to cross but her greeting was friendly enough, if somewhat gruff. When he complimented her on her garden – the border was full of interesting-looking plants – she softened and pointed out a few of which she was particularly proud. He praised her gardening skills and compared her to her sister but she strongly denied being in the same class, as her husband had predicted.

'Oh, no, Lord Edward. Hermione is . . . was the gardener in the family. Even as a small child, she had her own patch which she called her allotment or rather, since she could not manage the word, her "lotment".'

They went into the house where Mrs Booth took off her gardening apron and straw hat and washed her hands under the kitchen tap. There was no servant in evidence and she seemed unembarrassed at letting Edward follow her into the kitchen. He wondered if it was some sort of test.

'You have come a long way for a cup of tea,' she said, filling a utilitarian brown teapot from the ancient-looking kettle simmering on the Aga. Edward put her down as one of those women who prided themselves on their no-nonsense approach to life. He could imagine her saying, 'I don't stand on ceremony,' but instead she asked, 'So you are a friend of Charlotte's?'

Edward spoke warmly of the Hassels, and Mrs Booth allowed herself to say that she had always liked Charlotte but could not abide her books.

'I know she is very clever but I can't understand them. I prefer Dorothy Whipple. Have you read *Greenbanks*?'

'Perhaps having known the author as a child makes it difficult to read her as objectively you would a stranger,' Edward ventured.

'Maybe, but I blame it all on that Mrs Woolf. I bought one of hers – *Mrs Dalloway*, I think it was called. I couldn't get past page thirty. Gibberish! And now everyone has to write like that.'

They went into the drawing-room, a light, attractive room with a good view of the garden. 'Sugar?' she inquired, as though he would be judged on his response.

'No, thank you.' Edward cleared his throat. 'I think Charlotte will have mentioned why I wanted to talk to you.'

'You think my sister was deliberately poisoned?' she said forcefully but, underneath the bravado, he could see that she was upset.

'I'm afraid I do. I don't want you to think I'm muckraking. I believe there's a dangerous man at large who has killed at least two other people in addition to your sister. And he has to be stopped.'

'You're sure?'

'Didn't you think it odd when you found that piece of paper in the pocket of her boiler suit?'

'The one with . . .?'

'Yes.'

'I did think it odd but . . .'

'I know – it's a big leap from finding that quotation to thinking someone murdered her, and it might be best if I tell you why I have come to that conclusion.'

He recounted the whole story of his dentist's murder and the link with the deaths of General Lowther and James Herold. She listened without interrupting.

'I see what you mean,' she said thoughtfully.

'Was there nothing that puzzled you when you were cleaning out your sister's house? By the way, what is happening to it? The garden's famous. Is someone going to take it on?'

Mrs Booth shrugged her shoulders. 'What can I do? We can't afford to keep up two houses and my husband's work is here. He has been the local doctor for . . . ever since he qualified. His whole life is here. This is his family's house, where he grew up. We couldn't move and, to be frank, we would be very grateful for the money from the sale of her house. A place like this is expensive to keep up.'

'Has your husband always lived here? I mean, presumably he trained in London.'

'Yes, at Guy's.'

'And university?'

'Alfred didn't go to university and, before you ask, he was educated in Burnham Market. The Booths were an old family but never rich. Why are you interested?'

'Sorry, I was being nosy – a bad habit of mine. May I ask . . .? Your husband mentioned that there were three of you . . . three sisters.'

'Yes. Daphne died many years ago with her husband – in a motor accident.'

'They were in India, your husband said?'

'Yes, but the accident occurred when they were back in England on leave – outside Godalming. Fortunately, Isabella was not with them. So that just leaves me – the youngest. Does that make me a suspect?' She attempted a smile but it faded into a grimace of pain.

Edward was non-committal. He wondered why she had thought to give the exact location of Daphne's fatal accident. It was as though she wanted him to know every last detail – as though she was punishing herself.

'Isabella was where?'

'They had rented a house near Smithfield in the City – Cripplegate. Isabella was there with her nanny.'

'And you can't think of anything curious . . .?' he persisted.

Mrs Booth held up her hand almost as though she was warding him off. 'Just let me think for a moment.' She wrinkled up her eyes as she thought back. 'I really can't remember anything odd,' she said finally. Edward leaned back in his chair, disappointed. 'No, wait! I noticed that Hermione had been looking at her photograph albums. They were all spread out on the table. I would never have thought of my sister as nostalgic. If she went to her albums, it must have been for some reason – not just idle retrospection.'

'Have you got the albums here?'

'Yes. I didn't know what to do with them. I couldn't sell them and I couldn't destroy them.'

'May I see them?'

'Of course. They're in one of the outhouses with the rest of my sister's belongings.'

Mrs Booth took Edward to the outhouse – little more than a shed – and they looked gloomily at the pile of odds and ends she had not liked to sell or burn. He was inclined to wax philosophical about how little was left from a long life but changed his mind. Hermione Totteridge's true legacy was her garden and the books she had written.

'Some people compared her to Gertrude Jekyll,' her sister said, as if he had voiced his thoughts, 'but that's wrong. Jekyll was a garden designer. My sister was more interested in the science of gardening. She knew so much about the way plants work. She discovered several new species and bred literally hundreds of new plants. In the end, I believe her work was more important than Jekyll's but of course I'm prejudiced.'

'You admired her a great deal?'

'I did but I won't pretend she was easy. It's no surprise that she never found a man who could live with her. There was an authoritarian streak in her which could be . . .' Mrs Booth hesitated before settling for 'off-putting'. She pointed to an old tin trunk. 'I put the albums in there.'

'May I take it into the house?'

'If you want to but I don't understand why . . .'

'Nor do I,' Edward replied, lifting the trunk and finding it heavier than he had expected. 'But if we can find . . .' He grunted. 'How many albums are there?'

'Seven or eight.'

In the kitchen, Mrs Booth opened the trunk and took out seven battered morocco-bound albums.

'Can you remember if your sister had been looking at one in particular?'

'No, I don't recall any of them being open. I looked through one or two myself. I confess, I'm not a sentimental person but, now both my sisters are dead, I had to weep a little when I found a photograph of our parents. Looking at it, it suddenly struck me there's no one else alive now who remembers them or me when I was a child. Oh dear! You must think I'm being very maudlin.'

'Was your sister a keen photographer?'

'She liked photographing her garden – keeping a record. She was given a box Brownie – one of the early ones – when she must have been about seventeen. She was very proud of it and took to photographing all of us.'

'Where you were brought up?'

'In Kenya, but I was the only one who was born there. My father was a farmer and he took advantage of a government offer of assisted passage to Africa and the promise of free land for would-be farmers. Despite having a sickly wife and two small children, he decided to take the risk. He ended up trying to create a farm out of uncleared bush – back-breaking work. I was born a year

110

after they arrived. I must have been an "accident" and doubt I was very welcome as it was difficult enough to feed two children but, if that's what they felt, they never showed it. In many ways it was a paradise for children. Not for adults, though. We were too young to know about it but it was terribly hard for my parents. Mother got sick and died – a mosquito gave her malaria and we didn't have quinine. My father struggled on but eventually the farm failed and he died of what I suppose the Victorians would have called a broken heart. It was particularly hard on Daphne. As the eldest she had to take on Mother's role and look after Hermione and me, at least until my father died.'

'What happened then?'

'We were taken in by a nice old couple called Cunningham – it was they who gave Hermione the camera – and we all decamped to England.'

'When was this?'

'1874 when I was ten and Hermione was fifteen and promising to be a beauty. Daphne was seventeen and mad about boys. I remember hating England. It was gloomy and so cold after Africa and we had to go to boarding school. We hated it. Daphne and I both got married but Hermione became . . . well, I'd almost say obsessed with gardening. She had caught the bug early. We'd all got interested in gardening as children in Kenya. It was a wonderful place to grow plants. There were diseases, of course, and Hermione was always trying to find ways to keep her crop healthy. We mainly grew vegetables. Our parents encouraged us to help the family economy. I was made responsible for some chickens, I remember. How I loathed them! Anyway, Hermione got keen on the science of it all.'

'She didn't get distracted by men?'

'I don't know,' Mrs Booth replied, uncertainly. 'There weren't many for her to get keen on, at least not in

Africa. I think there was a young man in England but nothing came of it as far as I know.'

'And Daphne?'

'Well, as I said, we both got married about the same time. I didn't have children but she did. Just the one – Isabella.' She was clearly unhappy at having to recall what happened next.

'Your husband told me,' Edward said gently. 'You brought her up after your sister died . . .'

'Yes,' she said abruptly, obviously not wishing to discuss it. 'Then Isabella went to Kenya – she said she wanted to see where her mother had been brought up and visit her grandparents' grave.'

'And she fell in love out there?'

'Yes. She married a young man called Peter Lamming but he died shortly afterwards. We never even met him.'

'I was telling your husband,' Edward said hesitantly, 'that I knew Peter in Kenya. Until I saw his grave this afternoon I had no idea he was dead.'

Mrs Booth looked at him with renewed interest. 'You knew Peter?'

'Not well, but I liked what I saw of him. I must have left Kenya before your niece arrived.'

'Africa's a cruel country, Lord Edward. My husband will have told you . . .?'

'He did,' he said gently. 'And then your niece came back to England to live with you?'

'Yes, but she was never happy again. Her grief was . . . was shocking. Most people fight their way through grief but Izzy could not manage it.' She looked at Edward challengingly.

'She died of a burst appendix, your husband said.' He saw her expression. 'Forgive me. I did not mean to . . .'

She looked at him, her eyes fierce, wet with tears. 'I would once have said that it was sentimental hogwash to talk of dying of love but that's what Izzy did. She died of grief for her lost love. The appendix . . . that was just what she chose to die of.'

'I am very sorry,' he said gravely. 'Can I just go back to when you were children? After your father and mother died, you said you all came back to England with the Cunninghams?'

'Yes, they were very good to us and adopted us like the true Christians they were. They had no family of their own. When they died they left Hermione enough money to buy her house in Henley and start her garden business . . . I don't know why I'm telling you all this. I can't think it's . . .'

'Any of my business?'

'Relevant to Hermione's death.'

'Probably not, but you never know . . .'

Mrs Booth was sorting through the albums. 'This must be her most recent one. That's Izzy . . .'

Edward took it and looked at the photograph. 'She was very pretty.'

'She was, wasn't she?'

He began to turn the pages but stopped and went back a page or two. 'That's funny. Do you see? A photograph has been torn out.'

'So it has,' she agreed. 'I wonder why Hermione did that?'

'I don't think she did,' Edward said grimly. 'I think it was her murderer.'

Edward returned to London feeling that his journey had not been wasted. Mrs Booth had given him the names of her sister's two maids, her cook and her two gardeners who, she said, would have seen and challenged any strangers prowling around the house. They were fiercely protective of their mistress, she told him, and would certainly know if anything peculiar had happened in the weeks before she died.

It was strange being back in town after his time in Henley. He found he had rather missed the urban bustle and the familiar places of his London life – his flat in Albany, his club, Piccadilly, Jermyn Street, Bond Street. He noticed that, since Anthony Eden's resignation and subsequent fall from grace, men had given up black Homburgs – which had become known as 'Edens' because the Foreign Secretary always wore one and anything he wore was regarded as the height of fashion – and gone back to wearing 'bowlers'.

As the crowd streamed past him, he thought how narrow most people's lives were and how their daily routine was restricted to a few familiar streets or, in the case of Hermione Totteridge, to her garden. However much he travelled – and he travelled far more widely than most people – home, as Dr Booth had said, was just an acre or two of familiar country. Or was he being condescending? Verity would say so. One could travel and still be narrow-minded. Better, perhaps, to travel in one's imagination. How did the poet have it? 'Put a girdle round the earth in forty minutes.'

It occurred to him that another thing which appeared to link the murder victims – and, indeed, himself – was Africa. Apart from his dentist, they had all been in Africa – and Kenya in particular – at some time or other. He could not help wondering if Harry had anything to do with it. His invitation to stay at Turton House had been fortuitous. The murders had taken place in or around Henley – except for Silver's and that was different from the others. He was not ready to challenge Harry about his suspicions quite yet. He would merely be laughed at but he must be on his guard.

Edward was in a cab on his way to Victoria to meet Herr von Kleist-Schmenzin's train. He had travelled via

114

Brussels and, although his visit was informal and nobody was supposed to know he was in the country, Edward had no illusions that anyone who mattered would not be aware of his arrival and watching his every move. The German Embassy would have him followed as, no doubt, would the secret services of several other European countries. One or two of Fleet Street's more enterprising papers would certainly have got wind of his visit and Edward was frankly dreading that there would be a scrum of interested parties on the platform to greet the German politician.

Major Ferguson had informed him that Kleist-Schmenzin would be arriving at 8.35 p.m. – an awkward time from the point of view of eating but, as usual, the train was running late so he decided he had time for a Dover sole at Overton's, just outside the station. He was beginning to wish he had refused to act as Kleist-Schmenzin's nanny. It was probably all going to pass without mishap but he had an unpleasant feeling in the pit of his stomach which spoiled his enjoyment of the fish. He was about to leave when, glancing out of the window, he thought he saw a journalist he knew slightly. He buried his head in the evening newspaper and ordered a second cup of coffee.

Ten minutes later, feeling it was safe to show his face, he bought a platform ticket and paced up and down feeling conspicuous. The train was signalled at last and, with a whistle and a puff of smoke, steamed to a halt. He found the first-class carriages and was alarmed to see no sign of anyone resembling a German landowner and aristocrat. He looked round wildly as the last of the passengers streamed past him issuing imperious commands to porters labouring to balance trunks and suitcases on their barrows. Then, to his great relief, he saw Kleist-Schmenzin. It could only be him. He wore a thick overcoat with the collar up despite the evening being uncommonly warm. He was clasping a heavy suitcase and looked lost.

'Herr von Kleist-Schmenzin?' Edward ventured, suppressing a smile. *'Ich bin Lord Edward Corinth. Welches ist Ihr Gepäck?'*

'Ach! Lord Edward. We shall speak English, if you please, so as not to raise suspicion. And you must call me Mr Kleist.'

He smiled as though he had made a clever joke but Edward, whose German was still not fluent, was relieved although he doubted Kleist-Schmenzin could ever be mistaken for anything other than what he was. He knew from Ferguson that Kleist was forty-eight, a lawyer and an ultra-conservative politician who hankered after a return to the monarchy. He despised Hitler as a jumped-up adventurer who was gambling Germany's future on a war he could not win. He had never made any secret of his views and had been arrested twice in the dying days of the Weimar Republic for speaking against National Socialism. He represented a small group of conservative politicians and army officers whose leader was Ludwig Beck, army chief of staff and a career officer. Beck had endeavoured without success to persuade his brother officers to resign *en masse* in order to make Hitler see sense.

'Kleist-Schmenzin's a brave man,' Ferguson had opined, 'but he won't succeed in persuading us to support him. Even if we wanted to, we could do nothing to help. We have to face the fact that Hitler enjoys the support of the great majority of the German people and the army. Army officers now have to swear an oath of allegiance to Hitler personally – not just as head of state – and they are never going to betray their leader. Kleist-Schmenzin will be seen by most of the army as an out-and-out traitor and dealt with accordingly.'

'So why are we taking so much trouble over him?' Edward had asked.

'Because he is a brave man and because we ought to investigate any group within the Reich who could unseat – or at least unsettle – the Führer. There aren't so many good Germans that we can afford to ignore them.'

So it was that Edward told himself not to dismiss Kleist as a buffoon. He might be backing a losing horse but his courage could not be doubted. He wondered, if he were in Kleist's shoes, whether he could act with so little regard for the consequences for himself and his family.

He bundled him into a taxi and sank back with a sigh of relief. At least he had performed the first part of his duties by scooping Kleist up safely and delivering him to Claridge's.

'I did not see you get out of a first-class carriage?' he said, trying to make conversation.

'I did not travel first class,' Kleist answered gruffly. 'I did not want – how do you say? – to draw attention to myself.'

Edward did not like to point out that, dressed as he was, he was much more likely to draw attention to himself in second class.

As he paid off the taxi and prepared to enter the hotel, he saw out of the corner of his eye a man with whom he had crossed swords a year or two back. Major Stille – a deadly enemy of Verity's – was officially an under-secretary at the German Embassy in Carlton House Terrace, but Ferguson had confirmed Edward's suspicion that he was in fact a major in the SS and in charge of monitoring the activities of German subjects on British soil. When he looked again Stille had disappeared but Edward was worried. What if his charge was snatched by Stille's men or even assassinated? He told himself he was being melodramatic. This was London after all, not Sofia or Bucharest.

Once he had checked Kleist into Claridge's, he thought about going home but his charge had other ideas. He asked Edward to join him for dinner and his face clouded over as Edward started to explain that he had already eaten. Seeing this, Edward changed his mind and said he would find out if they were too late for dinner in the hotel restaurant.

No, Kleist said, he wished to see something of London. Was there not a nightclub nearby? Edward, remembering Stille, suggested that Kleist might wish to keep his head down. After all, wasn't that why he had travelled second class? Kleist pooh-poohed this, telling Edward what he had already told himself – that this was London, not some Balkan capital.

'But you must be tired,' he inquired hopefully. Kleist said he was *taufrisch* – fresh as a daisy – so, reluctantly, Edward telephoned Ciro's which was about the most respectable nightclub he knew. He went back to Albany to bath and change, promising to pick up his guest in an hour.

As soon as they arrived at Ciro's, Edward ordered himself a cocktail from George at the bar and then a second. Thus fortified, he began to feel he might survive the evening. Kleist looked around the attractively decorated room, softly lit by candles, with a smile of satisfaction. Many couples had finished eating and were on the dance floor. Billy Cotton's band was proving a big draw and the club was crowded. Edward summoned a waiter.

One of the advantages of Ciro's was that there was no *table d'hôte*. You chose from an elaborate menu card at one guinea a head or from a shorter menu at twelve shillings and six pence. Edward consulted his guest before ordering but Kleist was too busy soaking up the atmosphere to be able to concentrate so Edward ordered for both of them. He wasn't very hungry so settled for caviar, *Consommé double, Suprême de Volaille* and, to finish with, his favourite savoury *Anges à Cheval*. The chef, Monsieur Rossignol, late of the Deauville Casino, was an old friend so he knew the food would be perfectly cooked as well as being inexpensive. He did not yet know Ferguson's views on expenses but thought he could run to the Veuve Clicquot 1911. With the soup, he settled for a 1926 Puligny-Montrachet, Château Montrose 1920 with the chicken and a bottle of Cockburn 1912 to settle his stomach after the angels on horseback.

Kleist dug into his caviar and, when he had finished, put down his fork with a sigh. *'Kennen Sie Herr von Trott,* Lord Edward?'

'Yes, indeed. Adam is a friend of a friend of mine. We saw a lot of him when he was in England a year ago. You know him well? I gather he's now in the Far East?'

'Gut! Ja, he is my friend too. But you are wrong. He is not in the Far East – not any more. He is in Berlin. I saw him last week. We make a conspiracy together.' Kleist winked roguishly. 'We will throw out this peasant Hitler and restore the Kaiser. Can we count on the help of the British government? *Werden Sie uns helfen? Was denken Sie?'*

He looked at Edward with the earnest stare of a man who had drunk too much. With Edward's help, he had downed a bottle and a half of the Montrachet and they had had to order a second bottle of claret. As they made inroads on the port, Edward began to think the evening might not have been such a wash-out after all. He was feeling benign and expansive. Even his German seemed to improve. *'Das hätte ich nicht für möglich gehalten . . .'* He decided it was his duty to tell his new friend the truth – that the British Government would not lift a finger to aid Kleist, Adam and his co-conspirators.

He recognized, as soon as he finished expounding his views on world affairs, that this had been a mistake. It was not his business to pontificate on British foreign policy and he wiped the sweat off his brow with his napkin as he imagined what Ferguson would say if he ever came to hear of it. He hurriedly explained that he had no authority to speak for anyone but himself but Kleist did not seem to be listening. Having been so relaxed only moments earlier, he was now becoming agitated and talked loudly about Hitler and the vital importance of 'getting rid of him'. Edward decided he must try and deliver him back to Claridge's while he was still standing but, just at that moment, Kleist saw a face he knew.

'*Blicken Sie!*'

Edward followed his gaze and saw Jack Amery with a girl wearing too much make-up and not enough clothes who, on closer inspection, proved to be Una. He really did not want to have to socialize with them again but it appeared he had no alternative. It wasn't entirely Amery's fault. He was doing his best to pretend he had not seen them but Kleist was not so easily put off. He rose from the table, upsetting his wine as he did so, his napkin still tucked in his shirt. He touched Amery on the arm and, as he turned, embraced him in a bear hug which almost brought them both to the floor.

Speaking in German too fast for Edward to follow, he dragged Amery over to the table. 'Lord Edward Corinth, Herr Amery – my friend Jack. Do you know each other?' Kleist reverted to English for Edward's benefit.

Edward had risen. 'We do,' Edward admitted, shaking Amery's hand and smiling at Una. 'How do you come to know . . .?'

'Ewald? We got to know each other in Berlin. He's a good chap,' Amery said vaguely, 'but he ought not to be here. I won't tell a soul, Scout's honour, but they'll know about it at the Embassy and they won't be happy. Not at all happy.'

'I tried to persuade Jack not to back Hitler,' Kleist said boisterously. 'I told him he was after the wrong horse. Is my English correct?'

'Quite correct,' Amery assured him. 'We disagreed on that point but Ewald took me to his estate in Pomerania and we shot bear or peasants or something.'

Kleist snorted with laughter. 'He is such a joker – is he not, Lord Edward?'

'A joker,' Edward agreed drily. 'You had a meeting with Hitler, Mr Amery?'

'I was so fortunate, yes.' He spoke defiantly. 'He is a great man. Do not believe the lies you hear about him.'

Kleist turned away to talk to Una and the two of them went on to the dance floor. Amery frowned and seemed about to object. Instead he suddenly asked, 'What are you doing in Ciro's with my friend Ewald?'

Edward, who by this time had given up any hope that Kleist's visit could be kept a secret, said, 'He wants to put his views across to the British Government – as a private citizen, you understand.' He wondered if he had been indiscreet. Two dinners and rather too much wine had loosened his tongue. 'Keep it to yourself, will you, Amery?' he added, guiltily. 'We don't want to get him into trouble. From what he has told me I get the feeling that he has already put a noose around his neck just by coming here.'

Kleist was clutching Una to him like a lifebelt but Amery, who was now halfway through a bottle of Barsac, appeared not to notice.

It was very late before Edward was able to prise Kleist off the obliging girl. Amery had disappeared but

Una professed not to be worried. She said she frequently had to find her own way home. After having had too much to drink, she said, her husband would often spend the night walking the streets 'to avoid his enemies'.

'What enemies?' Edward asked.

Una shrugged her shoulders. 'Real or imagined, he has plenty of enemies,' she joked. Edward asked if she had enough money – they were apparently staying with her father-in-law. She took ten shillings off him without compunction and Edward, when he got his bill, found that he was also paying a substantial sum for Jack's gallant attempt to empty Ciro's wine cellar. He paid up and contemplated putting the cost of the evening on an expenses form and giving it to Ferguson. It would be worth it just to see his face.

Edward was exhausted, as he bundled Kleist into a taxi, and he wondered at the man's stamina. He had travelled for two days and could still drink and dance half the night. As he said goodnight in the hotel lobby, he asked, 'When did you say you got to know Mr Amery?'

'When he was in Berlin seeing Hitler. He had to wait many days until our beloved Chancellor had time to meet him.'

'What did he want with Hitler? Do you know?'

'There was no secret why he was in Berlin. Jack could not keep a secret if he wanted – not when he has had a few drinks, you understand.' Kleist mimed gulping down a drink. 'Anyway, he was proud to have been given such an important job.'

'Which was?'

'Sir Oswald Mosley had sent him to beg for money.'

'And did Hitler gave him any?'

'So he claims. That's why he's celebrating tonight. He takes – what do you say? – the cream for himself.'

'He steals from Mosley?' Edward wasn't sure what shocked him most – that Hitler was financing the British Union of Fascists or that Amery was creaming some of it off for himself.

'It's commission. It is the way things are done. There is much corruption at the court of King Hitler,' Kleist said bitterly. 'That is why he must go. He is not an officer . . . not a gentleman.'

Edward turned up at Claridge's prompt on nine the following morning expecting to have to dig Kleist out of bed but he was waiting in the lobby, bright-eyed and sober. They shook hands but avoided mentioning the previous night's festivities. They reached the Foreign Office ten minutes early and had to kick their heels until Sir Robert Vansittart was ready to see them.

Vansittart had been the administrative head of the Foreign Office but had resigned when Anthony Eden resigned as Foreign Secretary. The Prime Minister had 'kicked him upstairs' and given him a rather vague job as chief adviser on foreign affairs to the government. Edward had had dealings with him before and admired him. He had assumed he would wait outside while Vansittart and Kleist talked but Vansittart insisted that he join them.

As soon as they were seated, Edward was made aware that Vansittart had only grudgingly agreed to meet Kleist. He looked at his watch on two occasions as Kleist spoke – eloquently, Edward thought – of the growing opposition to Hitler among army officers and the aristocracy. He admitted they had made a mistake in thinking they could control Hitler. They had tried to use him but he had used them. Now, he was out of control and had to be stopped.

'But what do you want us to do about it?' Vansittart asked testily.

'Money to help us organize and a message of support . . .'

'That's quite out of the question,' Vansittart responded, almost angry. 'The British Government can only be seen to deal with the government of another country. We cannot stoop to conspiracy.'

Now it was Kleist's turn to get angry. He told Vansittart that he and his friends were the only opposition to Hitler and, if they were not supported on some legalistic pretext, there would be war by the end of the year.

'Hitler is a mad dog,' he said, leaning forward and jabbing the air with his finger. 'There is only one way of dealing with a mad dog. You must put it down.'

Vansittart raised his eyebrows. 'You are asking us to support political assassination? That is not possible. It is not . . . it is not English.'

Edward thought Vansittart was being rather absurd. To play by rules your opponent does not recognize is a sure way to defeat. However, it was not his place to say anything.

'What about Julius Caesar?' Kleist appealed to the classicist in Vansittart. 'Brutus was an honourable man but he detested tyrants and tyranny.'

'And that led to a savage civil war,' was all Vansittart would say.

The meeting was over in half an hour and Kleist came away dejected. There would after all, Vansittart had told him, be no meeting with Lord Halifax, the British Foreign Secretary. They were not due to see Churchill until the afternoon as Kleist had naively imagined that he might spend the whole morning with Vansittart.

On an impulse, Edward invited him to lunch at his club. They sat in the morning-room talking quietly of Hitler and the situation in Berlin, Edward growing ever more gloomy. Kleist spoke movingly of his estate in Pomerania, north-east of Berlin. He had opposed Hitler long before he came to power and had steadfastly refused to fly the Nazi flag over his *schloss*. He had been arrested twice but never held for long yet Edward sensed that, in the end, the Nazis would kill him. He had a son in the army, who was also an outspoken critic of Hitler, and was more fearful for his son than for himself. He was convinced that, once the German generals had decided on peace, Hitler would be over-thrown within forty-eight hours and a monarchist government restored.

When it was a reasonable hour to move to the bar, Kleist asked for bourbon – a taste he explained he had acquired on a visit to the United States – but had to settle for Scotch. Edward ordered champagne which he thought might lift his spirits. He was mistaken.

Over lunch, Edward tried to discover more about Jack Amery's visit to Berlin but Kleist could add little to their conversation the previous evening. One odd fact he did discover – quite by chance – was that James Herold had been an early enthusiast for the Fascist cause and had met Hitler in 1932, before he had come to power.

'Hitler has always been obsessed by mountains,' Kleist explained. 'He says he only feels free in the mountains where he can breathe fresh air.' When Hitler heard that the celebrated mountaineer was in Berlin, after climbing in the Alps, he had insisted on meeting him. Kleist said the two men had got on well and Herold had met Hitler on two further visits to Germany.

Edward mused on the attraction Hitler held for otherwise decent men. They could not see beyond the image he presented to the world – the idealized image of the blond Aryan, the emphasis on healthy exercise. A British public schoolboy, educated to believe in the Roman ideal of *mens sana in corpore sano*, could – Edward supposed – by closing his eyes to the racial hatred that condemned thousands of Germany's citizens to a squalid death in what were now being called concentration camps, mistake Hitler for a heroic figure who had risen above the corruption and compromise of democratic politics. Jack Amery – like Churchill – had been educated at Harrow but with very different results.

In the afternoon, rather the worse for drink, Edward decanted Kleist at Morpeth Mansions, Churchill having declined to meet him at the House of Commons. This time, Edward refused to be there while Kleist again begged for public support for the conservative opposition. He thought he knew what Churchill's answer would be. He would listen with sympathy and tell him that, if Germany attacked Czechoslovakia – which seemed increasingly likely – England 'would not stand idly by'.

In fact, Churchill went further and gave Kleist a letter laying out his views which he could show to the army officers if it would persuade them openly to oppose Hitler's mad gamble. He ended by saying that, once Britain went to war, it would fight until the bitter end. Victory or death were the only options. Churchill also promised to pass Kleist's views on to the Foreign Secretary.

Kleist came out of the meeting much happier but Edward, who by now knew Churchill quite well, hoped that his 'bullishness' had not misled Kleist. Edward was convinced that Britain would never go to war to defend Czechoslovakia but, of course, it was not up to him to say so.

It was with some relief that he delivered Kleist to his train that evening. There had been no assassination attempt, no journalistic debacle, nothing in short to which Ferguson could object. However, when he left Victoria, he again saw Major Stille who eyed him with such cold hatred that a shiver ran down his spine. When he looked back the man had gone, but he was aware that he now faced two deadly enemies – the murderer of his friend, Eric Silver, and at least three others as well as an agent of the German Government who must now know that he was working for Special Branch or MI5. Edward did not make the mistake of underestimating his enemy. He knew Stille of old as a ruthless man who would not hesitate to kill if he thought it necessary.

When he got back to Albany he felt drained and even Fenton's offer of lamb cutlets did not make him feel much better. He opened a bottle of his favourite claret and when Fenton came into the drawing-room to tell him that his supper was ready, he found him fast asleep in an armchair.

7

On his return to Henley, the first thing he did was visit Verity. He found her very much better and she said she was feeling stronger.

'The last time they examined my sputum, Dr Bladon said I was much improved.'

'Good, I'm glad,' Edward responded weakly.

'You know, if I don't improve, they'll have to collapse my lung.'

'Collapse your lung?' he echoed, feeling ill himself. 'That sounds unpleasant.'

'You can say that again! They take away your ribs . . . well, not *your* ribs, *my* ribs, and press the lung down. You see, the bacilli can't live if the lung doesn't work. Oh, I'm sorry. You've gone quite pale.'

'I . . . Please don't tell me any more, V. It makes me feel . . .'

'I don't see why you should feel ill just because I tell you what I'm in for,' she said with something of her old combativeness. 'Oh well, let's change the subject. You remember Kay Stammers?'

'Of course!'

'Well, she's invited me to see her plane. There's an airfield not far from here. Or rather it's just a field at the moment but they are beginning to convert it into an aerodrome in case – if there's a war – the RAF need it.

Kay flies all over the place. That's what I'm going to do when I'm better.'

'I thought you were going to be a tennis player.'

'I can do both, can't I? Look at Kay. She cheered me up no end by telling me about Alice Marble.'

'Remind me who she is. I know her name.'

'She's a tennis player – one of the best. She collapsed on court during the French championships in 1934 and the doctors diagnosed TB. They said she would never play again. She refused to believe it and returned in 1936, fitter and faster, and beat Kay in the Wimbledon finals 6–1, 6–1.'

'That's right! I remember now.' Edward knitted his brow. 'I say, Kay's not going to take you up in her paper bag, is she? I know you are much better but . . .'

'Don't worry! I won't take any risks. I want to get better so I know I must be good and not do too much.' The idea of Verity being good made Edward raise his eyebrows but he said nothing. 'Kay's been wonderful. She's going to introduce me to her friend Phyllis King. She won the Queen's Club ladies' singles in '33 and '34 and was in the finals last year. Kay thinks she'll win again this year.'

They were walking in the garden and sat down on one of the seats scattered about so patients could enjoy the sun without tiring themselves.

'So what else have you been doing, V, while I was gallivanting?'

'Yes, I want to hear all about your gallivanting.' Seeing his face fall, she added lightly, 'I mean, my favourite secret agent, everything you are *allowed* to tell.'

'I can tell you everything,' Edward replied, excusing himself for the white lie. 'I saw an old enemy, as a matter of fact.'

'Not Major Stille?'

'How did you guess?'

'What did he say?'

'Nothing, but he looked daggers at me. That's the only phrase for it.'

He went on to tell Verity about the twenty-four hours he had spent with Kleist and their meeting with Jack Amery at Ciro's. She looked up with interest when he mentioned the name but did not interrupt until he had finished.

'What a coincidence you running into Amery again! I met him too.'

'You met Amery! How on earth . . .?'

'Mary's father took us out on the river and we picnicked on Mr Amery's lawn. They seemed to be close friends. Amery gave him a bag. I don't know what was in it but it was heavy.'

'You mean you don't think your picnic was spontaneous?'

'No, I think it gave him an excuse to visit Amery without anyone noticing. Unfortunately, he made the mistake of inviting me along. He had forgotten, or didn't know, that Amery and I had been on opposite sides over Spain. I happen to know quite a lot about that man and the more I know the less I like the look of him. In fact, you should tell Major Ferguson that, if he wants to catch a traitor, he would do better watching him than my friend Claud Cockburn.'

Edward made her go over the whole expedition again, including everything she could remember Mr Black saying to her, but Verity had to admit that she had spent so much time asleep or dozing that there was not much to add.

'Oh, well – let's forget Amery for a moment. Do you think you are getting anywhere with your investigation? Was your visit to Miss Totteridge's sister useful? What's her name . . .?'

'Violet Booth. Actually, it was rather illuminating and I'm grateful to Charlotte for providing me with an entrée. I had another stroke of luck. I discovered I had known their nephew-in-law in Kenya and I think it meant they could speak more freely to me than if I had been a complete stranger.' He went on to tell her everything he had learnt in Burnham Market.

'So, do you have a picture of the murderer yet? Any idea who you are looking for?'

Edward thought for a moment. 'I think I do. He's probably about my age and I may even have met him in Kenya because I believe all this originates there. I think he may have climbed with James Herold in Africa and elsewhere. He could be anti-Fascist because the message left on Herold's body implies that he did not like his political views. I think there is some connection with Peter Lamming. The photograph torn out of Miss Totteridge's album may turn out to be Lamming or the murderer or both of them . . .'

'That's a clue,' Verity interrupted. 'When and where were the other photographs on the same page taken?'

'They were quite recent . . . all taken about five years ago and mostly in Miss Totteridge's garden.'

'But that photograph – the one that was torn out – couldn't be of Peter Lamming because Mrs Booth told you she had never met him and presumably neither had Hermione.'

'True. Well, maybe it wasn't of him.'

'Perhaps Isabella gave her the photograph,' Verity suggested.

'It's possible.'

'What does General Lowther's death tell us?'

Edward was so pleased to hear her refer to 'us' that he had difficulty in suppressing a smile. '"As flies to wanton boys, they kill us for their sport . . ." I think that's fairly clear. The General was no doubt responsible for the deaths of many young men in the war and the murderer took his revenge for one in particular.'

'Right, so go on with your description of the murderer.'

Edward considered. 'Well, I think that – paradoxically – he doesn't like killing and blames Miss Totteridge for killing insects . . .' he hesitated, thinking aloud, 'or killing someone . . . someone the murderer loved. I am guessing, of course, but the message Mrs Booth found on her sister's body is a clue. "So shall thou feed on death that feeds on men . . ."'

Verity looked doubtful. 'I think you are supposing quite a lot on very little evidence. The big question is, were all the murders done by the same person or was Eric Silver killed by someone quite different? If they were all committed by the same person, we must conclude he's a sadist and *does* like killing.'

'I keep changing my mind about that – whether we are looking for one person or two.' Edward sighed. 'There was a moment when I thought we were making progress but now I'm not so sure. Stille is certainly brutal enough to have killed Silver in that way.'

'But why?'

'He was a Jew, for one thing. But, no, it must have been because the murderer heard what Silver said to me.'

'But how could he have got into the building?'

Now I think about it, I never heard the front door lock behind me. It's one of those modern ones. You talk into a phone and Silver pressed a button that opened the door. When I was in, the door swung back and should have locked itself but maybe it didn't.

'Anyway V, I want you to keep your eyes open. I don't like your story of picnicking on Amery's lawn. I would guess he's hand in glove with Stille. I might try and do some digging on that.'

'You think Amery's working for the Nazis?'

'Don't you?'

132

Verity furrowed her brow. 'Yes, I think I do, but what can we do about it?'

'I've sent a report to Ferguson. Special Branch will try and keep an eye on him but they've got a lot on their plate. They can't watch him twenty-four hours a day. So, I repeat, keep a weather eye out for dirty tricks. Stille hates you even worse than me ever since you fooled him at that party in the German Embassy.'

Edward was referring to an incident three years earlier when Verity had been invited to dinner by Hitler's personal envoy who had no idea she was a journalist and a Communist. Stille took revenge by killing her little dog in the most horrible way and Edward had no doubt that he was capable of every sort of wickedness. It was one of the few advantages, Edward considered, of Verity being in Spain and, more recently, Prague – it kept her out of Stille's way.

'So, to recapitulate,' Verity said, calling the meeting to order, 'the murderer is probably in his late thirties, has lived in Kenya for some years in his youth and may be anti-Fascist. We, or at least you, probably know him because he almost certainly lives around here. Who do you know who fits that description?'

'Well, I can only think of one person.'

'Who?' Verity demanded as she saw him hesitate.

'My host – Harry Makin, Lord Lestern.' He thought for a moment and added, 'I must try to get an idea of his political views. He's a friend of Amery but that proves nothing. He probably doesn't have any "views", political or otherwise. He's far too selfish to be a political animal.'

Verity looked up at him very seriously. 'Edward, you've been warning me to be careful but it seems to me that you're the one who needs to keep a weather eye out. Do you have to stay with him? Why not go back to London and do your investigating from there?'

'And leave you here unprotected? You must be joking, V. I need to stay here for a few more days – at least until after the regatta. I think it will all come to a head then or not long after. I don't know why but I have a hunch that the murderer has one more victim in mind to complete his killing spree and I need to stop him.'

'You certainly do if that one person is you!' Verity exclaimed. 'I'd like to meet this friend of yours – Makin or Lestern or whatever he's called. Can you bring him over to visit me?'

'I might do that. I can't see it will do any harm and he did say you sounded like his sort of girl.'

'Charming! He doesn't sound like my sort of man.'

'I disagree, V. I think in many ways he is your sort of man.'

Verity considered this. 'Why? Do you think I like selfish, amoral men without any political views?'

'No, but he is . . . well, he's got something women like. Perhaps you'll be able to tell me what it is.'

'I've often wondered what would make you betray your country.'

'Me?'

'I was thinking of Jack Amery.'

'The same reasons you would need to commit murder', Edward said gravely. 'Money, revenge, blackmail.'

Verity frowned. 'So what next?'

'I want to go and see Miss Tiverton.'

'Miss Tiverton?'

'She's a village schoolmistress – a friend of General Lowther's. And tomorrow I am going to talk to Herold's wife. She must know something.'

'Is she a Fascist too?'

'I don't know but I intend to find out.'

'What is it about the mountains and Nazis?' Verity

asked, taking his arm and leaning on him. 'She won't mind talking about it – the murder?'

'We'll have to see. It depends what sort of person she is. From what I hear from Treacher, she's not the shy, retiring sort.'

Verity looked glum and Edward wondered what he could say to cheer her up. 'Look, V, I know it's hard for you being stuck here but, if it's any consolation, I think this is where the whole thing has its – what shall I say? – its core. I mean, there's evil about and I believe it originates in this sleepy little town, odd though that seems. There's no need for either of us to dash about the country.'

'Henley won't be so sleepy next week . . .'

'No, it won't. The town will be invaded by a host of . . . I wonder what you call someone who loves rowing – a philremex . . . philremigium? I don't know. What an opportunity for someone who intends to kill without being noticed.'

'So why look so cheerful about it?'

'I don't know, V. I suppose I'd like to bring this business to a head.'

'You say there's evil here but what can I do to help you uncover it? I feel so useless . . .'

'You're not useless. I couldn't do without you. I need to have you to talk it all over with. You point out when I'm going off track.' He had an idea. 'You are feeling stronger, aren't you?'

'Yes.' She looked at him hopefully.

'Well, why not go over to Phyllis Court – perhaps Kay would take you – and listen to the gossip. My instinct is that our murderer is familiar with the club. You may pick up something there.'

'Give me a cigarette, will you, Edward?'

He put his hand to his breast pocket but did not take out his cigarette case. 'Dr Bladon has forbidden you to smoke.'

'He's forbidden me to do all the things I enjoy. I mean, when are we going to be able to . . . you know . . .? Can you keep yourself pure for me?' She was trying to joke but it didn't quite come out as she had hoped.

'Darling V. Of course I can keep myself pure for you! You don't seem to understand. I'm not interested in anyone else. There's only you and I can wait for as long as it takes. I won't pretend that it's not difficult, you being so close and yet . . .'

'So far. Forbidden fruit! I suppose we can remain chaste for another month or two. Give me that cigarette now.'

It was a command Edward did not dare refuse. He sensed that she was very near the end of her tether.

'I haven't told you that when Mary and I got back from our picnic we found Jill had gone.'

'Gone?'

'She had a relapse. We haven't been allowed to see her so it must be bad.'

'I'm so sorry.' He hesitated. 'V, you mustn't worry . . .'

'I try not to but of course I do. It's like having a cloud in the corner of your eye. Most of the time I can't quite see it but then suddenly I can't see anything else. Especially just before I go to sleep, when my are eyes shut. Would you mind holding me?' She looked up at him, wide-eyed, appealing for comfort. He tossed away his cigarette and gathered her into his arms and held her tightly. In sickness or in health . . . he thought, I love this girl and I'm not going to let her go.

When she had said her farewell and watched the Lagonda disappear down the drive, Verity returned to the clinic tired and dispirited. Edward had done his best to make her feel part of his investigation but she accepted that she could contribute very little. Listen to the gossip at Phyllis Court! Was that all she could do? She had other reasons for feeling useless. The papers were full of a great battle in Spain – probably the Republicans' last effort to beat back the rebels – and she would have given anything, life itself, to be there. She still had many friends in Spain and longed once again to be part of that shining brotherhood who had set out in 1935 to defend the Republic. She knew, of course, that nothing now remained of that Arthurian band of brothers, that it had all – or almost all – been an illusion, but they had been glorious days. And if she were in Prague, she would be reporting on the Czechoslovak crisis. The Germans were making impossible demands on the Czechs, attempting to humiliate them. They seemed to hope that the Czechs would be forced to a point where they could not accept any further demands and so provide Hitler with the excuse he was seeking to invade.

Just as he was leaving, Edward had urged her to 'buck up' and 'look on the bright side'. She had snapped that she did not need his platitudes and it was stupid to tell her to look on the bright side when the world was tottering on the brink of Armageddon. He had apologized, pained and unhappy, and she had burst into tears. It wasn't just the world crisis that depressed her. Dr Bladon had told her that Jill was desperately ill and likely to die. It was all too much and she had clung to Edward but all he could do was stroke her head. There was nothing he could say to comfort her. They had long ago promised not to lie to one another and, although Edward had occasionally broken the rule – at least by omission – he was certainly not going to try and soothe her with false promises and idle talk of a quick recovery.

8

Edward returned to Turton House depressed and almost ready to give up the investigation. It all seemed so pointless when the world was crumbling under his feet. So it was that, when, at dinner, Harry plied him with very good wine and listened without interrupting as he spilled out his fears for Verity and his thoughts on the murders he was investigating, Edward found that he was telling him rather more than he had intended. He had always found it easier to think aloud when he was on a case. So be it, he thought bitterly. If Harry was a murderer, let him do his worst. He poured himself more wine. Would it be poisoned like Lowther's? He thought he knew what Herold might have felt. There was no point in trying to avoid his fate. Best to meet it head on and damn the consequences.

'Did you know Mrs Herold back in the old days, Harry? I suppose you must have done.'

'You mean his first wife?'

'He was married before? I didn't know that.'

'Oh yes, to the lovely Gwynnie,' he replied, pouring them both brandy. Edward refused a cigar but Harry took one out of the humidor and went through the whole ritual of cutting off the end, removing the band and lighting it before continuing. 'Sure you won't have one? The very best Havana, I assure you. No? Well – where to begin? It's quite a story. Gwynnie was a mountaineer, better than any of us, better even than Jimmy Herold and he'd climbed all over the world. In fact, they met for the first time at base camp on Everest. Then, as I expect you know, Gwynnie died in a climbing accident. They had only been married for five years. I told you I knew Herold in Africa but I didn't tell you the whole of it. We had a bit of a tussle for the favours of the delightful Gwyneth Jones when he brought her out to Kenya.'

'You mean before she married him?'

'You know me, old boy. When did I ever let a thing like marriage get in my way if I wanted a woman?' He spoke lightly but Edward felt there was a lot of pain and anguish just beneath the surface. That was the thing with Harry, he thought. You could never tell if he was really capable of loving a woman or if the pleasure was all in the chase. Were the ones he regretted the ones who had got away?

'After she died on the Eiger, I never spoke to Herold again.' Harry expelled a cloud of smoke which scented the room and made Edward wish he had taken a cigar after all.

'You blamed him for his wife's death?'

'I did. In my view, he was criminally careless fitting out that expedition. The equipment – even the tents – was not up to standard. I held him responsible for Gwynnie's death and I wrote and told him so.'

'Did he answer your letter?'

'Not a word. I expect he was too busy writing that sentimental load of tosh that made him so much money and netted him a new wife.' He shuddered. 'It still makes me sick to think of it.'

Harry explained that Cathy Bartlett, as she then was, had been working for the publisher who had brought out Herold's account of climbing the highest peaks, including the attempt on Everest which, though unsuccessful, had been judged a brave battle against atrocious weather. But what had really turned the book into a bestseller was the moving account of his – in the end unsuccessful – efforts to save his wife on the north face of the Eiger. His story of being caught on the mountain in a blizzard and having to spend the night in Gwynnie's arms, cuddling together for warmth on the narrowest shelf of rock, had captured the public's imagination. *The Fall: A Love Story* had been a notable Book Society Choice and had made Herold rich.

Cathy had been in charge of taking him around bookshops and arranging lectures and lunches. He had been the main speaker at a Foyle's Literary Lunch attended by the Prime Minister who had praised Herold as a credit to British manhood. In the two weeks they had spent together going round the country, they had fallen in love. It was almost a cliché – the handsome explorer, widowed and, whether he was aware of it or not, in search of a new mate and a pretty, clever girl who saw how famous he was and believed she alone recognized his loneliness and vulnerability. Her uncritical hero-worship appealed to his lust and vanity. They had married shortly afterwards and enjoyed three years of bliss before she discovered that climbing mountains frightened and bored her.

When he had finished speaking, Harry was silent for a minute or two and then, refilling Edward's glass, rather surprisingly suggested that they might go and see Cathy Herold together.

'What say we go tomorrow? It's only ten minutes in the car. Better sooner rather than later, eh? You never know, old man, I might see or hear something which won't mean anything to you but which will ring bells with me.'

'So you never met Cathy?'

'No fear! I took care to keep out of their way when they came to Kenya on honeymoon. I didn't want to get into a public row with Jimmy. By that time, my name in the colony was mud – just a few too many adventures, if you take my meaning. Lord D told me he would have me run out of the colony if he heard one more complaint about me. I couldn't risk that.'

It crossed Edward's mind that Harry might be lying. Perhaps he did know Cathy. Perhaps he was having an affair with her. Perhaps he had killed Herold to get her for himself. It would be consistent with his behaviour to other women . . . other wives.

As it turned out, his suspicions were unfounded. Cathy Herold had truly loved her husband and had not conspired to murder him in order to marry her lover. Edward was convinced of this when they met the following day. He introduced himself and then Harry. No one but a consummate actress could have counterfeited the surprise she showed when he mentioned that Harry had known her husband years before when he was married to Gwynnie.

'You knew Jimmy in the old days?' she exclaimed, looking at Harry with interest. 'I wonder why he never mentioned you.'

The almost visible flicker of physical attraction which passed between them was obvious to Edward. Clearly, Harry's magnetism for the opposite sex had not dimmed with the passing years. They both looked younger as they talked about Herold and Kenya. It wasn't just flirting, Edward thought. It was pure animal attraction. For several years before his death, Herold had been husband only in name and, whether she recognized it or not, his widow was now ready for a new man in her life. And why not, Edward thought to himself. From everything he had heard, she had been a good wife and was still young and physically in her prime. As for Harry – well, the female of the species was his meat and drink.

141

Edward guessed that Cathy Herold, when she had gone out to Kenya in her early twenties, must have been stunning. Her hair was dark and rather wild. Her eyes were bold and bright, her nose rather thin but her figure was still boyish. She must keep herself in trim, he thought.

After five minutes, during which he could not get a word in, Edward decided that he must explain why they were there. Mrs Herold had so far not asked that obvious question.

'I was so sorry to hear about your husband . . .' he began but Harry cut him short.

'Take no notice, Mrs Herold,' Harry joked. 'He's not sad at all. The fact is he's a sort of policeman and he thinks Jimmy might have been murdered.'

Edward looked at his friend and began to expostulate. 'I say, I didn't exactly . . .'

'You see,' Harry continued remorselessly, 'he doesn't think Jimmy – in his state – could have pulled over those hives and they certainly didn't do it on their own. Then there's the business of that scrap of paper you found with the quotation from Shakespeare.'

Clearly taken aback, Mrs Herold grasped at this last point. 'I never knew it came from Shakespeare – "buzz, buzz".'

'Nor did I but Corinth is much better educated than either of us and he tells me it's from *Hamlet*.'

'You're a policeman . . .? Mr Treacher seemed quite satisfied . . .'

'I'm not exactly a policeman but Inspector Treacher has given me permission to go over the facts . . . I don't want to upset you. Please don't feel you have to answer my questions. It's just that . . .'

'I've got nothing to hide, Lord Edward. Ask me anything you like. I agree about the hives. It puzzled me too.' She spoke defiantly but Edward thought he saw a glimmer of fear in her eyes. 'Come and sit down – both of you – and I'll make some tea. Then you can ask me anything you like.'

Cathy Herold was not quite what Edward had expected. For one thing, she was unashamedly not grieving for her husband – or not in any obvious way that required her to wear black and weep. She did love her husband but, after they had stopped climbing together, his long absences were difficult to bear. She was often bored and lonely. Then, when he was at home, he developed a sudden and, she thought, un-healthy interest in the politics of the far right.

She told them that she became increasingly uneasy about his unquestioning admiration of Hitler and was horrified when he announced in public that he shared Hitler's view that the Jews were to blame for England's moral and economic bankruptcy. She could see that her own hero was becoming increasingly deluded. He told her that he believed England had become decadent and needed someone like Hitler to bring back the nation's self-respect. He said the young needed discipline and hard work. He wanted to start training camps where boys could test themselves in demanding sports such as mountaineering. He wasn't alone in believing that the youth of England needed hardening if the country was to hold on to its Empire and Oswald Mosley for one, welcomed him as an ally.

If she ever took issue with him over his attitude to race or the infinite superiority of the German people, he refused to listen or dismissed her with a patronizing or pompous remark along the lines that she was a woman and could not know anything about politics. Despite this, she loved him more than she was angry with him for not quite being the man she thought she had married.

When he had his first heart attack, it was almost a relief. It made him more dependent on her and meant he could no longer disappear for months on end to climb far-off mountains. However, after his second, more severe attack, he could do no more than sit in a chair and look out of the window. He became a burden and she admitted that she sometimes longed for him to die. But when he did die, she had surprised herself by being angry. She genuinely grieved for the man she had married – not for the chair-bound cripple – and hated the thought that he had died alone and in agony. Or had he been alone?

Although she could not explain it, she was quite sure that the scrap of paper she had found on his body meant that someone else was involved in his death. It was hard to believe that he had got himself out into the garden when he could hardly stumble into his bed on the ground floor. Something or someone had propelled him outside and set his bees on him. The police would not take her seriously and she took the hint that Inspector Treacher was doing his best to protect her from incriminating herself. She realized he believed that she had helped her husband commit suicide and, if she made any trouble, she would be accused of murder.

She explained that she had no option but to go along with the view taken by the police. It was made clear to her that she should be grateful that her husband's death would be treated as an accident and at first she had been. It was a relief to have her life back and to be able to do what she wanted. However, a growing sense of unease – of unfinished business – had undermined her pleasure at being rich and single. She was delighted to receive Edward's telephone call. It was clear she had a penchant for attractive men in the public eye and, if Lord Edward was trying to discover who had killed her husband, she was more than happy to help him.

Although Mrs Herold didn't say all of this over tea, she spoke frankly enough and Edward was able to guess the rest. He put his slice of Dundee cake back on his plate and looked at her. He saw she was feeling guilty that she had not been there when her husband had died and not been able to protect him. However, that certainly did not mean she was not determined to enjoy her youth while she still had it. She was, he thought, in the mood to do something stupid – perhaps to celebrate her new-found freedom with a rash new relationship – but, paradoxically, she was not stupid.

'Did anyone come and see your husband in the weeks before he died? Or did he get a letter that disturbed him?'

She did not answer him immediately but sat thinking. After a minute she said, 'No, I don't think so. As you know, the police thought he committed suicide – that he got stung to death on purpose.'

'You don't think he did?'

'It was hell for him living in a useless body when he had always been the fittest of the fit. He certainly made it hell for those who had to live with him.' She could not resist adding, 'But I've told you – he couldn't have overturned his hives.'

'Did you have any help looking after him – friends, relatives?'

'A few friends and there was a nurse – Mrs Paria – who came in to bath him. I couldn't manage it on my own.'

'Where was the nurse when your husband died?'

'It was her day off.'

Edward made a mental note to speak to the nurse. 'What about relatives?'

'We haven't a relative between us – well, not so as you'd notice.' She sounded almost defiant. 'We are . . . were both only children. Jimmy's parents died . . . God knows when. Before I knew him, anyway. My mother is in a nursing home in Sussex. I go and see her when I can but she doesn't recognize me any longer.'

'That must cost a pretty penny?' Edward ventured.

'If you are implying that I might have murdered my husband for his money . . .'

She had immediately seen what he was driving at and, once again, Edward warned himself not to under-rate her. 'No, of course I didn't mean that,' he back-tracked.

'We had plenty of money,' she said vaguely. 'I don't have to worry about that. Jimmy made a lot from his books and lecturing and his parents were well off.'

'What about you?'

'I wasn't rich when we married but I wasn't poor either. My father had left me and my mother reasonably well off. Still, I'm not denying it made life easier being married to a rich man.'

'So nothing upset him in the weeks before he died? You said he had no unexpected visitors.'

'I was thinking about that. As it happens, he did have a letter which seemed to disturb him.'

'Did you see who it was from?' Edward asked, excitedly.

'I'm sorry but I didn't.'

'You haven't still got it?'

'He burnt it, I'm afraid.'

'Well, that suggests it was something he didn't want you to see.'

'It must have been very tough for you looking after Jimmy when he was ill for so long,' Harry said as they sipped their tea.

'It was tough for him,' Mrs Herold corrected him. 'I loved him – I really did. As I told you, it was no hardship looking after him. Not at first anyway. We thought he might improve. The doctor said it was possible but in fact he went downhill quite rapidly. I don't pretend it wasn't a blessed relief when he died but not because I resented looking after him. I didn't but it was horrible to see him suffer the way he did – hardly able to walk a yard or two without stopping to get his breath. I came to realize what a gift life is. We breathe without a thought. We walk without considering how to take our next step. When that is taken from us, it's not possible to think of anything else.' She saw Harry smile. 'I mean it. Your whole life is narrowed down to the pain and the effort of living one moment more.'

'Did he talk of . . . of ending it all?' Edward ventured.

'Yes, often in those last few months. We talked about the mountains we had climbed and he spoke more and more about Gwynnie and how she'd died . . .'

'And that made him sad?' Harry broke in.

'Not sad exactly. Resigned – grateful for the life he had had. As he said, he could just as easily have died on a mountain and had always considered the risks well worth taking. God or fate had chosen to take him a different way but at least he hadn't wasted his time on earth.'

'You said you climbed with him when you were first married?' Edward asked.

'He taught me,' she said simply. 'I loved it – at least at first. To rest on some peak, exhausted but triumphant, with Jimmy beside me and his arm round me – that was as near to heaven as I'm ever going to get. But the truth is that I wasn't good enough. I wasn't strong enough – unlike Gwynnie, so he said. I badly frightened myself a couple of times so in the end I gave up.'

'But you still keep fit?'

'Yes. I play a lot of tennis and . . .' she hesitated, 'and so on.'

'At Phyllis Court?'

'Yes.'

Edward looked at her and beneath her short-sleeved shirt he could see how strong her arms were. She would have had no difficulty overturning the hives.

147

As if reading his thoughts, she asked whether they had finished their tea and would like to go and see the apiary.

'Are you going to keep the bees?' Harry asked.

'For the moment. To tell you the truth, I'm not sure what I'm going to do. I may even go back to Africa. I rather hanker after some sun and this house . . . I don't know . . . I suppose it hasn't been such a happy place – with Jimmy being ill . . .' She tailed off before adding, 'Who knows? It's too early to say.'

'Of course,' Edward agreed. 'You have someone to help you?'

'With the bees?'

'Yes.'

'There's a boy – he's probably there now – Bill Watkins. We were lucky to find him. He's devoted to them. I certainly couldn't manage without him. He looks after the garden too.'

In the sunshine, the garden looked beautiful – a classic English cottage garden, its borders a blaze of colour. Lavender and rosemary scented the air and, at the far end near the hives, there was a small orchard where ancient apple trees leant for support on stout wooden poles. Roses rambled over the cottage walls and peeped in through the windows. The scent was intoxicating and Edward imagined that many of the flowers and shrubs had been chosen for the bees. Mrs Herold confirmed this.

'If you want your honey to taste of anything you have to give the bees a cocktail of good nectar plants – nothing fancy – just traditional English garden flowers.'

Edward thought she was making a great effort to remain calm. She couldn't quite decide how much of a grieving widow to be, he decided. He caught Harry's eye as they strolled across the lawn. A brief smile signalled that he too thought something was not quite right.

The young man who tended the bees was tongue-tied with shyness but when Edward got him on to the subject of the damage done to the hives he became almost loquacious.

'So many bees killed, so much waste! It took me most of that day to tempt them back. I had to rebuild the bases of the hives and . . . I don't know, it was a bloody marvel it weren't worse.'

'Why weren't you here the day Mr Herold died?'

'I sent him to Reading to pick up the new mower,' Mrs Herold answered for him.

'And when I got there I found there'd been a mix-up and it wasn't ready for me to collect,' Bill added, still annoyed at the memory of an afternoon wasted. 'There's so much to do at this time of year. Not just the bees . . .'

'So what had happened?' Edward asked with mild curiosity, turning to Mrs Herold.

'I telephoned Hale's in Reading and ordered a new Hayter. I said I would send someone over to collect it and, when Bill arrived, they pretended they had never got my message.'

'You don't remember who it was you spoke to?'

'At Hale's? No. I realize now that I ought to have taken a name but it never occurred to me.'

'And when you got back, Bill, did you find your bee clothes had been moved or were they just as you had left them?'

'No, they were on the floor of the shed in a pile. My hat had been badly dented and the veil torn. I couldn't find my wellington boots.'

'And you've still not found them?'

'No, Mrs Herold had to buy me another pair.'

'May we see them?'

'My clothes? Yes, of course, they're hanging up in the shed.'

They walked over to a garden shed behind the bee-hives. It was full of machinery and buckets, funnels and other bee-keeping equipment.

'Have these been cleaned since Mr Herold's death, Bill?' Edward asked.

'No, they weren't dirty so why should they be cleaned?' Light dawned. 'You think they were worn by whoever it was pulled over the hives?'

'It seems likely,' Edward said, examining the clothes. 'Presumably you needed them to recapture the bees?'

'Yes, when I got back from Reading I found poor Mr Herold had been . . . you know.'

'So the police had been and gone by the time you got back?'

'Yes,' Bill looked at Mrs Herold apologetically. 'All I could do was set about clearing up the mess and try to get the bees to come home. It was a day I'll never forget, that's for sure.'

Edward thanked him and apologized for disturbing him. He thought it odd that there had been no mower to collect at Hale's but, if she had wanted him out of the way while she killed her husband, surely she would have made sure there *was* a mower for him to pick up. Perhaps it was just one of those things. The shop either never got the message or mislaid it.

When they returned to the house they sat on the terrace on some ancient-looking garden chairs. 'Better than being inside on a day like this,' Mrs Herold said apologetically. 'It's been so hot . . .'

'Do you go on the river?' Harry asked suddenly.

'No, I never have.'

'I'm getting a small party together for the regatta. A picnic – a launch to watch the races from . . . I would so much like it if you could come. There's so much to talk about – the good old days . . .'

'Oh, I . . . I'm not sure. It's so soon after . . .'

'I'll telephone you.'

Edward wanted to go over everything one final time. 'So, forgive me,' he pressed, 'can I just get this straight. The day your husband died, you telephoned Hale's in the morning?'

'Yes, about ten and then about eleven I went shopping in Henley.'

'Your husband was all right when you left him?'

'No, he was worse than usual. It had been getting very bad – his breathing. He had an oxygen cylinder but it didn't seem to make much difference. I knew he couldn't go on very much longer so the cliché about his death being a blessed relief is true.'

'You'll miss him?' Harry asked.

'Of course! I told you, I'll miss the man he was. When I first met him, he was a marvellous man. So handsome and such a sportsman. He could shoot and climb and swim. Well, you remember, Lord Lestern. He was everything I thought a man ought to be.' She grinned. 'My hero.'

Harry made a moue of pretended hurt. 'He was a good man. I never pretended to be his equal.'

'But you're alive and he isn't,' she said roughly.

'Getting back to the timing,' Edward said quickly. 'You returned from your shopping when?'

'About twelve. I had a cup of coffee with a friend.'

'Oh yes, a Miss Latimer?'

'How did you know that?' Mrs Herold looked surprised.

'Inspector Treacher gave me permission to read his notes. You don't mind, do you?'

'No, I don't mind,' she said slowly.

'And, when you got back, you found your husband on the lawn . . .?'

'Dead,' she said grimly, 'and still covered in bees.'

'What did you do then?'

'You must know if you've read what I told the Inspector.'

'Forgive me, but would you mind going over it again? I don't mean to upset you but . . .'

'I screamed, dropped my shopping and went over to him. I could see the bees covering his face like a mask. I tried to brush them away but I couldn't. I think they had attached themselves to him with their stings and died with him. It was terrible . . . disgusting but, in the end, I . . . I've come to realize it was for the best. The doctor said it would have been instant . . .' She looked doubtful.

'And then you telephoned the police?'

'Yes. I didn't know what to do, who to call. I could see he was dead. His face was all . . . all of it that I could see . . . swollen and black . . .' She shook her head as if trying to dislodge the memory.

'When did you notice the piece of paper with the writing on it?'

'Not until they moved his body. I think it must have been pushed under him or something.'

'It wasn't on top of him?'

'No, I don't think so . . . it might have been . . . I don't know. I wasn't thinking straight. I just saw the piece of paper and the pen.'

'It was his Parker?'

'Yes. It was his pen – the one he always had in his breast pocket.'

Edward furrowed his brow. 'It seems odd, don't you think, that whoever killed your husband took his pen out of his pocket and wrote "buzz, buzz" in capital letters when his body was covered in bees.'

'He was probably wearing protective clothing.'

'You saw Bill's protective gloves? They are thick and stiff – so it would be rather difficult to remove a pen from the inside pocket of a jacket covered in bees. Why didn't he use his own pen?'

'We are certain it was Jimmy's pen?' Harry asked.

'According to Treacher's notes,' Edward replied. 'A Parker is quite distinctive but, I agree, it needs checking.'

'Perhaps he wrote in capitals because he was still wearing gloves,' Harry hazarded. 'Much easier than writing normally.'

'Good point! Mrs Herold, would you mind if we borrowed Bill's gloves and did a little experiment. I don't know that it is significant though. Once the murderer had the pen and was away from the bees, he could have taken his gloves off.' He turned back to her. 'And the paper was torn from . . .'

'I don't know.'

'Is there a book of some kind in which Bill records how the bees are doing on – the honey yield – that sort of thing?'

'Yes, Bill has it. Do you want to see it?'

'Please.'

Mrs Herold stood up and called across the orchard. Bill lifted his head from the mowing, turned off his machine and came over. She asked him if he had the bee book and he said it was in the shed.

'Could we see it, do you think, Bill?'

'It's not quite up to date,' he said defensively.

'Don't worry, we just want to see if anything has been . . .'

Edward stopped her. 'We'd be most grateful,' he said with a smile. 'Oh, and could you bring your gloves – the ones you use to deal with the bees.'

Bill looked doubtful but nodded and ambled off to fetch the book and the gloves.

'You didn't want me to say what we needed them for?' Mrs Herold queried.

'Better not.'

'Mrs Herold – Cathy . . . I'm so sorry.' Harry had taken her hand and she let him stroke it. 'This must be awful for you. Forgive us for opening it all up again.'

'No, I want to know the truth.'

'I think someone killed your husband,' Edward told her. 'Don't you?'

She looked at him wide-eyed. 'But who would want to do that?'

'That's what we must try to find out,' he said gently.

Bill returned with the gloves and a small, cheap notebook – the sort you could buy in any stationer. Mrs Herold put out her hand to take it but Edward was there before her.

'Thank you, Bill,' he said soothingly. He leafed through the pages, which were full of measurements and brief, dated comments on the condition of the bees. He came to the final page.

'You haven't written up the damage to the hives yet?' he asked, looking up at Watkins.

'I didn't know what to write,' he whined, almost wringing his hands.

'Of course not, Bill,' Mrs Herold said. 'We'll think of something together, shall we?'

Edward was not listening. He had found what he was looking for – a jagged tear where a page had been roughly torn out. 'Do you know anything about this?' he asked. Bill scratched his head as though thinking hard how much he should say. 'You must have noticed this page had been torn out? Did you do it?'

'No, sir!' He sounded aggrieved. 'It were an empty page. I didn't think nothing of it.'

'Very well. You can go now. I'll return these to you in a few minutes.'

'Don't blame me for nothing,' Bill cried. 'It weren't me what killed the master. He loved the bees . . . we both did. I didn't set them on him!'

'We don't think you did, Bill,' Mrs Herold said placatingly. 'We're not accusing you of anything.' She patted his arm and he seemed reassured.

After he had gone back to his mowing, Edward and Harry both tried to write while wearing the gloves. It was difficult but not impossible.

As they were about to leave, Mrs Herold said, 'So my husband was murdered?'

'I'm sure of it,' Edward replied gravely. 'By the way, one last question. Was your husband a friend of Jack Amery?'

'We knew him, of course. He was . . . is a neighbour and he and Jimmy shared the same political views.'

'Do you like him?'

'No. I can't bear him. He tried to kiss me once, in the passage with Jimmy in his wheelchair only a few feet away.'

'So you've seen him recently?'

'The last time he came was four weeks ago. He didn't stay long when he saw the state Jimmy was in and I knew he wouldn't ever come again. He doesn't like illness and he was too selfish to pretend otherwise.'

'Well, thank you so much, Mrs Herold. You have been most kind. By the way, may I borrow a copy of *The Fall*? I'd be very interested to read it.'

'Of course.' She went over to a bookcase full of works on mountaineering and two or three, Edward saw, about Hitler and National Socialism. She took out her husband's book and handed it to him. Edward thought how odd it was to have found a second wife through an extended love letter to his first. 'Will you find the person who did this?' she asked quite fiercely.

'I will indeed. Have no fear of that,' Edward answered, her hand in his. The look in his eyes seemed to convince her because she nodded as though satisfied and turned to say goodbye to Harry.

9

Verity had not seen as much of Kay Stammers as she would have liked because Kay was in training for Wimbledon. She believed she had a good chance of reaching the finals and even of winning. So it was a delight for Verity when her friend breezed in one morning and said she had Dr Bladon's permission to take her on the river.

Kay said she despised motor launches and insisted on a rowing boat. Verity protested that she was not up to rowing but Kay said she would provide the muscle if Verity would steer. For fifteen minutes Kay rowed hard and Verity enjoyed watching her. Occasionally, Verity would forget what she was supposed to be doing and put them in the path of a motor launch or into the bank. The trouble was she found Kay fascinating and distracting. She was just the sort of woman she admired – independent, adventurous, intelligent and physically in her prime. The sweat began to pour off her forehead and she had to wipe her eyes almost every time she took a stroke so that Verity finally begged her to rest.

'We're not going anywhere.'

'You're right, we're not. I'm sure you wish we were.'

'You mean . . . I want to escape from the clinic?'

'Well, yes.'

'Actually, I think I may be getting institutionalized. I'm not even sure I could cross a road by myself any longer, let alone a continent.' Verity hesitated. 'I expect you think it's rather childish – my wanting to rush around the world when I should be tucked up with Edward in some baronial hall.'

'No, of course not. I admire what you have achieved – Guernica, for example. Your report did more than anything to make people realize the tragedy that was taking place in Spain.'

'Oh, gosh! It's only by the wildest stroke of luck that a reporter is actually on hand to describe a convulsion – a significant moment in history – a landmark which stands out even in our horrible century.'

'Like me being born left-handed. Most people think it's a disadvantage being left-handed but it's a real stroke of luck for a tennis player. Believe it or not, my teacher forced me to write with my right hand until my mother made a fuss. She thought I was crippled or something. Sorry, I didn't mean to go on about me. I say', Kay rested on her oars, 'do you mind talking about it . . . about Spain, I mean?'

'No, I feel like talking.'

'Well, let's tie up under that willow over there and rest awhile.'

When they were safely moored, Kay joined Verity in the back of the boat and they lay together like lovers enjoying the sound of the water and the wind rustling in the willow above them.

'May I ask you something Verity, if it won't make you cross?'

'Go ahead.'

'Do you think your lot can really win?'

'Last winter, I thought there was a chance. We . . . I mean the Republicans,' she corrected herself with a wry smile, 'won a great battle at Teruel.'

'I read about that. It's a city on the Guadalajara front, isn't it?'

'Yes. The battle was fought in the most terrible conditions. One thinks of Spain being so hot but you have no idea how cold it gets in winter. There was snow, frostbite, starvation and, as usual, not enough guns but the town was taken.'

'And lost again.'

'Yes. It was a great blow and now they are fighting on the Ebro river and we seem to be losing.'

'Do you know one thing that surprises me?'

'No, what?'

'You'll think me cynical but why has it taken Franco so long to win? I thought it would only be a matter of weeks before the Fascists took Madrid but the war still drags on. Is it just that the Republicans fight so fiercely?'

'They do but that's not the reason – at least so my friends there write to me. They say – and I'm inclined to believe them – that Franco doesn't want to win too quickly. In fact he wants to go as slowly as possible, never giving up an inch of the territory he gains, like some sort of awful meat grinder. He wants to spread terror, squash any sign of dissent and annihilate as many Republicans as possible. It's said that Franco told Mussolini, who asked the same question, that the military occupation would be useless if Spain wasn't "pacified" at the same time. He knows that the roots of anarchism there are very deep. To put it another way, he wants to eradicate anything which will be an obstacle to the survival of his dictatorship. I think, beneath the cynicism, he really believes that he is God's agent on earth.'

'How chilling!' Kay said. 'What help is there when such monsters roam the world?'

'We must face it down. That's all there is to it,' Verity replied gloomily.

'You won't believe this because I'm not brainy or anything like that but a friend took me to a reading by a poet called W.H. Auden in London last week. I thought I wouldn't understand a word but he read a poem about Spain and it really moved me. It made me think of you, of course!'

'Can you remember any of it?'

'Not that I can quote. I'm afraid I don't have that sort of memory but I do recall one phrase. He talked about the deliberate increase in the chances of death and – this was the phrase I remember – "the conscious acceptance of guilt in the necessary murder". I wonder if that is how Franco sees it?'

'Auden is a supporter of the Republic.'

'Yes, but that is what's so tragic. The other side seems to view the war in the same way you do. I mean, are ideals the most dangerous thing? Worse than greed or nationalism?'

'I don't know what you mean, Kay. We have to believe in something otherwise we might as well be animals.'

Kay thought for a moment or two and decided to change the subject. 'It must be wonderful to have your reputation. You know people trust you. When you describe some battle or whatever, people know that was how it was.'

'It's kind of you to say so but I don't fool myself. Many people *don't* trust me and they're probably right. I don't pretend to be omniscient. On the ground, it's all such a muddle. I never know the whole truth and, if I did, no one would publish it. From the air – as it were – I could probably pick out some sort of pattern but I can never see more than a small part of what's going on. We have to leave it to the historians to make sense of it all. I try not to generalize or make pronouncements. I have to stifle my doubts even about small things. Am I really seeing what I think I'm seeing?'

'How do you mean?'

'Well, take Guernica. I thought I knew what happened, but did I? I saw an undefended town destroyed by German aircraft but was I being manipulated? Did I simply see what the Communist Party wanted me to see? I'm pretty sure now – though I have no proof – that the Communist leadership had notice of what was going to happen. Stalin has his spies in the enemy camp just as there are German spies inside Russia. They – my trusted leaders –' Verity spoke with heavy irony – 'allowed it to happen to alert the world to the plight of the Republican cause.'

'And it did.'

'Yes, but they could have saved many innocent lives if they had given the city some warning. Still,' she added sheepishly, 'I'd like to think that, even if what I write isn't the whole truth and doesn't lead directly to action, it at least has some effect on public opinion. I mean, I know whatever I say won't change our government's policy of non-interference. However, I hope that what I write – what I *wrote*, I should say – makes people a little more receptive . . . a little more aware of what is happening.'

'It's all such a muddle – Spain, I mean,' Kay said, thumping her hand against the side of the boat. 'Who is good? Who is bad? Both sides kill innocent civilians.'

'The thing to remember – what I hold on to over and above the muddle and cynicism – is that the war in Spain is fundamentally a class war. It's the people against the ruling class. Whatever else, that's true.'

'You aren't fed up with journalism?' Kay asked after a pause.

'No, it's good for me. I have only to go to another country with a different sky and a different language to feel that life's worth living. There are things for my mind and eyes to feed on – actual sights rather than things I've read about. I'm one of those people who have to see something before they can imagine it. Doubting Thomas is my saint. And I meet people I would never have met otherwise. The boys I met in Spain – particularly from the International Brigade – were from all sorts of backgrounds but united by their hatred of Fascism.'

'So you learnt something – in Spain, I mean?'

'I learnt that you can be right and be defeated,' Verity replied bitterly.

'I suppose you must have had to sacrifice a lot?'

'You mean husbands and babies and things? No, as a woman I count myself very lucky to be able to do what they call a man's job. Most women can go nowhere and see nothing. They become tame rabbits and their husbands get bored with them. I like the long, cold train journeys listening to people talk. I like sharing the discomfort of the men at the front. I think it is not disgusting to look at the world and see it for what it is. I reported on the war in Spain and, if I am spared, will report on the war to come because there must be witnesses. I have trained myself to observe. I'll never see enough but I will report what I see. Journalism is an honourable profession.'

'You must be sick of war.'

'It's a solution to life,' Verity said sadly.

'Well, that's one thing you haven't seen before, I imagine.' Kay lifted her head and pointed across the river. 'Isn't that Edward – the one in front? Or do I mean stroke?'

Two men were sculling up the river in a pair. They were going fast but both seemed relaxed, their long, level strokes taking them quickly past the little rowing boat. Neither man turned his head and the two women watched mesmerized as the slim, fragile craft disappeared upstream.

'Very impressive,' Kay commented but Verity merely bit her lip.

How near am I to losing him? she asked herself. Should I burden him with a sick wife who cannot even do the job she was trained for? Silently, she spoke to him: My life is not long enough to love you properly. Shall I ever sleep in your arms as your wife, Edward? Oh God – if I believed in your existence – give me courage.

Kay, sensing her dejection, kissed her quickly on the forehead, sat up and took hold of the oars. 'Come on, Verity. Get a grip on the tiller or whatever they call it. It's time we went back.'

It had been at breakfast that Harry said to his guest, 'You know, Corinth, you look jaded, pooped, not to say tuckered out. It's time I took you out on the river. I can fit you up with a rigger or . . . I know . . . much better – a pair. There's one in the boathouse. It's not in the first flush of youth but it's perfectly sound.'

'Oh, no!' Edward said weakly. 'I don't think I'm up to it. It's been a lifetime since I did any serious rowing.'

'Nonsense! Have you finished breakfast? Right then – meet me at the boathouse in twenty minutes in kit suitable for messing about on the river.'

It pained Edward to have to admit it but he *was* jaded and desperately in need of exercise. As soon as they were on the river, he felt better. He had been worried that he would be an embarrassment and catch a crab or worse, but it was like riding a bicycle – something which, once learned, your body never forgot. His hands were soft, of course, and his breath not as good as it had once been but he was one of those lucky people who remained reasonably fit without taking regular exercise.

'Where shall we go?' Harry had asked as they slipped the oars through the rowlocks.

'Do we have to go anywhere in particular?' Edward responded. Then an idea occurred to him. 'I tell you what. We might go up to Amery's house if we can identify it and it isn't too far.'

Verity's report on the picnic with Mary Black's father had interested him. He had decided he might do a spot of espionage and this seemed as good a time as any.

'It's quite a distance,' Harry demurred. 'It'll take us three hours – more probably. We'll have to go through at least three locks but I'm game if you are. You're sure you're up to it?'

'I think so,' Edward said bravely. He felt he couldn't back out now without losing face.

'What happens when we get there?'

'I don't know. If the Amerys are there, we can beg a drink of water.'

'And if they're not?'

'Roam about a bit. You know the house, don't you?'

'I've been there a few times for a drink before going on somewhere.'

'But you know the lie of the land?'

'Yes, I suppose so.' Harry looked dubious. 'You're not suggesting a spot of housebreaking, are you?'

'Why, does that bother you? I seem to remember you doing some pretty similar stuff in Kenya.'

'But that was Kenya and I wasn't planning to steal anything,' he said defensively.

'Only a woman's virtue,' Edward replied sententiously. 'Anyway, we're not going to steal anything.'

'And if we're caught?'

'I don't know, Harry,' Edward retorted with some irritation. 'Pretend it's a joke or something. I hope you haven't lost that dash or whatever-you-call-it that got you thrown out of so many places in the Nairobi neighbourhood.'

Stung, Harry said, 'Come on, then. I thought you were the one who had become so law-abiding.'

Edward laughed. For some reason, he was feeling reckless. What did a bit of burglary matter when the whole world was about to go up in flames? Hitler had been thwarted in his attempt to swallow Czechoslovakia in May by a rare moment of spine-stiffening on the part of the French and British governments. They had threatened – though not promised – to stand by the Czechs if they were attacked. The Czechs, for their part, had gallantly declared that they would resist a German invasion and mobilized their armed forces. Hitler had very publicly ordered a huge increase in Germany's armed forces and announced his intention of humiliating the Czechs even if this meant going to war before his military chiefs were ready.

It was clear to Edward, as it was to everyone who could read a newspaper, that war was imminent and Britain needed to redouble its efforts to strengthen the Royal Air Force. Gas masks had been manufactured and distributed. Trenches were dug in Hyde Park and sandbags heaped against Whitehall ministries. But it turned out to be another false alarm. Neville Chamberlain – 'a man of peace to the depths of his soul', as he put it – had retreated and, in a speech to the House of Commons, almost apologized to Hitler for standing up to him. The French, too, had retreated, saying in effect that they would not go to war if Hitler decided to absorb into the Reich the Sudetenland, the German-speaking part of Czechoslovakia. Hitler bared his teeth but whether it was a smile or a snarl no one could say.

With an oar in his hands, Edward felt his blood stir and he determined to show his friend that he was as tough as he was. Harry, too, felt his spirits rise. He loved an escapade and had, he told himself disingenuously, been boringly well behaved since arriving in England to claim his inheritance. He said as much and Edward was amused to find Harry was still the amoral man he had encountered in Kenya and of whose antics he had eventually tired. He and Jack Amery were both rascals in their different ways, he thought, although Jack had even less to recommend him than Harry.

'That's it,' Harry said at last. 'Next stroke, easy oars.' Edward was devoutly grateful. He had started gamely and continued out of pride and bloody-minded determination but did not think he could have carried on much longer without collapsing. His lungs were bursting and, at first, he could do no more than sit where he was, panting and sweating.

It had been a lot further than he had reckoned and his hands were blistered and every muscle in his body ached. The thought of rowing all the way back appalled him. They had rested, necessarily, while negotiating the locks and had stopped at Marlow for a drink and a sandwich at a riverside pub. At Boulter's lock, Edward had decided the expedition was madness and they ought to turn back but, quite suddenly, they were at journey's end. He saw a white house with a lawn stretching down to the river and a low brick wall against which they secured their craft. They scrambled ashore and walked up to the house. Harry knocked on the back door but there was no reply. They went round to the front door and knocked again but there was still no answer. Edward sighed with relief.

'What do we do now?' Harry asked.

'There's a window open on the first floor. Why doesn't one of us shin up the creeper and have a look inside?'

Harry looked at him with interest and shook his head in ironic disbelief. 'And I thought you were so respectable. What if we're caught?'

'We'll think of something,' Edward replied airily. He wasn't quite sure why but he had an overwhelming desire to search Amery's house. He had no idea what he expected to find – something linking him to the Nazis perhaps? He wondered if the bag Amery had given Mr Black was money he had brought back from Germany to fund the British Union of Fascists. It would be something to report to Major Ferguson if he could find some proof.

'Who's doing the shinning?' Harry queried.

'Well, it's very much up your street, isn't it – climbing trees, lamp-posts, drainpipes and so on?'

'I don't know why you say that.' Harry sounded put out to be so remembered. 'However, give me a lift up and I'll see what I can do.'

Edward clasped his hands together to make a stirrup into which Harry put his foot. Grunting with the effort, he lifted him as high as he could. Harry scrambled up the creeper without too much trouble and put his head through the open window.

Looking about him to see if they were observed, Edward called, 'Can you see anything?'

Harry turned. 'It's their bedroom, I think. Wait there a minute. I'll climb in and come down and let you in.'

Edward was about to tell him not to but Harry had already scrambled over the sill. His enthusiasm for burglary had seeped away and it now hit him that what they were doing could land them in a police cell. He heard the bolt on the door being drawn back and Harry appeared, looking rather dishevelled with leaves in his hair.

'Come on! There's no one here. We can look over the place at our leisure.'

'I don't know – perhaps we shouldn't . . .'

'Look here, old chap. I've climbed up some pretty unpleasant creeper and torn my trousers getting through a window so the least you can do is take advantage of my efforts.'

Edward entered and found himself in the kitchen. It didn't look as though a great deal of cooking was done there or much cleaning either. Dirty breakfast plates lay soaking in mud-coloured water in the Belfast sink. The store was an ancient cast-iron affair with a large kettle sitting on the hotplate. He touched it and found it was still warm.

'They can't have been gone long,' he said.

'Well, let's be quick then. What are we looking for?'

'I'm not sure – documents – anything that might tell us what Amery's up to. Look, you go upstairs and I'll do down here.'

Harry ran up the steep wooden staircase. Edward heard him walking overhead and the sound of drawers opening and furniture being moved around. He went through into what seemed to be the sitting-room. A substantial wireless set dominated the room – a wooden cabinet through which, Edward thought drily, only the BBC was worthy to broadcast. However, when he looked more closely, he saw that the needle was set to Hamburg rather than London. There were magazines scattered all over the place – the *Quarterly Review*, the *Tablet*, the *Listener* and, somewhat surprisingly, *New Verse*. Newspapers, including *The Times* and the *Mail*, lay in piles on the floor but there was nothing suspicious, nothing overtly political and no German publications.

He was particularly interested to see that Amery read the *Tablet*. This was in effect the official organ of the Roman Catholic Church in England and was edited by a snobbish, fat man called Douglas Woodruff whom he had met once at the Hassels' and thoroughly disliked. He was a strong supporter of Franco and welcomed his rebellion against the virulently anti-Catholic 'Popular

Front'. Edward picked the magazine up and saw an advertisement for an article by Graham Greene on the cover – an author whose novels he had rather enjoyed.

Tossing it back on a table, he looked round. The house was little more than a cottage but there seemed to be a small study across the passage from the sitting-room. His heart missed a beat. If there was anything to find, it would surely be in there. A battered-looking typewriter sat on an even more battered desk. Beside it were two or three photographs including one of Amery's father, Edward was pleased to see. He noticed a neat pile of journals and pamphlets including *Blackshirt* – the paper of the British Union of Fascists – and General Fuller's *What the British Union has to offer Britain* as well as a noisome leaflet entitled *What shall we do with the Lion of Judah?*.

Feeling rather ashamed of himself, he opened the desk drawers but there was nothing of interest except a cheque book. He flicked through it but Amery was one of those feckless people who could not be bothered to fill in the stubs. He was just putting it back in the drawer when he noticed a sheet of paper which had been pushed right to the back. He looked it over and whistled. It was a bank draft for twenty thousand pounds made out to Amery and signed by someone whose name he could not decipher. However, on the back it bore the official stamp of the German Embassy in London. To his amazement, the stamp authorizing the payment was signed by the ambassador himself, Herbert von Dirksen. It was the absolute proof he sought of Amery's dealings with the Nazis.

He turned to call to Harry to come and see what he had discovered and found himself looking into the muzzle of a revolver.

'Major Stille!'

Stille was dressed like any English holidaymaker in

shorts and an open-necked shirt, though perhaps his hair was cut a little too short and his eyes were too hard and narrow for comfort.

'Lord Edward Corinth,' he said with a sneer. 'The amateur private eye.' His accent had a faint American twang and there was something not entirely English about the way he pronounced his 'r's. 'The busybody – *der Wichtigtuer, der Schnüffler*. What are you looking for?'

'What are you doing in Mr Amery's house?' Edward thought he would try sounding superior.

'What am I doing . . .?' Stille laughed. 'What are *you* doing – or are you going to tell me he invited you to look through his desk? Give me that, please,' he added sharply.

Edward was attempting to put the sheet of paper in his trouser pocket. 'This . . .?' he said in as innocent a voice as he could manage. 'I can't give it to you because it doesn't belong to you. It is a bank draft made out to Mr Amery. I found it on the floor and was going to return it to him.'

'Please do not joke with me.' Stille waved his gun threateningly. 'I think I am going to kill you but not here. I do not wish to cause my friend embarrassment. I think we will go to the river where I see your boat and there I will kill you. But first give me that paper.'

He held out his hand and, reluctantly, Edward took the bank draft out of his pocket. To distract him, he tossed it on the floor and Stille bent down to pick it up. As he did so, Harry came up behind him and hit him hard over the head with an iron poker.

'I've always wanted to do something like that,' he said with satisfaction. 'Is he dead?'

Edward knelt down beside the unconscious German. He touched his head and saw blood oozing. 'What disgusting hair lotion the man uses,' he exclaimed, drawing back. 'Thank you, Harry. No, he's not dead but you certainly hit very hard.'

'No point in taking chances. He was going to kill you, no doubt about it.'

'Yes, I know,' Edward said grimly. 'My heart was in my mouth. I thought he must have heard you coming down the stairs.'

'I was as quiet as possible.' Harry looked pained.

'You did well, thank you again.'

It occurred to Edward that Harry could commit murder without too much soul-searching.

'Who is he?' Harry asked.

'Major Horst Stille of the SS. He is in charge of German agents in this country. He is based at the German Embassy where he's called an Assistant Secretary or some such but, from what I hear, he works for Himmler and is quite independent of the ambassador.'

'You seem to know a lot about him.'

'Our paths have crossed before,' Edward said lightly.

'I believe you work for . . .'

'No one employs me,' Edward interrupted. 'I do have connections with Special Branch,' he added, seeing Harry's look of disbelief, 'but I'm not a policeman.'

Harry shrugged. 'So what do we do with the body?'

'Leave it for Amery, I think. He can bandage up his head.'

'You think he's a friend of Amery's?'

'I think Amery works for him,' Edward said flatly. 'In effect, he's Stille's agent in the BUF.'

'Jack passes German money to Mosley?'

'Yes, and this bank draft pretty well proves it. Why else would the German Embassy be transferring twenty thousand pounds to him?'

Harry looked at the piece of paper and whistled. 'What now?'

'We get out of here.'

'Will Stille tell Amery who knocked him out?'

'He never saw you although I suppose – given that

I'm staying in your house – it won't take him long to work out who gave him such a headache. It doesn't matter if Amery knows I have my eye on him. I would much rather he stopped doing what he's doing than he ends up in prison or worse.'

'You think he *will* stop?'

'Probably not. He strikes me as almost mad but you know him better than I do. By the way, you'd better keep a lookout from now on. I'm afraid your name will be added to Major Stille's list of people he would rather have dead than alive. If it's any comfort, mine and Verity's have headed that list for three or more years and we're still here.'

'Touch wood!' Harry said. 'What shall I do with the poker? Throw it in the river?'

'No point in that. You never know, Amery might need it. Wipe it clean of your fingerprints and leave it here. We'll not add theft of household implements to our misdemeanours. By the way, I never asked, did you find anything of interest upstairs?'

'Only this,' Harry replied, passing him a photograph.

10

'Call me Bill,' Bruce-Dick said, ushering Edward into a small hallway.

The secretary of Phyllis Court was very correct with a straight back and a firm handshake. He was clean-shaven and balding, his grey hair swept back to reveal a fine intellectual forehead. His shirt cuffs were showing the regulation half-inch beyond the sleeves of his pin-stripe suit. A white handkerchief peeped out of his breast pocket and his tie – a sober red and green – was secured by a gold pin. Edward had no doubt that such a neat man was also a meticulous administrator. Mrs Bruce-Dick came forward and he introduced Harry.

'My friend, Lord Lestern. We were at school together and then Kenya.'

'Yes indeed,' Bruce-Dick said as though he was about to add that he knew the colony well. 'I was in oil. No oil in Kenya.'

Edward chuckled but Harry's attention had strayed to a young woman dressed in white standing in the background.

'My daughter, Sybil,' Bruce-Dick said as if explaining a puzzling phenomenon, and Sybil was indeed very different from her mother and father. She was beautiful for one thing. There was no other word for it and she knew it. She smiled and the twinkle in her eye captivated Harry.

'Alberta, show our guests into the drawing-room.'

Theirs was a large flat on the Phyllis Court estate but Bruce-Dick was quick to tell Edward that they also owned a London flat in Elm Park Gardens. A mob-capped maid served them canapés and Edward had the impression that they were waiting for some other guests. As the minutes passed, he could see Bruce-Dick was getting increasingly anxious. He had a habit of twitching his trousers at the knees, presumably to ensure they did not lose their knife-edge crease. Twice he took surreptitious glances at his watch, and when at last the bell jangled his face cleared. He was on his feet calling to the maid that he would open the door before anyone else had moved. He left with mumbled excuses and they could hear him welcoming someone in the hall. Edward had rather expected that the guests would include a woman to even the numbers but, when the drawing-room door opened, they were joined by a father and son.

Edward and Harry rose to greet them. 'I don't think you know Roderick Black, Lord Edward, but I believe he has met your friend, Miss Browne. And this is his son Guy. Roderick, Guy . . . Lord Edward Corinth and Lord Lestern.'

The introductions complete, it was made immediately clear that Guy was Sybil's acknowledged suitor. He went over to her and held her hand for a moment longer than was necessary before turning to her mother. He was a dark, good-looking boy of about twenty-five with a fine moustache with which he had obviously taken some trouble. He had wide, frank eyes but his chin, Edward thought rather unkindly, was distinctly weak. Harry was put out to find that Sybil was already spoken for and did not hesitate to show it. If he was to be done out of a pleasant evening of flirting, he would make Guy pay for it. Instinctively, the two men began preening their feathers in front of Sybil who merely looked amused.

Roderick Black came over to Edward and said how glad he was that his daughter had found a friend in Verity. 'Mary tells me that you are engaged.'

Edward blushed. He was pleased but embarrassed that Verity had confided their secret to her room-mate. He had no idea how to deal with his new status. Somehow, it felt rather ridiculous to be engaged. It was something that happened to young people – like Guy and Sybil – not to middle-aged men. Black, seeing his confusion, added, 'Oh, I'm sorry. Have I been indiscreet? I didn't realize it was a secret.'

'Not really a secret. It's just that we wanted to keep quiet about it until Verity – Miss Browne – is better. We don't want to tempt fate.'

'Of course, I quite understand. I will tell no one.'

Bruce-Dick, who had been listening, added his congratulations. 'There have been rumours,' he said coyly, 'but we'll be as quiet as the grave, won't we, Alberta?'

It was possibly this rather unfortunate mention of the grave which made Black say, 'It's a lonely, worrying business for Mary and, I imagine, for Miss Browne. I'm sure it's only a matter of time before they find a cure . . .'

He looked genuinely distressed and Edward felt for him. 'I know . . . it's wretched.'

Any friend of Jack Amery had to be suspect but he was prepared to keep an open mind as far as Roderick Black was concerned. Over rather indifferent mock-turtle soup followed by over-cooked beef washed down by watery claret they talked about the impending regatta. This, rather than Wimbledon or Lord's, was Bruce-Dick's passion and, encouraged by Black father and son, he became rather a bore about it. Harry, who had obviously done his homework, was able to keep his end up as his host recalled past regattas and records were rehearsed and argued over at – for Edward at least – tedious length and detail.

Guy was modest about his chances of winning the Diamond Sculls, or the Diamonds as he called it. He explained that there was an American by the name of Joe Burk from Penn Athletic Club who was said to be unbeatable.

'I saw him on the river yesterday as a matter of fact. He's very fit and very fast,' he said ruefully. 'And don't forget, there's also Habbits. I've never seen him scull badly and on a good day he can beat any of us.'

'Habits?' Edward queried.

'L. D. Habbits of Reading,' Guy laughed, 'though, I suppose inevitably, we call him "Bad Habits".'

'Oh, I see,' Edward said smiling. 'And why is he so good?'

'I don't know, he just is. Mind you, he has very long arms.'

'That helps?'

'Yes. Normally when a man stands with his arms stretched out sideways, he's as wide as he's tall. If your arms are longer than normal and you stretch wider than your height you have greater leverage and, if you are strong enough to keep it up, then you go significantly faster. The instant the blades are covered, the whole weight must be lifted from the stretcher and applied to the oar handle and must stay like that until the hands come into the chest. I'm sorry, I'm being a bore.'

'No, certainly not,' Edward reassured him, impressed by his enthusiasm and scientific approach to the sport. 'And do you name your boat? I mean, I know Trinity – that was my college – always call their boats *Black Prince*.'

'Some are given names and some aren't, there's no rule. I always think that an eight pounding upstream with blades flashing is one of the most exhilarating sights you could ever hope to see.'

175

'What is good rowing?' Edward asked.

'Well, to get pace, it's what happens *between* the strokes that matters. A boat that wins is one that travels faster when the blade is out of the water so a good "finish" is essential. A prolonged feather against the wind and a lightning entry of the blade into the water is what makes the difference.'

Guy's eyes blazed and even Harry smiled. Guy Black was clearly a young man to reckon with.

After dinner, Bruce-Dick asked the men if they would mind joining the ladies for coffee and to try some quite passable port. Edward had the feeling that he preferred not to risk an all-male inquisition although what he might have to hide he could not imagine. No one objected so they returned to the drawing-room. Guy, blushingly, invited Sybil to walk with him in the garden and she agreed, lowering her eyes and giving a shy nod.

Inevitably, the conversation among those left behind turned back to rowing and the regatta. Roderick Black had been a 'useful oar', as he put it, in his youth but now subsumed his own ambition in his son.

Taking Edward to one side, he said, 'I don't know whether Miss Browne mentioned it but I took her and Mary on the river.'

'Indeed, it was most kind of you. She told me how much she enjoyed it. You picnicked, I gather, on Mr Amery's lawn?'

'Yes, that was tactless, I'm afraid. I had forgotten that Miss Browne was on the opposite side of the fence – a Communist, I mean. Do you know him?'

'I do,' Harry broke in. 'We saw something of each other in Kenya.'

'You were in Kenya, Lord Lestern? What a small world! I used to have some business interests there.'

'But that's not where you met Jack Amery?' Edward asked.

176

'No, I met him through his father, in the House.'

'But politically . . .' Edward probed.

'Politically, he is to my right. There's much about Sir Oswald Mosley I admire but he's gone too far. I've told Jack that but he won't listen. Were you involved with the film he was making in the colony, Lord Lestern? What was it called?'

When Harry told him Edward had the impression that Black knew its title but did not wish to appear too intimate with Amery.

'He's rather a wild young man, is he not?' Bruce-Dick said, disapprovingly.

'Do *you* know him too?' Edward asked, intrigued.

'Not really but I see him sometimes on the river. He rows well but he won't put his back into it.'

'Yes,' Black said, 'he was wild at Harrow. He was always doing outrageous things and whenever the police raided the Hypocrites Club, the '43 or the Blue Lantern there were always Harrow boys there, usually including Jack. Discipline was very slack at the school at the time – so his father told me,' he added as an afterthought, again, perhaps, not wanting to look as if he knew Jack well.

'At least there's no politics in rowing,' Edward remarked.

'I wish that were true,' Black replied. 'You obviously don't remember but there was an almighty fuss last year when the victorious eight from Rudergesellschaft Wiking gave a Nazi salute in the Stewards'.'

Everyone looked glum for a moment.

'I say,' Edward said, as though he had just thought about it. He took out the photograph Harry had found in Amery's bedroom. He had intended to show it to Bruce-Dick to see what he made of it but why not show it to Black as well? Presumably, he had never been into Amery's bedroom so he would not have seen it before

177

and would not know its provenance. 'I found this photograph in an album belonging to a friend of mine', he lied. 'I borrowed it because it showed some of the Kenya crowd and I'm almost sure . . . that *is* Jack Amery, isn't it?' He pointed to a face in the back row.

'Yes, that's him, all right,' Black agreed. 'It must have been when he was making *Jungle Skies*.'

Bruce-Dick had got out his monocle and was examining the photograph. 'Surely that's Peter Lamming?'

'Yes, that's what Harry and I thought. It must have been taken – when? – fifteen years ago?'

'What happened to him?' Bruce-Dick asked. 'I just remember he had that extraordinary year at Henley when he won the Diamond Sculls. It must have been just before he went out to Kenya. What did *The Times* call him? Of course! The Diamond Boy.'

'He died – malaria, I believe. He'd only been married a year. A tragedy,' Edward answered him. It suddenly struck him that he did not know for sure *how* Lamming had died.

There was an awkward silence until Bruce-Dick moved on to talk about the regatta which began in two days' time.

'The first day's always the best,' he said. 'There are so many races – never a dull moment. There are always one or two very close ones whereas on the last day the finals can be something of an anticlimax.'

'And Guy is in with a chance of lifting the Diamond Sculls? You must be very proud,' Edward said to Black. 'May I ask,' he continued, turning to Mrs Bruce-Dick, 'are he and Sybil engaged? I hope I'm not being impertinent but they seem so well suited.'

He knew he was chancing his arm but he was interested to see what reaction he would get and, damn it, he'd had to confess to being engaged to Verity.

Perhaps 'confess' was the wrong word, he thought guiltily. Mrs Bruce-Dick seemed hardly able to answer him but eventually murmured that there was no engagement.

The party broke up early. Guy was sticking to a strict regime which involved no alcohol, early nights and two hours on the river early in the morning when most of Henley was thinking about breakfast. Bruce-Dick, too, had a busy day ahead of him. During the regatta, Phyllis Court was completely booked out and there were parties every night. As they left, he touched Harry on the arm and said in a low voice, 'Dashed sorry about the time it has taken to get you a membership here. I think I can say you won't have to wait much longer.'

As they strolled back to Turton House, their path illuminated by the light of a full moon, Harry was cock-a-hoop. 'It's all thanks to you, old boy. Can't say how much I appreciate it. You know, I might stay in England after all. It's not such a bad place once those toffee-nosed friends of yours stop acting as if my presence left a nasty smell under their collective nose.'

Edward pooh-poohed the idea that he had played any part in getting his friend into Phyllis Court but privately he offered up a prayer that Harry would not do anything outrageous and get himself thrown out. The people who mattered in a place like Henley were much stuffier than in Kenya. In Happy Valley, you could get away with murder if you were moderately discreet but not in England and certainly not in Henley.

The regatta was held from Wednesday 29th June to Saturday 2nd July. The first day was blessed by a cool breeze and high cloud, ideal for rowing. There had been a brief shower in the early morning but that hadn't put anyone off and by midday the Stewards' Enclosure and the Phyllis Court stands on the other side of the river were almost full. The Committee chairman, Lord Desborough, was well pleased. Along the booms that marked out the course, a host of small boats – mostly punts and rowing boats but including a few slipper launches – nuzzled one another for a view of the first heats. Two by two, like the animals entering the Ark, eights, fours and pairs dipped their gaily painted oars in the river, glacially calm but for the occasional wash from some large motor launch.

Along the course, progress boards recorded the state of the race. It was almost cruel, Edward thought, to watch two eights rowing their hearts out. Parallel at the start, one would forge ahead of the other – and once an eight was a length ahead, it was rare to see it overtaken. At the winning post, the dejection and exhaustion of the losers was in stark contrast to the elation of the winning crew. He remembered a coach telling him at Eton that he always exhorted his crew to row well even if the other crew seemed to be drawing ahead. 'If you remember to row well,' he opined, 'you are much more likely to win than if you panic and try to row faster.'

'And if you still lost?' Edward had asked.

'Then at least you will have given pleasure to those watching who know what it means to row well,' was the somewhat *Through-the-Looking-Glass* response.

'Which end do you pole from?' Verity had asked as Edward tucked her into the punt Bruce-Dick had kindly lent him.

'At Cambridge we pole from the flat end,' he told her, 'but at Oxford they pole from inside the punt.'

'How absurd you men are!' Verity giggled. She was feeling very much better and, when Edward had suggested watching a few of the races from a boat, she had been excited. She had never been in a punt before and enjoyed being so close to the water, sliding, swan-like, across the river. She began to understand the popularity of punting with young men as she lay back and studied Edward. From below, his beak-like nose and strong chin were more than usually evident. Each time he pushed against the pole, his biceps bulged, obliging her to admire his athletic physique. He had taken off his jacket but refused to remove the Old Etonian tie Harry had lent him. When she scoffed at him, he told her he felt underdressed without one and that, outside Eton, Henley Regatta was one of the few places it was quite legitimate to wear it. He knew he ought to be wearing a cap or a straw boater but he had never been a member of a rowing club and didn't want to pretend he was something he wasn't.

Edward didn't know a great deal about the sport but he was particularly keen to see if Guy could do anything in the Sculls. As he, rather skilfully he thought, attached the punt to a boom without falling in, he noticed an acquaintance, George Bushell, who – according to the programme – was the regatta's official photographer. Bushell had his apparatus in a launch and was positioning himself to record the first race.

'George . . . I say, George!' Edward called, inviting a disapproving look from a man in the neighbouring punt.

Bushell looked round to see who was calling his name. 'Corinth! What are you doing here? I didn't know you were a rowing man.'

'I'm not – just an interested spectator.'

'Can't stop and chat, old boy, but here – let me take a picture of you and your lady.'

Without waiting for permission or introductions, he took his photograph. 'Come to the exhibition on Friday,' he shouted as his launch moved off. 'In the Stewards' tent . . .'

They returned to *terra firma* for a late lunch and, as the band played, ate smoked salmon and drank champagne. It really wasn't what a good Communist should be doing, Verity told herself, but she suddenly realized that she didn't care a damn. For the first time in months she was happy. Without being aware of it, she found that she had lost her faith in the Communist Party – not in Communism but in the *apparatus* of Communism. Like a Catholic who no longer went to Mass, she felt guilty but defiant. She was hearing from friends back from the war who wrote to her or visited her that the Party had intensified its efforts to destroy its allies. SIM, the Servicio de Investigación Militar, the Republic's secret police, was now nothing more than a branch of Stalin's NKVD. Many of Verity's old friends and comrades had been 'liquidated'. Conscripts – mostly boys of sixteen or less – were now trying to halt Franco's inexorable advance. It was murder on a grand scale.

'And is the "Old Coll" on display today?' she asked Edward with heavy sarcasm.

'Indeed. At four o'clock, if you care to look at your programme – in The Ladies. It should be a good race against Trinity College, Dublin.'

'The Ladies? That's wonderful! I had no idea there were women rowing at Henley.'

'Don't be silly, V,' he said crossly. 'Of course there are no women's eights. It would be physically impossible. It's the Ladies' Challenge Plate.'

'I don't see why . . .' She saw his face and decided not to pursue the matter. Why shouldn't women row? They had proved themselves in other 'male' sports but she recognized that this wasn't the moment to speak her mind. It amused and annoyed her that Edward – in common with all men of his class as far as she could see – talked about *our* school, university or regiment long after ceasing to be a member of whichever institution was being discussed. It confirmed her view that the English – she did not know if were true of the Scots or the Irish – held tight to their authority and their place in society by tweaking on one string or another, like a skilled harpist, to obtain the desired effect. 'Everyone' knew someone you knew – that is if you had been born into a certain class.

She had noticed that, when Edward met a stranger, the conversation almost always began with the weather but that was not what was being discussed. After a sentence or two, he would know precisely what class the new acquaintance belonged to and even the school at which he had been educated. Once, provoked by Verity, he had admitted that he was more relaxed with other Old Etonians although, of course, he had friends who had been educated at other schools and at no school at all. It was as if, with a fellow Old Etonian, there was a sub-text or hidden language that made communication easier and so many things could be taken as read without having to be put into words.

'So what are the prizes?' she asked instead.

'Some very impressive silverware,' Edward said, a trifle pompously. 'The cup for The Ladies is . . .'

'I meant prize money.'

He looked shocked. 'There's no prize money. We are talking about a gentleman's sport, I'm glad to say. I hope you aren't going to ask where you can place a bet on a race.'

Verity ignored his sarcasm and persisted. 'So they race their hearts out for the honour of it?'

'Yes.' Edward sounded surprised. 'What did you think?'

Had he thought about it, he might have concluded that Verity was definitely feeling better if she was up to ragging him.

They decided to watch Eton and Trinity College fight it out from the stands. She was surprised to find Edward became quite agitated. It wasn't until the last half of the race that he could see through his binoculars that the two crews were neck and neck. As they drew towards the finishing line, the crowd lost its inhibitions and began to shout and applaud. This seemed to release something in Edward. To Verity's amazement, she watched him shouting himself hoarse for his old school, applauding enthusiastically as Eton won by a whisker.

'Bad luck, old chap,' he said to the man next to him who wore the black-and-white striped tie of the Dublin University Boat Club. 'Your chaps did jolly well. Just up against a better crew, I suppose.'

His neighbour scowled and went off mumbling under his breath.

'Did I say something wrong?' he appealed to Verity. 'I was just trying to be polite.'

That first day of the regatta was almost perfect and Edward looked back on it with some pleasure even though it was tarnished by what happened later. He met friends and acquaintances from Eton and Cambridge and enjoyed jawing about the old days. To a man, they all expressed surprise at seeing him at Henley and delight that, at his age, he was becoming a rowing enthusiast. Verity was quickly bored by all this back-slapping but her day was saved by the unexpected arrival of Kay Stammers who had been knocked out of Wimbledon in the second round. Verity found her on her own in the tea tent looking morosely at the river and eating strawberries and cream.

'Kay! What are you doing here? I'm so pleased to see you.'

'I've been kicked out of the tournament so I thought I'd come and find you. Where's Edward?'

'He went off with some "chums",' Verity replied, a touch acidly. 'He said he would be back in a minute but that was half an hour ago. But what happened? Tell me. I thought this was going to be your year.'

Kay was philosophical about her unexpected exit from the tournament. 'I played rotten tennis and I deserved to be beaten.'

'Who beat you?'

'A French girl I had never heard of and who turned out to be young enough to be my daughter.'

'Not really?'

'Well, not quite that young but she seemed a child to me. Still, there's always next year.'

'So who's going to win?'

'Helen Wills Moody as usual, I suppose . . . but,' she added, brightening, 'she's first got to beat Hilde Sperling – the German girl who could be dangerous – and Helen Jacobs. But Helen Moody will win. She's ice-cool, a robot on court.'

'Kay, you're my saviour. I'm so pleased you came to find me. Edward's been sweet but really, I've decided rowing isn't my sport. It's all very pretty and everything and some of the men are gorgeous but it's so repetitive. You see that island with the temple thing on it? A cannon goes off when a race starts, and that's about the most exciting thing that happens. They parade down the course in parallel, sweating slightly, and one is declared the winner. I know I'm being unfair but it's not like tennis where there's so much variety . . . so gladiatorial.'

Kay laughed. 'I don't think you are a sports person at all, if the truth be told. I believe you see all sport as a trivial distraction from the real world of war and politics.'

'I suppose I do really.' Verity stuck her chin out defiantly. 'I never liked that story of Drake insisting on finishing his game of bowls even though he had been told the Armada was in sight of Plymouth. It's such a *man* thing – so English – always wanting to be "amateur", as though trying too hard or preparing too well isn't *sporting*, not "playing the game".'

The contempt with which she spoke made Kay laugh. 'That includes me, does it?'

'No! Of course it doesn't. You are serious – in fact you're wonderful. I really don't know what I would have done without you encouraging me and setting me a good example. I mean,' she added, feeling that she was being disloyal, 'Edward has been simply splendid and I owe him everything but . . .'

'But you need a woman friend sometimes.' Kay laughed again but gently. She seemed to have a thought because she said suddenly, 'I tell you what! We've talked about it for ages but, now you are so much better, this is the time to do it.'

'Do what?'

'Take you up in the Tiger Moth. We can do it tomorrow. I've got nothing planned as I expected to be playing tennis and the weather forecast is good. Just for half an hour. It can't do you any harm and might do you some good.'

'Oh, that would be wonderful!' Verity said, clapping her hands. 'I'd love that but . . .'

'What?'

'Don't tell Dr Bladon or . . . or Edward. They might try to stop me.'

'Our secret then.' She clasped Verity's hand. 'It'll be a lark. Just say you are having a day off from the regatta and I'm taking you for a drive. That won't be a lie because I am going to take you for a drive – to Booker Aerodrome.'

Edward seemed more relieved than anything to know that Kay was going to take Verity off his hands for a day. It wasn't that he didn't enjoy being with her. He loved her devotedly but she did demand his full attention otherwise he saw that look on her face he dreaded – that 'what-are-we-going-to-do-now' look – and if he failed to come up with anything, she became bored and fell to teasing him. He had an idea that when they were married – if they ever did get married – he would need to find something to occupy her. He began to think that a world war was just what she needed and then felt ashamed. It wasn't really like that, he reminded himself. It was more like being the only person who knew that Mount Vesuvius was about to explode and bury the light-hearted, pleasure-seeking Pompeians in molten lava.

There was to be a party that night at Phyllis Court and Edward had taken a table. There would be dinner and dancing, of course, but nothing too dramatic. The fireworks were kept to celebrate the end of the regatta. To Verity's chagrin, Kay and Edward both insisted that she was not yet well enough to stay up late and drink champagne.

'If you want to come out with me tomorrow,' Kay said meaningfully, 'you must get some rest.' With bad grace, Verity accepted her fate and Kay took her back to the clinic. Edward had invited Kay to join him and Harry at Phyllis Court. Kay was doubtful at first but Verity said she should go. 'I want a full report in the morning. If Edward misbehaves, I want to hear about it.'

Harry and Kay took to each other immediately, which was hardly surprising. Kay looked stunning in a long white dress, long white gloves and diamond choker about her slim neck. Harry was just the sort of man she liked. He had seen as much of the world as she had so they compared notes on America, Africa and exotic places in between. They were both keen flyers and decided there and then to take to the skies together as soon as the regatta ended. Harry's dubious reputation with women – Edward had thought it his duty to warn Kay – merely amused her. She was challenged and, although she did not trust him, she loved his rakish, devil-may-care attitude to life – and it didn't hurt his being a lord.

Edward looked on – a touch morosely – as the two of them danced the night away to the music of Jack Palmer and his orchestra. He knew it would please Verity to hear that he had been sidelined and, shortly after eleven, he made his excuses and left. Harry and Kay hardly seemed to notice.

When he got back to Turton House, he sat nursing a whisky and soda. Idly, he took up a photograph in a silver frame of Harry arm in arm with a beautiful woman. As he studied it, he thought he recognized the woman as Christobel Redfern. She and Harry were both carrying guns and were clearly about to go into the bush to hunt game. There was something about the relaxed, intimate way they stood together, not touching – not *needing* to touch – that said as clearly as words that they were lovers. On a whim, he opened the frame to see if there was a date or inscription on the back of the photograph but found nothing. However, there was another photograph secreted behind it. It was of Peter and Isabella Lamming. In contrast to the other, it was a formal, posed study which had obviously been taken at their wedding. Isabella had a posy of flowers in one hand and the other was tucked under Lamming's arm. He was wearing some sort of uniform.

The next morning, Edward left the house before his host was awake and strolled towards the Stewards' Enclosure. The races did not begin until eleven but there were already crowds milling around – some hiring punts at fifteen shillings and six pence for the day. He met several acquaintances, one of whom introduced him to Lord Camoys – a Senior Steward and, inevitably, an Old Etonian. Camoys invited him aboard the *Arethusa*, one of the umpires' launches, to follow a heat of the Stewards' Challenge Cup. Leander, the oldest and most prestigious boat club, was rowing against Magdalen College, Oxford. Half an hour later, Edward found himself sitting next to the Magdalen coach as the launch ploughed downriver towards the start with all the superiority of a swan among ducks. He had a strong temptation to trail his hand through the water, as he had done as a child, but remembered being told that anything which could be construed as a signal from someone in the umpire's launch might allow the losers to challenge the result of a race.

As the *Arethusa* rounded Temple Island, Edward admired the elegant folly which, with the church and the ancient bridge, gave Henley its air of serenity. The folly had been built in 1771 by Sambrooke Freeman of Fawley Court, one of the fashionable houses near the town. It was designed by James Wyatt and boasted, Camoys told him, wall paintings in the Etruscan style. The Victorians had added, rather unfortunately Edward thought, a heavy wooden balcony. Part of the island had been dug away when the new straight course had been made in 1924 but it was a delightful place to start a race – particularly if all one had to do was watch from a motor launch as other men laboured over their oars. He wondered idly if the captains of Roman triremes had viewed their galley slaves with the same detached satisfaction.

Back on dry land he thanked Camoys and went off to get a drink. The band of the Grenadier Guards was playing lustily and he stopped to listen. He was tapping his fingers to an overture by Suppé when Guy Black came out from behind the bandstand, deep in conversation with none other than Major Stille. What the German was doing at Henley, Edward could not imagine and what he had to say to Guy was something he did not want to think about. Roderick Black was, he suspected, to the right of Genghis Khan but it had never occurred to him that he – or, worse still, his son – might actually be a Fascist. Stille, who was dressed like almost everyone else in white ducks and a coloured cap, disappeared into the crowd. Edward hesitated for a moment and then decided he might as well make his presence known to Guy. Perhaps he did not realize that Stille was a Nazi agent pretending to be an Assistant Secretary at the German Embassy. It would be a good idea to warn him before Guy compromised himself.

'Hello, Guy,' he said, touching him on the arm. 'You are racing today, aren't you?'

'Corinth! Yes, I am – this afternoon.'

'I couldn't help noticing that you were talking to Major Stille. You do know who he is?'

'Of course, I do,' Guy replied roughly. 'He rowed for Rudergesellschaft Wiking just after the war. He helped coach them to win the Grand Challenge Cup last year.'

Edward was taken aback. He had no idea Stille was an athlete but, then, why shouldn't he be? 'Wasn't that the time they gave the Nazi salute?'

Guy shrugged. 'I don't see what all the fuss was about. After all, we have the National Anthem or,' he added as the band struck up the Eton Boating Song, 'your old school song.'

'That's not the same thing at all. I happen to know that Stille is a nasty piece of work. He's a member of the SS and responsible for German agents in this country.'

'You're not accusing me of being one, are you?'

'Of course not, but I thought I ought to warn you.'

'What do you expect to happen? Do you think Stille will suborn me or something? Perhaps you think he'll sabotage the *Hornet*? My heat today is against a German, Ricard Gustman – one of the best. That's what we were talking about, if you must know. Though what business it is of yours, I really don't understand.'

'The *Hornet*? Is that what your boat's called?'

'Yes, why?'

Edward hesitated. To mention the murders and their links to the insect world would sound ridiculous. 'Just a coincidence. I'm sure Verity told me that was the name of the launch she went on with your father and Mary.'

'That's right, the *Henley Hornet*. We call all our boats *Hornet*. A family tradition.'

'Yes, well, do be careful, Guy. Despite what you say, I know Stille better than you and he's not a man your father would want you to associate with.'

'On the contrary, it was my father who introduced us. Now, if you'll forgive me, I have things to do. Goodbye.'

Edward let him go without another word. He had heard enough to make him worried. The calm of just a few minutes ago had been replaced by an undefined anxiety. Something bad was about to happen and he ought to be able to prevent it – if he could only work out what it was.

11

Verity and Kay had not spoken much on the drive to Booker Aerodrome but an air of suppressed excitement emanated from both of them. Verity had the same feeling she remembered having as a schoolgirl when she embarked on one of her – usually ill-advised – escapades. It was a perfect day for flying. The cloud was high, the wind light and there was a freshness in the air after the previous night's showers. It was so good to get away from the clinic and forget she was supposed to be ill – forget everything except that she was free.

Kay parked the car and led Verity into a huge hangar. The doors, which were wide open, framed the sky so the clouds appeared to scud across the blue as though across a vast cinema screen. There were several small planes parked around the perimeter, some with men working on them, the others silent, expectant, like dogs waiting to be let out of their kennel.

'Here she is,' Kay said, leading Verity up to her Tiger Moth and patting it. 'Bert – my mechanic – has done all the hard work but, if you don't mind waiting a few minutes, I'd like to give her the once-over.'

Verity sat quietly on a broken-backed chair while Kay checked the plane and fuelled her up.

'Did you say you'd flown before?' Kay asked, passing Verity an empty can before jumping down from the engine cowling.

'Only as a passenger. Edward's a flyer. He says you have to fly in Africa if you want to get anywhere and he once flew us back from Spain.'

'And you didn't feel sick?'

'Not at all. Has it ever made you sick?'

'No. When my father taught me to fly, I was always concentrating too hard to feel anything.'

'Will you teach me?' Verity asked wistfully. 'I'd like that more than anything.'

'Of course, once you are quite well.'

Verity scowled but said nothing. She was well now, she thought, if only she had more energy. 'Can I ask how much it costs – a Tiger Moth, I mean?'

'A thousand pounds,' Kay replied airily. 'Less if you buy one second-hand. The problem is getting one. They're all going to the RAF. De Havilland just can't make enough of them. You see, it's not just us who want them but other air forces – the Canadians, even the Portuguese, I'm told.'

'I didn't realize. So the government is at last spending money on new planes?'

'It seems so. The RAF likes Tiger Moths because they are so easy to repair. Everything important is readily accessible, as you'll see.'

'They're not fighters?'

'No, they're trainers but that's vital. This country's desperately short of trained pilots.'

'Are all Tiger Moths the same?' Verity inquired naively.

'I should say not! Mine's a DH.82A, if you want to be technical. To be honest, it's not that different from the biplanes they used during the war – improved of course. For instance, the wings and bracing have been stiffened up so you can do quite violent aerobatics even when heavily laden. Barrel rolls, loops, nose dives, bunts – anything you can think of. She's so strong. I bought her two years ago and I love her.'

'What's a bunt?'

'A sort of loop. Maybe I'll show you.'

'Can you fly upside down?'

'Certainly! But not with a passenger on board.'

Verity was silent as she tried to imagine what it must be like to fly such a machine. 'She's definitely a "she"?'

'Yes. I love men but I love women even more,' Kay said, stroking the propeller, not looking at Verity.

'Have you given her a name?'

'I call her *Free Spirit*.'

Kay dispensed sugared buns and hot coffee from a Thermos while Bert and another mechanic rolled the Tiger Moth out of the hangar on to the grass. After they had finished, she locked their handbags in a metal cabinet. 'Right! Now let's get you togged up.' She had a spare flying suit which she said would fit Verity. 'It's cold up there, you know,' she said, pulling at a zip. 'You look very dashing. All you need now are some goggles. Some flyers won't use them but I do.'

When Verity was properly kitted out, Kay produced a camera. 'I'll get Bert to take a photograph of us beside the plane. You'll meet him properly in a moment. He's a first-class mechanic. I don't really need to check and refuel her myself but I like doing it. It's sort of intimate – like grooming a horse. You can ride a horse someone else has groomed but you don't have the same relationship with it.'

They reached the plane and Verity shook hands with Bert. 'She looks so fragile. Is that just wood under the canvas or whatever it is?' She prodded a silver wing with her finger.

'Just wood covered in Irish linen coated with dope to give it rigidity,' Bert confirmed. 'You've got to be careful when you're working on her but in the air she's very forgiving, if you understand me, miss. That's right, isn't it, Miss Kay?'

'Quite right. You can treat her quite badly in the air – do all sorts of things you shouldn't and she doesn't mind. I mean, she might tremble a bit in protest but she won't crash or anything. That's why the Tiger Moth is so good for training. Right, here we go. Everything OK, Bert?'

'Nowt to worry about, miss. She's just wanting a run. You see, miss,' he said to Verity, 'I think of her as being like a racehorse. She needs regular exercise to keep her fit.' He helped her into the seat in front of Kay.

'I'm in the front?'

'Yes, in the instructor's seat. When we are in the air, you can take over for a minute or two if you like. Get a feel of her. Now, just flick those switches on the side in front of you, will you? I'm afraid you won't be able to hear me during the flight but, if you press your ear to the Gosport tube, you might catch something if I shout. When I want to point something out to you, I'll waggle my stick from side to side and you'll feel your stick move between your legs By the way, if you don't like anything I'm doing or you want to go back, just put both your hands on the top of your head like this.'

Verity smiled. 'I feel quite safe in your hands, Kay. Do what you like with me.'

She felt very snug in the little cockpit. When she stretched out her legs, she felt the pedals move as if *Free Spirit* were alive. The stick between her legs wiggled without her touching it as Kay made herself comfortable behind her. She looked at the instruments. They had a worn appearance as though they had registered a lot of height and speed in their time and nothing could now shock them. The compass seemed simple enough but, when she tried to read it, she found she could not understand it. It was like a small ship's compass and you had to look down on it. She admired Kay so much for being the master of such a machine and it made her relax to feel she was in the hands of an expert. There was absolutely nothing she need do but see what there was to see and feel what there was to feel.

Bert hopped up and locked her into her safety harness. 'Good luck, miss. Your first time in the air?'

Verity felt unable to answer and merely smiled.

When Kay was satisfied everything was ready, she signalled to Bert – acting as prop swinger – and he pulled down on the propeller. She had explained to Verity earlier that the prop swinger had to 'suck in' by swinging the propeller four times while the switches were off to suck the fuel from the carburettor into the engine. When Bert had done this, he shouted 'Contact' and Kay switched on the pair of magnetos. After three more tugs on the propeller, the engine roared into life. As it warmed up, the noise engulfed Verity and she felt as though the life force was flowing through her.

At a signal from Kay, the chocks were removed and they rolled over the grass. When they reached the end of the runway, she turned the Tiger Moth and prepared for take-off. They began to trundle over the grass. At first, Verity could see nothing ahead of her because the nose of the plane pointed upwards and blocked her view. Then the tail went up and she could see down the runway. Even when *Free Spirit* began to gather speed she could not believe they would ever leave the ground. Suddenly they were airborne. There was no sense of 'taking off'. It was as though they just floated into the sky. A shiver of excitement went down Verity's spine and she laughed aloud. Although she had flown in small planes before, she had never been in one as small as this. It was, she thought, like riding bareback. She could feel it alive between her legs.

A gust of wind caught the Tiger Moth and tossed it to one side. Instinctively, Verity reached for one of the metal struts but stopped herself and relaxed. *Free Spirit* seemed so fragile, like a moth blown about by the wind. She had wanted to be free – free of her illness, free of the earth, free even of Edward – and now she *was* free. She had to suppress an insane desire to unfasten her harness, get up out of her seat, force herself through the wind between the struts and leap into nothingness.

Perhaps it was the disease which had attacked her lungs that made her so light-headed. It was fortunate that Kay could not see her face or read her thoughts. She felt the stick move between her legs and remembered that this was how Kay had said she would get her attention. She turned with difficulty and saw that Kay was pointing right and downwards. There, far below, was Henley. As they swooped lower over the town, she could see the river glinting in the sun and, as they went even lower, boats and then people looking up at them. Verity wanted to wave but thought Kay might not approve. The bridge, the temple on the island, the church and the Phyllis Court tennis courts swung below them and, once again, she was overwhelmed by a sense of exhilaration close to hysteria. She struggled to remove her goggles but the wind made it difficult to see without them and, as the plane turned, the sun blinded her. The noise of the engine and the wind was much greater than she had imagined and her mind was bludgeoned into a state of pleasant numbness which made coherent thought almost an impossibility.

All too soon, they were back over the aerodrome and below her she could see the little painted aircraft on the grass. Kay signalled for her to hold on. She was going to try a loop. The Tiger Moth began to dive and Verity was thrust back against her seat hardly able to breathe. Then *Free Spirit* – living up to her name – climbed away to begin the loop. At the top, the little craft began to spin and she felt rather than saw Kay try desperately to pull out of it. The plane seemed to lose momentum

197

before, quite suddenly, rearing up into a climb and entering a fast unbanked turn, its wings parallel with the horizon.

Verity realized something was wrong and that the Tiger Moth was spinning like a spider being flushed down the sink. It came into her mind that these might be her very last moments of consciousness but oddly enough – and when she thought about it later, she could not explain it to herself – she was not frightened or apprehensive. She did not scream or wave her hands about but merely smiled as though – if this was her fate – she would welcome it as a friend, as a blessed relief from earthly chains. For a second or two, the little plane – every joint and strut humming with effort – appeared to hang motionless. Verity saw the needle of the air speed indicator flickering round the lowest point on the dial. She wanted to breathe but could not. Behind her, she could hear Kay grunting and shouting as she tried to regain control.

Kay hauled on the stick and kicked hard on the rudder pedal but nothing happened. The stick would not move. Sobbing with the effort, she tried to make her mind work and it suddenly came to her that she had not enlisted the aid of the engine. She slammed on full throttle. With some power restored to the elevators, the Tiger Moth almost instantly flipped into a normal spin and, just a couple of hundred feet above the ground, Kay regained full control. Relief flooded through her and the last reserves of strength left her. When they landed, she was very pale and her hands trembled as she taxied to a halt in front of the hangar and switched off the engine.

'Verity, are you all right? God, I thought . . . well, I thought we'd had it. I'll never forgive myself for putting you through that.'

It took Verity several minutes before she could speak. She sat where she was, smiling idiotically, wanting to tell Kay not to fuss but unable to utter a single word. All the breath had been drawn out of her and her head still spun. Bert ran up and climbed on to the wing to help her remove her safety harness. After another few minutes she felt able – with his assistance – to haul herself out of the little plane. At last, very wobbly on her feet and clinging to Bert, she stood on the grass.

'For Gawd's sake, miss, what happened up there? I do believe I thought you'd had it.'

'I really don't know, Bert. I've never known anything like it,' Kay replied. She took off her goggles and flying helmet and shook her hair free with an angry flourish. She was very shaken – no longer the cool, self-possessed woman of the world. 'Verity, I can't tell you how sorry I am. I must have frightened the wits out of you. I know I was as scared as I've ever been.'

'No, I . . . I wasn't scared,' Verity said, her voice gaining strength but sounding rather bewildered. 'I can't begin to explain it to you but I was . . . I was in another world.'

'You were within a few seconds of being in another world,' Bert said drily. Four or five uniformed men were running towards the Tiger Moth. 'Here they come! I'm afraid the powers that be are going to make life difficult for you, Miss Kay. You'll have to do a full report.'

'And you're going to have to do a full technical report. I just couldn't move the stick,' Kay responded crisply, regaining some of her customary poise and authority. 'Bert, could you please take Miss Browne to the mess to rest and recuperate. Feed her coffee and brandy while I deal with all this.'

A reaction had set in by the time Kay joined them in the mess. Verity's exhilaration had left her and she felt numb with fatigue. She lay back on a sofa with her eyes closed. Kay sat down beside her and put her hand on Verity's.

'Have another sip of brandy. Waiter – a double brandy, please. I need it myself!'

Verity opened her eyes and, seeing Kay's expression, made an effort to reassure her.

'I'm all right – just winded. Give me minute or two and I'll be as right as rain.'

Kay grimaced. She knew that Dr Bladon – and Edward – would blame her for taking Verity up in the Tiger Moth, let alone nearly killing her. That loop at the end had been a stupid idea but there was no reason why it should have gone so badly wrong. The Tiger Moth was a reliable plane in which she had performed much more risky aerobatics than a gentle loop. Bert would go over it nut by nut, bolt by bolt and she ought to have his preliminary report tomorrow but her immediate anxiety was to get Verity back to the clinic and make her confession to Dr Bladon.

Twenty minutes later, Kay helped Verity – half asleep and barely able to walk – into the car. She sank back and closed her eyes.

'Are you sure you're all right?' Kay asked, unnecessarily. It was plain she was not.

'It was the happiest day of my life,' Verity mumbled and fell into a profound slumber which Kay thought was too close to unconsciousness for comfort. She put her foot on the accelerator pedal and within the hour drew up with a spray of gravel in front of the clinic. Dr Bladon came hurriedly out of the front door accompanied by two nurses. It was obvious he had been waiting for them.

'Miss Browne, are you all right? Miss Stammers, I really must protest! I gave permission for my patient to go for a short drive but you have been gone most of the day.' He looked at Verity and felt her pulse. 'Good heavens! Nurse, quickly please. We may need a stretcher. What has happened? What have you done to my patient, Miss Stammers?'

Verity opened her eyes and, smiling sleepily, said she was quite all right. Leaning on the two nurses, she managed to stumble into the clinic without recourse to a stretcher.

Kay made as if to leave but Dr Bladon insisted that she accompany him to his office and explain exactly why Verity was so exhausted.

'I took her up for a spin in my kite,' she said, trying to make light of it but unable to hide her feelings of guilt. She told him how much Verity had wanted to go up in the plane and how she thought the fresh air would do her good.

Dr Bladon snorted contemptuously. 'Please don't be absurd, Miss Stammers. You know perfectly well that "fresh air" does not mean a wild adventure in your "kite", as you call it.'

'Well, it would have been all right except for . . .' Kay hesitated.

'Except for what?'

'I had a bit of trouble with the controls and got into a spin. Still, I got her out of it . . . the spin, I mean, so it ended all right.'

Dr Bladon looked at her, his eyebrows raised and his face red with anger. 'Miss Stammers, from what you say – and I am inclined to believe you have only told me half the story – you have been at the least grossly irresponsible and at the worst criminally negligent. Miss Browne is a very sick woman and, if you have delayed her recovery, or . . . or worse, you will not be forgiven. Good day to you.'

He opened the door of his office and Kay left, feeling that she had been severely but properly rebuked. She knew she had to tell Edward before he heard what had happened from another source and she decided to drive straight to Turton House, but he was not there.

Edward was troubled by a feeling of impending doom. He felt threatened on all sides. Major Stille clearly had some sort of a relationship with Roderick Black and his son Guy. Was that why he was here in Henley? Edward could not believe it was just an innocent visit to watch the rowing and meet old friends. Stille never went anywhere without a purpose.

Then there was Harry. Was he what he seemed, a generous host and loyal ally? Or was he devious and possibly murderous? It couldn't be ruled out. Then there were the murders he was supposed to be investigating. What had he discovered? Only that Hermione Totteridge, Ernest Lowther and James Herold had all been murdered and that their deaths were linked by the phrases or quotations left on their bodies. He reminded himself that he must telephone Chief Inspector Pride and see if he had made any progress with his investigation into Eric Silver's gruesome killing. If there had been an arrest, he was sure he would have been told. The newspapers which had paraded the dentist's killing on their front pages no longer showed any interest in it. Their crime reporters had been transferred to a Liverpool shipowner who had, it appeared, murdered a prostitute to stop her telling all his sordid secrets to his wife. However, Edward knew that when Pride did make an arrest, Silver's murder would once again be front-page news.

Mulling it over in his mind, he decided that, on the evidence available, Silver's murder was linked to the other three but tangentially. He was looking for a murderer who was far more savage than the killer of

Lowther, Hermione Totteridge or Herold – someone who knew about these murders but had not committed them. Blackmail? Revenge? Or merely a wicked joke? He was being taunted by the entomological connection. He was at that stage in an investigation when he saw parts of the pattern and knew that quite soon – in a matter of days – he might see the whole. Yet his instinct also told him that he was being observed and that there would be more death, more killing before the murderer could be stopped.

'Something wicked this way comes . . .' he muttered to himself.

Brooding on these and other matters, Edward strolled along the river bank acknowledging the greetings of coxes, coaches and rowers as they prepared their boats. According to his programme, on this second day of the regatta, there were three races he did not wish to miss. At five past two, Trinity – his old college – was competing against Leander in another heat of the Stewards' Challenge Cup and at a quarter to three Eton was due to meet Westminster School in the Ladies' Challenge Plate. That was followed by a heat of the Diamond Challenge Sculls with Guy Black pitted against L. D. Habbitts whom he had said he would be lucky to better.

With time on his hands, Edward decided to hire a skiff and explore Temple Island. As far as he knew, it was uninhabited although someone had told him that, until recently, an old lady had lived there in some style. He particularly wanted to see the two-faced god under whose protection the island flourished. Bruce-Dick had told him the story of the first regatta in 1839 when four races were rowed from the tip of Temple Island to Henley Bridge. Oxford's Old Etonians had trounced Brasenose College on that occasion and the same evening Trinity, having partaken of mutton chops and ale, had raced *Black Prince* – with the college's three crowns on her bow – against an eight made up of Old Etonians from several Oxford colleges and beaten them by a canvas. Now, almost a century later, Edward could only feel anguish that the regatta, along with so much he treasured about England, was on the point of being blown to smithereens by evil men – of whom Major Stille was a prime example.

There was not much river traffic round Temple Island as Edward bumped his skiff against the wooden jetty and jumped ashore, wetting his feet in the process. He swore but was soon entranced by the oasis of peace amid the bustle of Henley at the height of the regatta. The island was the shape of a ship and, in the sunshine, appeared to Edward as though it might at any moment set sail and float downstream. The folly itself was much smaller than it had seemed from the *Arethusa* earlier that morning. It consisted of a rotunda decorated with the Etruscan-style reliefs he had heard so much about. It was a charming room several feet above ground level, reached by wooden stairs. When he entered, he found it was a mere five or six yards across with curved windows giving views of the river and the green fields beyond.

Walking to a little lawn on the 'prow' of the island, he found a bench from which he could survey the folly. Above the rotunda was the statue of Janus, fenced in or perhaps protected by pillars and surmounted by a delicate cupola. All in all, it was almost perfect – quite useless but pleasing to the eye, beautifully proportioned, sufficiently arcadian to satisfy any romantic poet and reminiscent of paintings by Fragonard and Watteau.

On three sides, only a few feet of grass surrounded the folly and Edward was surprised how close it was to the river. He got up from the bench to look at a small plaque on the wall which marked the water levels reached in years gone by. He saw that on occasion the island must have been almost totally submerged and the little temple half drowned, but this was midsummer and the water was tame and subservient. He thought he might try and climb on to the roof to see the statue close to but the narrow stone staircase was behind a locked iron gate so he had to be satisfied with admiring it from below.

He returned to the bench thinking that he would enjoy the peace and quiet for a few more minutes before returning to his skiff. He closed his eyes and fell into one of those reveries where the mind drifts in shallow waters awaiting the call to return to the waking world.

The hoarse, unlovely cry of a seagull roused him. Stretching, he got up from the bench – noticing to his annoyance that it had left a stain on his white trousers – and went to examine the Janus statue one last time. It was frustrating not to be able to get closer. He pulled at the metal gate and, to his surprise, found it was not in fact locked. He was almost certain that it had been when he had tried it earlier but told himself he must have been mistaken.

He climbed up the stone steps and came out on a lead roof beside the statue. He saw that it stood on a pedestal which resembled a section from a Corinthian column but was much more recent than the statue itself. Now that he was eye-to-eye with it, he saw that Janus needed some attention. One of the statue's two faces looked towards Henley and the other over the little wilderness at the other end of the island. The stone was flaking and the faces crumbling. There was a melancholy about it which was satisfactorily poetic and Edward wished he had the talent to sketch it or pen some suitable verses in its honour. There was no expression on either face and he imagined that in the dusk they must look quite sinister.

He looked over the edge and wished that the Victorians had not surrounded the temple with such a clumsy wooden balcony. It was quite inappropriate, almost as if they had encumbered it with a chastity belt. He turned back to the statue and, as he was preparing to descend, noticed something metallic pushed between the feet of the god. Tugging at it, he found it to be an old cash box, large enough to hold a sizeable sum of money in banknotes. The box was unlocked and, his curiosity now fully aroused, he opened the catch. There were no banknotes inside but there was a large envelope. Edward was sure that he had stumbled on something secret, something he was not supposed to see. Without hesitation, he tore open the envelope and found inside a sheaf of papers. He had seen such papers before when working on a case in the Foreign Office. They were all marked 'secret'.

Before he could master the contents, he felt something cold and hard press against the back of his neck.

'I shall take those, Lord Edward – if you please.'

There was no mistaking Major Stille's voice.

'I might have guessed . . .' Edward growled. 'In fact, when I saw you talking to Guy Black, I knew you must be here for a reason. Are these papers his or his father's?'

For some reason he felt quite unafraid. He was standing on a slightly sloping lead roof with no guard rail of any kind. How easy it would be for him to slip and fall either on to the grass below or into the river. It flashed through his mind that he was completely at Stille's mercy and he knew from past experience that the man had no mercy. Clearly, he had stumbled on a *poste restante* where one of Stille's agents – probably

Roderick Black – left messages and stolen papers for him to collect when it was convenient. Stille was a patriot of sorts, Edward supposed – a man who would do anything to get what he wanted. When his body was recovered, Edward told himself, Major Ferguson or Guy Liddell might suspect who was behind his death but why should Stille worry? His work in England was almost done and he would have no reason to care about his activities being investigated. With diplomatic immunity, the worst that could happen would be deportation. Perhaps, Edward thought, this was his last success – his final coup – and Stille would be as ruthless as his master, Heinrich Himmler, with anyone who got in his way.

Edward glanced to either side and wondered if he could get behind one of the pillars, but that was quite absurd. They were slim and delicate. In any case, he could not move fast on the awkward little roof. He considered shouting but there was no one within earshot on the river – a situation which had delighted him just a few moments earlier. If he opened his mouth to shout, Stille would almost certainly shoot him. There was nothing he could do. He was trapped on a narrow ledge only accessible by a curved stone staircase which was difficult to negotiate at the best of times and he was alone with a man with a gun. He wanted to laugh.

'Turn round very slowly, please, with your hands in the air.'

Edward did as he was told. In one hand, he still held the papers he had taken from the cash box. Stille was smiling. He had obviously read Edward's mind as clearly as if he had spoken and had watched him come to the only possible conclusion.

'I've had just about enough of you, Lord Edward Corinth.' The scorn in his voice chilled Edward's blood. 'You and your precious *hure* – your whore – have caused me some trouble. I admit it. I can now take my revenge. I am going to kill you but, before I do, I want you to know that she is dead. I want you to live long enough to grieve for your lady friend.'

'I don't believe you,' Edward managed.

'Yes, you do,' Stille sneered. 'I wonder if there will be anything of her left to bury?' he asked meditatively, as though really wanting an answer.

'What do you mean by that, blast you?'

'Did she not tell you she was going up with Miss Stammers in her Tiger Moth? I see that she did not. Ah, well. There are worse ways to die. The instruments failed, the rudder jammed and . . .' He made a movement with his left hand to suggest a plummeting plane.

'I don't believe you . . .' Edward repeated but his voice faltered.

'Do you want me to say it again? I would be delighted to. I have killed Fräulein Browne. She once made a fool of me in our own Embassy and then took it upon herself to seduce one of our best young men . . .'

'If you mean Adam von Trott, he hates the Nazi Party and Hitler above all else.'

'When I get back to Berlin the first thing I shall do is report on the activities of Herr von Trott. Thanks to our friend Kleist-Schmenzin, I have put together a very full report on the traitor. Von Trott and Kleist-Schmenzin will both be shot. We have too many traitors but then . . .' he paused, 'so do you. Now, hand me those papers.'

Edward suddenly felt ice cool.

'If you want these papers you'll have to take them,' he said in calm desperation. It was an idle threat and he knew it. If he was shot before he had time to toss them off the roof, Stille would have no difficulty picking them up. There was only a light breeze. He readied himself to die as Stille barked at him once again to hand over the papers. Edward saw his finger tighten round the trigger. He thrust the papers at him but, as the German made a grab at them, they fluttered over the balcony on to the grass where the breeze caught them and blew them towards the water.

Cursing, Stille took his eyes off Edward for a second to see where they had landed. As he did so, Edward punched him hard in the face with one hand and knocked the gun out of his grasp with the other. It went sliding across the lead roof. Both men made a grab for it and missed. Edward saw it fall on to the balcony below. With a cry of anger, Stille lunged at his adversary but, as he caught him, he tripped over one of the lead ribs which cut across the roof. He fell, dragging Edward with him, and the two men ended up in an unscientific tangle on the very edge of the roof.

Edward was the taller and stronger and clutched Stille in a stranglehold, his arm around his neck. Stille struck out in desperation. He had to collect his prize while there was still time, before the river reduced the papers to an unreadable mush. He kicked Edward hard in the knee and the pain made him cry out. He let go of Stille's neck and held on to his knee in agony. As Edward released his hold, Stille got to his feet and made for the stone stairway. He ran down to the balcony and grabbed his gun. Uncertain whether to go back and finish Edward off or gather up the papers – some of which were starting to drift gently into the reeds – he chose his papers. Edward, he decided, could not go anywhere. He was crippled. He had no gun. He was trapped. He could wait.

Once on the grass, Stille began gathering up everything within his reach. By now, at least half the papers were in the river but he stuffed a dozen sheets in his pockets before giving up the chase. He turned to look up at Edward, his face disfigured by rage and hatred.

Now he would kill the man who had once again frustrated his plans and made a fool of him. By this time, Edward had hauled himself up but he was in considerable pain and could not put any weight on his injured leg. He listened as Stille began to climb back up the stone stairs. He looked round for a weapon. There was nothing. Leaning against the statue for support, he felt it tremble, as though it were alive. He looked down at its base and saw an empty space where the cash box had been concealed. A section had been dislodged, either by whoever had used it to hide the box or through natural wear and tear. It occurred to him that he might be able to block the entrance to the roof. He pushed harder and this time the statue definitely moved. Hearing Stille's feet on the steps, he pushed again and felt the statue spin on its plinth. For a second it almost righted itself but, as Edward gave it another shove, it toppled to one side and crashed over, blocking the top of the staircase.

For a few moments there was no sound other than the wind in the trees and the water lapping against the island. Edward hung on to a pillar and waited to see what Stille would do. At last, dragging himself over to the top of the steps, he saw blood and then, to his horror, what had been Stille's head. By some extraordinary stroke of luck or fate, the statue had caught him just as he climbed the final steps on to the roof and smashed his skull like an eggshell. Edward made an effort to lift the statue but it was quite unmovable. Even if he had been able to put any weight on his leg, he could never have raised it.

He sat down on the empty plinth and contemplated the havoc he had wreaked. His enemy, the man who had claimed to have killed Verity, was dead – that he could not regret. It had been a question of him or Stille. The German would never have let him leave the island alive. In the process, he had badly damaged an eighteenth-century statue which had stood guard over the island and the river for a century and a half. He wondered whether Henley would ever forgive him? But surely that was just it! Janus – protector of gates and passageways – had stood guard and, when his world had been threatened, had defended it, taking revenge on England's enemy.

It was Guy Black who came to Edward's rescue. He was sculling past the island – a gentle warm-up before his heat later that afternoon – when he heard and then saw Edward on the temple roof, shouting and waving. He sculled over and called up, 'What's the matter? Are you stuck or something? What are you doing up there, anyway?'

'I'll explain later, Guy. I'm afraid Major Stille has been killed. Could you call the police?'

'Major Stille? My father will be glad to hear it. Did you kill him?'

'In self-defence. Look, I can't have a conversation with you in your boat and me stuck on this roof. Can you go back to the Stewards' and get help?'

'Of course. But what about you? Are you all right?'

'I'm all right,' Edward said grimly. 'Just a dicky knee. Nothing serious but I can't get down from here.'

'Can't I help?'

'No, the statue has toppled over and blocked the staircase.'

'Gosh, yes! I thought something looked different. I'll go at once.'

'Thanks. And tell Inspector Treacher to bring something to lift it, will you? It's too heavy to move by hand.'

'Right. I won't be a jiffy.'

211

Edward collapsed on the cold lead roof, utterly exhausted. With his head in his hands, he thought about Verity. How could he live if she were dead? Nothing in his life mattered if she were not there to share it with him. All he could do was wait and torture himself, as Stille had intended. Perched on the narrow lead platform, he grimly recalled St Simeon Stylites on his pillar and groaned aloud.

12

Early the next morning, Fenton drove Edward over to the
clinic to see Verity. Now, more than ever, he hated not
having her in his sight at all times. Dr Bladon was brisk
with him, telling him to return at midday as she was still
asleep. However, he agreed, rather reluctantly, that, if she
felt up to it, Edward could take her to the last day of the
regatta as long as she watched the races from a deck-
chair in the Stewards' Enclosure. She was on no account
to be back late or he would never be trusted to take her
out again, and with that Edward had to be satisfied.

'So that's about it, V. Guy says Stille was blackmailing
his father and, when I saw them talking yesterday, he
was warning him off.'

'And you believe him?'

'Don't you?'

Verity had not been allowed to go to Edward when
she heard of his life and death struggle with Major
Stille. She was made to rest and, as she put it, 'guarded
day and night' to make sure she didn't abscond. When
he had at last been able to come to her, they had held
each other tightly. In a typically English way, they had
not said much – there was no need – though Edward
had muttered in her ear that he loved her and, half-
jokingly, that he would never let her out of his sight
again. They had quickly turned to discussing Stille's
spy network as an easier topic of conversation and

Edward noted with relief that, contrary to what he had expected, her experience in the Tiger Moth had left her stronger rather than weaker.

Verity, still in her dressing-gown, was sitting on a bench in the garden where Edward was confident that no one could overhear them. His knee was strapped up and he had to hop around on crutches but, as he told her, he had got off very lightly. Thanks in part to the painkillers the doctor had given him but more to the knowledge that Verity had miraculously survived the attempt on her life, he was feeling calm, almost serene.

'I can hardly believe it,' she said. 'Stille's dead and we have nothing to worry about any longer. I have hated and feared that man for so long, I can hardly take it in that he is no longer here to haunt us.'

'But, with his last throw of the dice, he as near as damn it did for both of us.'

'But he didn't,' she said, touching his hand. 'What's happening there now?'

'On the island?'

'Yes. I thought you might be under arrest or something. After all, you did kill a man.'

'It's all roped off. There's nothing more the police can do for the moment. Stille's body has been taken away. One good thing is the statue doesn't seem to have been badly damaged. It's tougher than it looks.'

'I might say the same about you,' Verity said, squeezing his arm.

'Treacher has spoken to Pride and also to someone high up in the FO. They've still got a lot of questions to ask me but they don't seem to doubt my version of events, which is comforting. For one thing they found Stille's gun only had his fingerprints on it. And he also had some secret papers on him.'

He could not tell Verity that Guy Liddell, the head of MI5, had taken a personal interest in Stille and would be in Henley the next day to catechize him but not, Edward got the feeling, to reprimand him.

'Surely the German Embassy will have something to say about the violent death of one of their number?'

'I doubt it, V. There's a pile of evidence to prove that Stille was up to no good and, in any case, with the PM flying to Germany to see Hitler, the Embassy won't want to rock the boat. Excuse my mixed metaphor!'

'Do you think Roderick Black will be prosecuted? After all, he was passing secrets to the enemy. Don't tell me! I can guess what will happen. It will all be covered up to avoid a scandal.'

'I'm afraid so. I doubt he will be charged with anything. As you say, they'll want to hush the whole thing up.'

'As usual,' Verity added cynically. 'To be honest, I'm quite relieved for Mary and Guy's sake. And . . . well, Roderick Black may have used me but he was kind to me in his way.'

'Let's forget about it, shall we? I'm determined to enjoy the last day of the regatta tomorrow – if you're feeling up to it.'

'Surprisingly enough, I am. I don't know why but I feel as though . . . what shall I say? As though my body was cleansed in that moment we hung in the air waiting to die. I don't want to sound melodramatic but I feel renewed in some way. I hope it's not all an illusion.'

'You certainly look different. There's a sparkle in your eye which I've been missing,' Edward said, leaning over to kiss her.

'Hey, watch it! I expect I'm still infectious.'

'I don't care. By the way, did you hear that Guy beat Habbits? I missed it, what with one thing and another, but I hear it was a near-run thing. It would be terrific if he could carry off the Diamonds tomorrow. He's a fine boy. You know, V, he had persuaded his father to go to the police and I think he would have done if events hadn't overtaken him.'

'If I understand it right,' Verity continued sceptically, 'you're suggesting that Roderick Black became so involved with Mosley and the BUF that he endangered his whole career. Was it really that serious? After all, many right-wing Conservatives have links to Mosley.'

'This was more than "links". Jack Amery went to Berlin to see Hitler and persuade him to fund the British Union of Fascists. Hitler agreed and Amery brought the money back in cash – or at least some of it. Amery knows he's being watched by MI5 so he persuaded Black to take a pleasure cruise to his house complete with sick daughter . . .'

'And naïve Communist journalist! What good cover,' Verity interjected.

'Black took the money and handed it over to Mosley at some convenient moment. If – when war breaks out – it emerged that Black had received money from Hitler, his political career would be at an end and he would probably end up in jug.'

'So Stille used the threat of exposure to get Black to pass him secret papers?' Verity still sounded dubious. 'I feel there must have been more to it than that. I mean, would he allow himself to be so easily blackmailed? If he had gone to your friend Major Ferguson at Special Branch, I bet they would have given him carte blanche to do whatever Stille asked so long as he kept them informed.'

'Well, you may be right.' Edward sighed. 'I've given up pretending I know all the answers. I sometimes think I don't even know all the questions.'

'So what next? Is this linked to the murders we're investigating?'

'I'm not quite certain, V. I rather think not.'

'So we've still got work to do?'

'Yes. I have an appointment with Miss Tiverton. I need to talk to her about General Lowther and then I'm going to see Chief Inspector Pride and Inspector Treacher. I want to be brought up to date with their investigations and I think they have a few questions to ask me. I'll call in this evening and report.'

Edward was touched that, even when she was still recovering from her brush with death and he was hobbling around on crutches, Verity thought of them as an investigative team. How inadequate, he thought. Why not leave it to the professionals? That was what he ought to do but a nagging demon was telling him that he could do better than the police – that he could see what they had missed. He was certain the solution to the murders lay in a Norfolk churchyard but how could he prove it? He touched his knee absent-mindedly and winced. He swore he would find out the truth before the pain went. Stille might be dead but an equally ruthless killer was still out there who, though he did not say as much to Verity, might be just as dangerous.

An hour or so after Edward had left, Kay put her head round Verity's door. Thoroughly chastened and far from her usual breezy self, she greeted Verity with a hug which almost squashed her. 'Will you ever forgive me?'

'Of course! I mean, what is there to forgive?' Verity replied, gently disengaging herself. 'It wasn't your fault. In fact, it is I who should ask you to forgive me. According to Edward, Major Stille was out to kill me and you sort of got in the way. Do you know how he did it yet?'

'Bert says someone must have interfered with the rudder between his getting the old girl ready and us turning up at the aerodrome. She would have been left unobserved for at least an hour which was plenty long enough for someone who knew what they were doing.'

'No one saw anyone acting suspiciously?'

'No, that would have been too easy! If you put on overalls and look as though you know where you're going and what you're doing, no one would challenge you. Although they would now. Security has been tightened up – after the event.'

Kay knelt beside her chair. 'I don't think you understand how I feel about you. You see, Verity, you're just the sort of person I want to be but I'd never have the courage or moral purpose to do what you've done.'

'Oh, but that's nonsense! You've achieved so much . . .' Verity began but Kay placed her finger to her lips.

'No, hear me out. I can play tennis a bit but so what? You show the world what is happening and what needs to be done. When you're better, will you take me with you – to the battle front, I mean?' She saw Verity's look. 'No, of course you can't. What am I saying? You can't take tourists to the front line.'

'Dear Kay, there's no front line any more – or, rather, we are all in the front line now. War's going to come to all of us sooner rather than later. There's no shame in enjoying these last days of peace. And you know,' she hesitated, 'that moment when I thought we were going to die – I was happier then than I have ever been. Isn't that terrible of me? I'm not suicidal but I wasn't frightened in those few seconds when we were spiralling out of control. I just thought here, at last, is death and it has come to me cleanly, in the air, not while I was rotting away in a hospital bed with some horrible disease.'

'Verity, can I ask you something? If we don't believe in an afterlife, shouldn't we be more frightened of death?'

'I don't think so. Anyway, what can we do? We can't *pretend* to believe. In my view, death hides no secret. It opens no door. It's the end of us. What survives is what we have given to other people, what stays in their memory. For me, that's enough.'

'Verity!' Kay whispered. 'We are alike. That's what I believe too but I would never have found the words to say it. Can I kiss you?'

'That wouldn't be a good idea.'

'Oh, I don't mean *that* way but . . .'

Verity blushed. 'I didn't think you did. I've always loved men – so far as I have loved at all. I just meant that no one is allowed to kiss me – not on the lips – in case they catch something.'

Kay got up and paced about the room. 'I don't care a toss about that. But kissing isn't what I meant now I think of it. You know how schoolboys have secret societies and passwords and so on? I'd like to cut myself and mingle our blood and swear to be friends for ever.'

Verity laughed. 'Kay, you are a romantic! I'd never have believed it. If I do get better, it will be mostly due to you – and Edward, of course. You encourage me and give me something to aim for. With you around, I won't despair.' She hesitated. 'You won't get into trouble about the accident? They won't try to stop you flying, will they?'

'They might do,' Kay replied, trying to sound unconcerned. 'It depends what they find. There has to be a formal investigation but, if they find the plane was tampered with, they won't be able to blame me. But they will want to know who did the tampering and why.'

'We're sure it was Major Stille. You heard that Edward killed him on Temple Island?' Verity looked at Kay with wide eyes.

'Of course I did! The whole of Henley's talking about it. You haven't seen the papers? I thought you might not have so I brought you some of the cheap rags – and the *New Gazette* of course. They have a picture of you and Edward looking quite dashing on the front page. Even *The Times* has the story.'

'Yes, I'm suddenly popular with Lord Weaver again. He rang me himself and I promised to write my account of it all for him – an exclusive, they call it. Dr Bladon is keeping the rest of the pack off my back.'

'I know. When I asked to see you, he looked at me as though I was a murderess and made me promise not to tire you. He told me his phone hasn't stopped ringing with reporters wanting to talk to you and they've even been banging on his front door.' Kay grinned. 'I think Edward's so brave. If you don't marry him soon, I think I'll have to. I say,' she added shyly, 'will you mention me in your article?'

'Of course! I'll tell the world how you saved my life.'

'I wasn't a hero but . . . Well, you're alive and that's what matters. I wonder if Edward will ever forgive me?'

They hugged and then Kay was gone. Verity was left feeling sad. She tried to get a grip on herself but, whenever she said goodbye to a friend, she always had a feeling that she might never see them again. Something to do with her time covering the war in Spain, she supposed. Once, when she had mentioned it to Edward, he said it was the same feeling he had when his parents left him at prep school after the holidays.

She picked up the *Express* and began to read a lurid and highly inaccurate account of Edward's fight to the death with Major Stille – a 'ruthless Nazi agent' as the reporter had labelled him. She put out a hand to the box of violet creams which Kay had bought her but hesitated when she remembered Edward warning her not to eat or drink anything which might have been poisoned. 'And don't dig into chocolates or fruit if you don't know who gave them to you. Remember what happened to Snow White,' he had said.

Verity had giggled but had promised not to take any risks. But she *did* know who had given her these chocolates – someone who loved her perhaps rather more than she was comfortable with – but still . . . She popped a violet cream in her mouth and picked up the *Daily Mail*. What a rag, she thought, as she read about Lord Edward's love for 'Communist war correspondent, now at death's door in exclusive TB clinic'.

General Lowther had lived in a pleasant house on the outskirts of Hambledon, a small village with a rather splendid church half an hour's drive from Henley. Miss Tiverton, the village schoolmistress, lived in a quaint flint cottage near the church. It was a great relief to be out in the country and, as far as Edward could see, free from reporters eager for an interview. Miss Tiverton had a telephone so he had been able to make an appointment but had not prepared her for his strapped-up leg and crutches.

'Oh, my!' she cried, opening the door to him. 'Have you had an accident, Lord Edward? Be careful of the step and . . . Too late, I was going to warn you about the low ceilings. You're not hurt, I trust? Please, sit over here.'

Edward was relieved to find that she knew nothing of the circumstances of his injury. She obviously did not read the newspapers and for that he was grateful. Twittering away like one of the small birds on the bird table in her garden, Miss Tiverton tried to make him comfortable in the largest of the armchairs but her house was that of a single woman – every surface was covered with knick-knacks and he hardly dared move for fear of upsetting a small regiment of ornaments and keepsakes. On the narrow mantelpiece a bone china St Bernard dog complete with brandy barrel round his neck was bracketed by the Lord's Prayer in a small frame and a photograph of a severe-looking couple in Victorian dress – Miss Tiverton's parents, he assumed.

'Forgive me for barging in on you like this but, as I explained on the telephone, I just wanted to ask you a few questions about General Lowther. I believe you were one of his few friends.'

'Oh, I would hardly call myself a friend, Lord Edward.' She smiled shyly but with a little pride, Edward thought, that she might be taken as the General's friend and social equal. 'There are not very many educated people around here and the General enjoyed our little chats.'

'You dined with him on a regular basis?'

'On a regular basis?' She sounded shocked. 'Once a month, certainly not more. He was a very kind gentleman.'

'Did he ever come here?'

Miss Tiverton looked even more shocked. 'Never! I could hardly have entertained a single gentleman in my house.'

Edward forbore to ask why not. Miss Tiverton was about fifty-five, he guessed, very short-sighted to judge from her pebble-lensed spectacles and thin as a garden rake. Only a very over-imaginative gossip would have seen anything improper in her inviting the General to her house, though she was a maiden lady.

'I gather from Mrs Venables that you and the vicar were the General's only visitors.'

'Well, if you put it like that, I suppose we were. There are other gentlemen in the neighbourhood but he did not accept any invitations.'

'Why was that, do you think?'

'He said to me once, Sylvia – that's my name and the General was the only man I allowed to call me by it . . .'

'Not even the vicar?' Edward teased.

'No, James is much younger than I, Lord Edward. It would hardly be . . .' she thought for a moment, 'appropriate to let him call me by my Christian name even though he is a man of God.'

'I'm sorry, you were saying . . .?'

'The General said to me, "Sylvia, seclusion is part of the price I pay for my mistakes."'

'What did he mean by that, do you think, Miss Tiverton?'

'I have no idea.'

'You did not ask him?'

'That would have been vulgar,' she said reprovingly.

'You must have been very shocked and upset when he died so suddenly.'

'I was, of course, but he had warned me something like that might happen.'

'He warned you?'

'Yes, he mentioned on two or three occasions. The very last time I saw him he said, "Sylvia, they are out for my blood and they will come soon." Of course, I refused to believe him but he said, "Don't be alarmed. It is God's will. An eye for an eye . . ."'

'Surely you must have asked him what he meant by that?'

'I did, Lord Edward, and he replied, "The kindly ones."'

'Good heavens! The kindly ones! Was he referring to the Furies, do you think?'

'I do, yes.'

'Did you tell Inspector Treacher this?'

'Mr Treacher?' She sounded genuinely shocked at the suggestion. 'No, I never would but he didn't ask me.'

Edward wondered once again why the Inspector had been so lax in his investigation of the General's sudden death. Why had he been so ready to accept the doctor's opinion that it was a heart attack? Was it because it was the easiest way of proceeding or was there a more sinister reason? Treacher seemed honest, but was he?

'I understand that the General left you all his money. Did that surprise you?'

'No, he told me he would,' she said, quite unruffled.

'Did he say why? I mean, was it because he liked you and had no close relatives?'

'Not at all. He wanted to do something for the children in the village and trusted me to use the money for that purpose.'

'I see. Are you . . .?'

'We're building a new school. There's no secret about it. The old one is quite inadequate. We'll name it after the General, of course.'

Edward decided to ask one more leading question. 'Did it ever cross your mind that the General might have been murdered?'

'Indeed, I was certain of it,' was Miss Tiverton's unexpected reply.

'You ought to have made your suspicions known to the coroner.'

'I don't think so, Lord Edward. Although the General warned me that he was expecting to be killed, the doctor said he had died of a heart attack. What was my word against the doctor's? In any case, the General wanted to die. He was an old man. He had no relatives, no friends, nothing to live for. I believe he welcomed death.'

Edward was beginning to realize that behind Miss Tiverton's thick spectacles there lurked a sharp-eyed, hard-headed judge of human nature.

'What sort of a man was he? I know nothing about him except what I read in the *Times* obituary. He was a VC – the first Battle of Ypres, if I remember correctly – so it goes without saying that he was a brave soldier.'

224

'He was a gentleman. He never discussed his VC. I think his view was that he had done his duty like so many of our other brave boys – nothing more.' There was a wistfulness in her voice that made Edward wonder if one of those 'brave boys' had been the love of her life.

'Had he made any enemies? I mean, perhaps there was someone who thought less well of him than you.'

'If he had any enemies, he never mentioned them to me.'

Edward sighed. 'So you have no idea who it was he feared?'

'I don't think he feared anyone.'

'But you said he expected to be killed.'

'That's true but, as I told you, he did not fear death. I never asked him why he *expected* to die. It was his business and, if he had wanted to confide in me, I'm sure he would have done so.'

'But you might have saved his life if you had warned the police that he was in danger.'

She looked at him scornfully. 'Do you really think I would have winkled out his secret and then gone to see Inspector Treacher?'

'No, I can see that would have been impossible,' Edward agreed. 'And he never talked of regretting sending someone to their death?' Miss Tiverton seemed puzzled. 'I was just thinking of another VC – General Sir Alistair Craig whom I knew some years ago. He was killed by someone who believed he was a mass murderer, not a hero.'

Miss Tiverton looked bewildered and then angry. 'The General did his duty,' she said primly. 'No one has ever said anything against his reputation as a soldier.'

Edward imagined these two lonely people looking back on their lives, waiting for death. She must have read his thoughts because she said sharply, 'I hope you aren't pitying me, Lord Edward, or the General. Both our lives have been lived to the full. I have taught several generations of children from this village to read and write and watched them grow into useful men and women. What more could a teacher ask?'

'No, I wasn't pitying you. Tell me, have you always lived here?'

'All my life. I was born in this cottage. But please don't think it means I have led a narrow, circumscribed life. I may not have travelled the world – as no doubt you have – but I have seen in this village a world of human and spiritual growth. Some tragedies, some failures but, on the whole, I have watched ordinary people deal bravely with whatever fate has thrown at them.'

'I understand that, Miss Tiverton, and I can also see that you are an intelligent, strong-minded woman.' Rather like Verity, he added to himself.

Taking no notice, she continued, 'Since the war there have been thousands of . . . old maids, people call us, and we are despised, laughed at or – worst of all – pitied. We may not have married and had children but many of us have still managed to lead fulfilled lives.'

'I don't pity you, Miss Tiverton,' Edward repeated. Changing the subject, he asked, 'Are you sure the General had no relatives? Mrs Venables thought he might have had a nephew in Africa or Australia.'

'I never heard him mention anyone. As far as I know, he had no relatives.'

'No one ever visited him? No strangers, I mean?'

'No. How many more questions have you got for me, Lord Edward? Really, I can tell you nothing.'

'There's just a couple more. I'm sorry to be a nuisance but no one knew the General as well as you.' She nodded her head in acknowledgement. 'When he went to London, do you know what he did there?'

226

'We never discussed it although I know he went to his wine merchant. Unfortunately, I am ignorant about wine – I do not even like it – so I wasn't able to talk intelligently to him about what he had purchased.'

'I understand he went every month but, surely, he wouldn't have needed to restock his wine cellar so frequently? He must have had a regular appointment with someone.'

'If you are implying that the General might have had some . . . some woman in London, all I can say is that I don't know and I don't want to know.'

'One last question, Miss Tiverton, and then I shall leave you in peace. Was he a native of these parts? Was he born in Hambledon?'

'No, indeed! He retired here because his wife was from this part of the world and, when she died many years ago, he stayed.'

'Do you happen to know where he came from originally?'

Edward wondered for a moment if she would say Norfolk but instead she replied, 'His family came from Godalming, I believe.'

After leaving Miss Tiverton with many expressions of respect and gratitude, he went to see the vicar. He proved to be a breezy young man who had nothing much to offer in the way of information about the General.

'I got on well enough with the old man. I used to tell him he drank too much and that he ought to get out more but he took no notice.'

'Did he go to church?'

'On high days and holidays – not every Sunday. He didn't want to be taken up by the local worthies, I believe.'

227

'And he got on well with Miss Tiverton?'

'Yes, they were two tough old birds who respected each other. He liked it that she didn't fuss over him – make cakes, that sort of thing – and I remember him telling me once that he respected her judgement.'

'Were you surprised when you heard he had left her most of his estate?'

'Not really. Who else had he got to leave it to? He left the church a thousand pounds – very generous and most welcome. God moves in mysterious ways.' A thought struck him. 'You don't suspect Miss Tiverton of murdering him, do you?'

'It had crossed my mind,' Edward admitted.

'That's quite absurd! I've known her for some time, Lord Edward, and I can assure you that she is not the murdering kind.'

'He's buried here, in the churchyard?'

'Yes. In fact, we reburied him two days ago. You know the police asked for him to be exhumed. It's very sad. I have never had a body exhumed before.'

'Did they tell you why?'

'I understand they feared he might have been poisoned but really, Lord Edward, you should speak to Inspector Treacher about it.'

'Of course! I'm sorry. I didn't mean to upset you.' Edward paused and then asked, 'At his funeral – the original funeral – were there many people?'

'A few villagers. Mrs Venables and Miss Tiverton, of course. He had no relatives that we know of.'

'No strangers?'

'None. Hold on, though, a wreath was left on the grave that no one admitted sending.'

'Who delivered it?'

'No one knows. We found it the day after the funeral. There was no card or anything.'

'You don't happen to know what the General did

when he went to London? I know he went to see his wine merchant but that can't have been the only reason?'

'A woman, you mean?' the vicar said with the easy frankness of the new, modern clergyman.

'Well, I . . .'

'The funny thing is when I did ask him once, he said he went to church. Somewhere in the City, I think he said.' He pursed his lips. 'Did he mention St Mary's, Cripplegate? I rather think he did but I took him to be joking.'

'That's interesting. Did he ever say anything to you about death? Miss Tiverton told me she was sure he expected to die sooner rather than later.'

'No, nothing.' He wrinkled his brow. 'Although, now I come to think of it, I do remember – it must have been the last time I saw him – he quoted Abraham Lincoln. "We cannot escape our past." Nor can we,' he added with a shrug.

After interviewing the vicar, Edward called in at the police station as arranged where he found Treacher and Chief Inspector Pride exchanging information. Treacher, looking uncomfortable, seemed to greet him with relief as a welcome distraction from the interrogation he had been suffering at the hands of his grim-faced senior colleague. He looked even glummer when Edward had given them his report.

'I would go to Cripplegate myself,' he ended up, 'but being a cripple . . .' he laughed weakly at his joke, 'I'll have to leave it to you, Pride.'

Pride nodded his head. 'You probably want to hear how I'm getting on.'

Edward listened while Pride brought him up to date with the investigation into Eric Silver's death. When he had finished, Edward sighed heavily. 'So we now know where we stand?'

'Yes, we do,' Pride said firmly.

'The writing on all the notes is in the same hand? We're sure of that?'

'Yes, even though there was an attempt to disguise it. And, what's more, our handwriting expert is almost certain it matches the writing you sent me, Lord Edward.'

'But there's still not enough evidence to make an arrest?'

'Not for a day or two. You must keep a weather eye open, though. The murderer will suspect you know his secret and may try to harm you before we can put him in handcuffs. How is your leg? Don't forget, you would be at a disadvantage in a scrap.'

Edward grinned. 'I know the danger I'm in. Still, I'm hoping to provoke an attack and force the issue.'

'A dangerous strategy, Lord Edward.' Inspector Treacher stroked his whiskers.

'Have you had the results of the post-mortem, Treacher?'

'It was cyanide. Not very much but enough to kill an old man. I can't think how we missed it.' Treacher looked down at the floor and Pride studied the calendar on the wall.

'So General Lowther was poisoned?' Edward tried to overcome the Inspector's embarrassment.

'Yes, my lord. I feel very much to blame. If the doctor hadn't been about to retire I would have had him struck off,' he added savagely.

'Hmm.' Pride looked as though he was going to say something unpalatable about the investigation so Edward broke in again.

"Treacher, did you find out anything when you re-interviewed Miss Totteridge's staff?"

'Yes,' he replied heavily, obviously chagrined to have to admit once again that he had missed something vital the first time. 'I've just been telling Chief Inspector Pride. Her gardener said a man from the chemical company had come round to find out what she thought of the new poison. They were in the greenhouse for some time and the gardener said he saw the man leave. My guess is our murderer took the opportunity to lace her tea with the poison. We've checked with the chemical company and, of course, they knew nothing about a visit from any of their people.'

'Would the gardener be able to recognize our murderer?' Edward asked.

'Probably, but it's still not quite enough to convict him.'

'And Eric Silver? I did think his was a different type of murder committed by someone else. Was I wrong?'

'I believe you were,' Pride said. 'Silver's murder *was* different because the murderer panicked. The killings of Lowther, Hermione Totteridge and Herold were all carefully planned. Silver's murder was hurried and unplanned. I think the murderer overheard what Silver told you, Lord Edward, and decided to kill on the spur of the moment. He must have wanted to involve you and thought it gave him the perfect opportunity.'

'You mean leaving the family motto on Silver's body?'

'Correct!' Pride replied. 'And it worked. You saw it as a challenge, just as the murderer hoped you would.'

'I'm afraid he hates me and that was another reason he killed Silver so horribly. He did not hate Lowther, Herold or Miss Totteridge – not in the same way, not to the same degree. It should have been me, not Silver, in that dentist's chair.'

Pride nodded in agreement. 'He'd say that he only killed those who, according to his perverted logic, deserved death and were ready for it. Herold and Lowther, certainly. Miss Totteridge was different. An obstinate old woman, I think he would say, who refused to give him the reassurances he demanded from her.'

'And the photograph he stole from her album?' Edward asked Treacher.

'I can't be sure but I think it was of Peter Lamming and Isabella. It wasn't taken by Miss Totteridge herself but sent by her niece from Kenya – probably so her aunt could see the man she was going to marry. I'm guessing but I think we'll find it once we start looking.'

'I think so, too,' Edward said thoughtfully. 'Well, let's draw the net a bit tighter and try to bring this whole nasty business to a head, shall we?'

The two policemen looked at him without smiling, fearing that the worst was still to come.

Edward closed his eyes for a moment. 'So wicked, so ruthless! It makes me sick to my stomach,' he muttered half to himself. 'We are what we do and this man has done evil.'

Arriving at the clinic, he half-expected to find Verity listless and weary once the exhilaration of surviving her ordeal in the Tiger Moth had faded. Instead, he found her jumping around in excitement.

'You're full of beans, V. What's happened?'

'I'll tell you what's happened. While you've been touring the countryside, I've been reading a book.'

'Glad to hear it. One of Mrs Woolf's socialist tracts?'

'I've been reading,' she said reprovingly, 'that book of Herold's you gave me.'

'*The Fall*?'

'*The Fall: A Love Story*. More precisely, I've been reading the account of the climb on which his first wife was killed.'

'On the Eiger?'

'Yes. It's very well written but there's something more.' She looked at him with shining eyes and Edward thought she seemed almost her normal self again.

'Don't tease! Tell me,' he smiled.

'James and Gwyneth Herold didn't climb the Eiger alone. There were several others in the party including your friend Harry Makin. That was his name before he inherited his title, wasn't it?'

'Good Lord, V! Why didn't I read that book before? From now on, you won't find me criticizing Inspector Treacher for not carrying out a thorough investigation.'

'When you went to see Cathy Herold, didn't Harry go with you? Why didn't she recognize him or at least know his name?'

'Because she had never met him before and because I introduced him as Lord Lestern. Why should she make the connection?'

'They had never met before?'

'No.'

'Well, hadn't you better tell her?'

'I suppose so,' Edward said meditatively, 'but not quite yet. I need to think about all this. Darling V,' he added, pulling himself together and taking her hand, 'you've done well – very well. Do you feel up to coming to the regatta tomorrow?'

'Try and stop me! I want to be in at the kill.' She realized what she had said and made a face. 'I didn't mean that. You know what I meant, don't you, Edward?'

'I do,' he replied, looking at her fondly.

'By the way,' she said, the thought striking her. 'Weren't you going to talk to Herold's nurse? What did you say her name was? Mrs Paria? Such an odd name.'

'Yes, I was, but the agency she worked for say that she has disappeared – gone abroad they think. They said she was . . . Oh God, of course! What an idiot I am! I'll never do *The Times* crossword again!'

13

'Miss Browne – or may I call you Verity? I can honestly say I have heard so much about you . . . from Edward,' Harry added unnecessarily.

Edward was curious to see if they took to each other at their first meeting. He could see Harry was putting on the charm and, though Verity was smiling, he knew instinctively that she did not like him.

The final day of the regatta could be something of an anticlimax. There were many fewer races than on previous days and the finals sometimes turned out to be a damp squib, but today was going to be different.

The sun shone and the breeze was light – nothing to worry rowers or spectators. The stands were already crowded and there was a general feeling of excitement in the air. Harry was in his element on the launch he had hired called, appropriately, *River Life*. Cathy Herold greeted Edward with suspicion and hardly deigned to take Verity's hand, fearing perhaps that she would catch something from her. As soon as they were on board, Harry made Verity comfortable with a rug over her knees. Edward had exchanged his crutches for a stick but he, too, was glad to sit down. When Harry had cast off, he called Cathy over to help him steer. This seemed to involve a good deal of horseplay and there was much giggling and holding on to one another which made Edward feel rather uncomfortable, as though he and

Verity were de trop. The *Henley Hornet* passed them driven by Roderick Black. Harry's party waved and Mary and the Bruce-Dicks waved back.

He focused his attention on Verity, making sure she did not tire herself or get cold until, rather ungratefully, she asked him not to fuss over her. Fortunately, it was a large launch with a cabin down two or three wooden steps where one could escape the rain or the company. Looking at his programme, Edward could see only two races he particularly wanted to watch – Eton against Radley in the finals of the Ladies' Plate at midday and, of course, Guy Black in the finals of the Diamond Sculls at two thirty. The American, J.W. Burk, was much fancied but everyone agreed that 'anything could happen'. Guy had confounded his critics by reaching the finals but he knew it would take a miracle for him to beat Burk. In a way, it took the pressure off him.

After the first race, Harry stopped the engine and knotted the rope round a willow which drooped over the river. Appearing to remember his manners, he came to sit beside Verity. Edward limped towards the prow where Cathy was leafing through the pages of a magazine without much interest. She didn't seem particularly pleased to be interrupted but commiserated with him politely enough about his leg and asked what it had felt like to kill a man even if it was in self-defence.

'Cathy,' Edward admonished her, 'what's got into you? Have I done something to offend you?'

'I'm just fed up with you asking questions and stirring up old scandals. From what Harry has been telling me, you seem to have put James down as the villain of the piece. My husband was a great man in his day – twice what you are,' she added belligerently.

'I think he was politically naïve but he was a brave man and he was murdered. I can't see why you should object to my trying to find out who did it.'

'No one murdered James,' she replied icily. 'You persuaded me to think someone had but I have come to realize that I was wrong to take you seriously. You're just a trouble-maker and as for Miss Browne, I don't know what she is doing here. She ought to stay in that clinic and not spread her germs around.'

Edward was angry but then became thoughtful. Who had been getting at her? Had Harry been talking to her about Herold? It seemed likely.

'I think I know who killed your husband,' he said in a low voice.

'You know?' She looked worried, even dismayed. 'How could you possibly know? I told you, he wasn't murdered. He was an ill man and he died from a heart attack.'

Edward treated this with the contempt it deserved and changed the subject. 'The nurse – how long had she been coming before your husband died?'

'A fortnight – maybe three weeks. We had another girl before that but she wasn't a trained nurse.'

'She didn't live in?'

'Mrs Paria?'

'That was her name?'

'Yes. April Paria. It was an odd name but she said it was South African – Dutch, I think.'

'You know she seems to have disappeared?'

'Disappeared?'

'Inspector Treacher hasn't been able to track her down. What did she look like?'

'I don't know. Anonymous. Smartly dressed, in her fifties I should say . . . I liked her. She was the no-nonsense type – strong too. She could lift James out of his chair . . . Oh, I say! You don't think she . . .?'

'In Latin a bee-keeper is an *apiarius* or, if female, *apiaria* – almost an anagram of Paria.'

'Are you telling me she murdered James? No, I don't

believe you,' Cathy said after a pause. 'I repeat, he wasn't murdered. I really don't want to talk about it any more.'

After an hour, during which they watched three races, Edward asked to be put ashore. He needed to stretch his legs. Although his knee was much better and he could bend his leg with relatively little pain, sitting in a launch even as large as Harry's had made it stiffen up. Verity insisted on accompanying him. Harry seemed relieved to be rid of them – perhaps wanting to have Cathy to himself, Edward thought.

'You're sure you're up to it?' he asked anxiously for at least the third time as he helped Verity out of the launch. 'Dr Bladon made me swear not to exhaust you.'

'I'm feeling very much stronger. I'd like to come, honestly. Anyway, you may need my arm more than I need yours.'

Not wishing to be accused of fussing again, Edward took her at her word and they strolled along the river bank enjoying the colourful scene. He could not walk very fast but then neither did he wish to. He wanted to enjoy the moment. How many more sunny days with Verity at his side were left to him, he wondered? 'What a couple of crocks we are,' he said aloud and she squeezed his arm more tightly.

'We have each other so it can't be all bad,' she said with a smile. 'You know, I do believe I'm happy. Isn't that amazing? I didn't think one ever knew one was happy until after it was all over.'

'And I'm happy too.' Then, not wishing to tempt fate, he added, 'So I suppose that means something bad is going to happen.'

'Pessimist,' Verity chided him. Suddenly, she stopped and pointed. 'You see that tent – they're advertising a photographic exhibition inside. Do let's have a look. Your friend . . .'

'George Bushell.'

'Yes, he took a photo of us on the first day – remember? Let's see if it's on show.'

It was dark inside the tent but the photographs fixed to wooden panels were well lit.

'There we are!' Verity called out, excitedly. 'Why, it's really rather good! I wonder if we can get a copy.'

Edward peered at the print. It was in black and white, of course, but it was so vivid it might have been in colour. The sun had cast an interesting shadow over the boats and punts around them so they seemed in some clever way, highlighted.

'That's quite a pretty girl I'm with,' Edward said at last.

'And that's quite a distinguished-looking man beside me,' she laughed.

A hearty voice hailed them from the back of the tent. 'Is that who I think it is? Edward, you seem to have been in the wars. What did you do – fall over a tent peg or have you been destroying more of Henley's heritage?'

'George!' Edward greeted his friend warmly. 'Yes, something like that. I say, did you overhear us saying rude things about your photograph?'

'It's very "period",' Bushell joked. 'In two or three years' time, they'll be saying this photograph sums up the last regatta before the war.'

'Don't joke, Mr Bushell,' Verity said, shivering.

'Sorry. But I wasn't joking. This is history, you know, and I'm recording it. Oh dear, I didn't mean to make you glum. Here, let me give you a copy. I've got one somewhere. I'll just put it in an envelope and then I must get back behind my camera. Won't be a jiffy.'

As they waited, Verity said, 'He's right, isn't he, Edward? These are the last moments of peace.'

'Maybe but, according to *The Times*, the Prime Minister is going to Germany to meet Hitler so there may still be a chance of delaying the inevitable. Chamberlain will find some other sop to pacify him. I don't doubt that he'll sacrifice Czechoslovakia to save our skins.'

'But that would be so . . . disgraceful.'

Edward shrugged. 'Let's have a look at some of the other photographs while we're waiting for George. Hey, look at this, V. Do you recognize anyone?'

The photograph showed two men talking earnestly to one another.

'It's Jack Amery with Stille,' Verity shuddered. 'Did he really try to kill me? It all seems rather fantastic somehow.'

'I don't think there can be any doubt of it,' Edward replied soberly.

'He was a wicked man,' she said, remembering the savage killing of her little dog when their paths had first crossed three years earlier. 'I'm glad you killed him.'

'Although I didn't really mean to,' Edward replied weakly, not much liking to be congratulated as a killer. 'But you're right. He was a wicked man who was working for a wicked regime. "By the pricking of my thumbs, something wicked this way comes." Compared to Major Stille, Macbeth was an innocent.'

Verity moved on, glancing at several other photographs hanging nearby. 'There's a lovely one here of Guy Black.'

Edward went over to look. Guy had just finished his first heat and was chatting to his father who looked justly proud. Edward examined the small crowd in the background.

'Hold on a minute, I'm sure that's Dr and Mrs Booth – Hermione Totteridge's sister and brother-in-law. They were the last people I expected to be here. I wonder, V . . . I think we should go back to the launch. I'd really like to talk to them. I might be able to spot them from the river.'

George Bushell reappeared and Edward took the envelope he proffered. 'Thanks, old chap. I'll frame it. Can't stay to chat. I've just spotted a photograph of some people I know who I didn't think would be here,' he explained. 'Very good photographs! As you say, the historical record . . . quite invaluable.'

Through his binoculars, Edward saw that Harry's launch was at the start near Temple Island so he and Verity flopped down in deck-chairs to await its return.

'You don't think they are in any danger?'

'The Booths? Probably not. I just had a moment of panic. I have to admit my tussle with Stille has left me rather nervy. I keep having to tell myself that now he's dead, we don't have anything to fear.'

'But I say, what about Roderick Black's launch? Isn't it called the *Henley Hornet* . . .? Oh, I say . . . Bees, flies, hornets . . . You don't think there will be another murder, do you?'

'No, it's just a coincidence but I need to get to the Booths before they do anything silly.' He smiled but Verity could see that he was worried. 'Stay with me, will you, V? I need to keep a close eye on you until I'm sure the man who has killed at least four people is behind bars.'

Glancing at his programme, Edward saw they were just in time to see Eton challenge Radley for the Ladies' Plate. 'Gosh, we almost missed this. I hadn't realized what the time was. You'll enjoy this, V.'

Verity pouted and was about to say she would go and see if she could find Kay Stammers when she changed her mind. If she loved Edward, as she had told herself she did, surely she could be patient and share his pleasure.

It was a few minutes before the two crews were visible through Edward's binoculars. 'They're neck and neck! Come on, Eton!'

As Edward watched the race, Verity watched him. She was surprised and touched to see the years fall away as he stood and cheered his old school. The weariness and strain which had marked his face ever since she had returned to England with tuberculosis were replaced – at least for a minute or two – by boyish enthusiasm and gathering excitement as the two eights fought their way down the course. To cries of 'Well wowed, Wadley!' from a stout gentleman on their left and 'Go for it, Eton,' shouted even more loudly by Edward, the two eights hove into view.

Suddenly Verity, too, was excited. 'Come on, Eton,' she heard herself screaming in a most unladylike manner. She wondered what on earth she was doing egging on a school she abhorred as embodying everything she hated about the English class system. Then she saw the eights, not representing anything but themselves – young men striving their utmost to overcome the opposition – as she constantly strove to overcome the obstacles that stood in her way to becoming a first-class foreign correspondent. She would cheer them for what they were – young men at the peak of physical fitness doing their duty as they might soon be called to do in a much more dangerous world far from the calm waters of the River Thames.

'Go for it, Eton!' she screamed again and Edward glanced at her in surprise and delight. The Radley eight were a canvas ahead at the halfway point. The race seemed to be over bar the cheering and flag-waving but then the Radley stroke caught a crab – or, if not quite a crab, slid on his seat and scooped up air instead of water. The Eton cox screamed his lungs out and a couple of minutes later the Eton boat crossed the winning line a whole length ahead of its rivals.

'That poor boy at stroke,' Edward said. 'He'll never forgive himself for letting his crew down. He'll dream about that mistake for as long as he lives. I feel for him, I really do.'

Verity was struck by his essential good nature and sympathy for the losers. She knew she would never care a toss how victory was achieved so long as it *was* achieved. She certainly wouldn't bother herself worrying about the losers but Edward – who so demonstrably wanted Eton to win – had immediately voiced his concern for the feelings of the Radley crew. It was a small thing, but it made her doubly sure that he would never let her down.

He saw her look at him and said, 'What?'

'I was just thinking how much I loved you.'

He looked puzzled. 'Because we won?'

'No, because you cared about what must be going through the minds of the losers.'

'Oh, V . . .' he began and then stopped suddenly. 'I say, isn't that Dr Booth over there?'

'I don't know. I've never met him.'

'Wait for me here. I'll just see if I can have a word with him.'

He walked quickly in the direction of the tent to which he thought Dr Booth was making. At first, he could not see him and was turning to go back to Verity when he heard a voice calling him.

At a little table by the tea tent, Violet Booth and her husband were sitting eating sandwiches and drinking lemonade.

'I thought it was you,' Edward said. 'May I join you for a moment?'

'Of course,' Mrs Booth said, waving towards a spare chair.

'I didn't know you were interested in rowing.'

'Oh yes, Lord Edward,' Dr Booth answered. 'Living where we do, on the coast . . .' His voice trailed off into silence.

'I think you know why we are here,' his wife said quietly.

'I think I do. It's because of your niece and Peter Lamming, isn't it?' She nodded her head. 'You were James Herold's nurse, were you not, Mrs Booth?'

'I was but it's not what you think,' she replied, looking intently at Edward as though interrogating him. She laid a hand on his arm but withdrew it quickly, perhaps fearing it was too intimate a gesture. 'It's not what you think,' she repeated.

'Is it not? By the way, I should tell you that Mrs Herold is here. I don't know if . . .'

'I'm going to talk to her . . . explain,' Mrs Booth said in a firm voice, 'but not quite yet. This evening perhaps.'

'You're staying in Henley?'

'At a bed and breakfast,' her husband replied, perhaps deliberately not saying exactly where.

'And General Lowther?'

'We had nothing to do with the General's death. You must believe me,' Mrs Booth said, a glass half-raised to her lips. 'Although we sent a wreath.'

'I don't quite understand . . .' Edward said gently.

'Of course you don't,' Dr Booth interrupted him. 'After you visited us . . . Violet and I . . . well, we had a good chat. We talked about things we ought to have discussed long ago.'

'You told me a lot I didn't know, Lord Edward,' Mrs Booth broke in. 'We felt we had to do it for my sister . . .'

Just as he was about to ask her to explain what she

meant, Edward sensed someone had come up behind him. Looking round, he saw it was Roderick Black. After he had been introduced to the Booths, Black said, 'I hope I'm not interrupting, Corinth, but I was wondering if you and Miss Browne were going to watch my son win the Diamonds.'

'Good heavens, is that the time?' Edward said, looking at his watch. 'Yes, if we can find Harry. We left him to stretch our legs and the last time I saw him he was up near Temple Island.'

'Well, why not watch the race from my launch? I wanted to have a word with you anyway.'

'Thank you. I wouldn't miss it for the world. I owe Guy for rescuing me from the island. Win or lose, he's a fine boy. By the way, I wonder if there would be room for Dr and Mrs Booth to watch it with us.' Black looked dubious and Edward wished he hadn't suggested it.

'I don't want to sound inhospitable but I rather doubt there would be room . . .' he began.

'It's a very kind thought, Lord Edward,' Dr Booth said, coming to his rescue, 'but we haven't quite finished our lunch. I think we'll watch from the stand. I gather your son has a good chance of winning, Mr Black. You must be very proud.'

'I am, Dr Booth. Even though I think Burk is likely to win, Guy will certainly give him a run for his money.'

Edward rose to leave. 'I'll see you both later. We mustn't keep everyone waiting.'

'Where's Miss Browne?' Black asked as they walked towards the river.

'She's just . . . Damn it, where has she gone? I left her sitting here while I went to talk to the Booths. I told her not to move and now she's vanished.'

'No, there she is with her friend, Miss Stammers.'

'Verity, I thought I'd lost you. Miss Stammers . . .' Edward's voice was cool. He still, unfairly, blamed her for taking Verity up in her Tiger Moth and almost killing her. 'I was just going to watch Guy's race. I don't know where Harry's got to but Mr Black has kindly invited us to watch it from his launch.'

'Roderick, please!' Mr Black insisted.

'If you don't think us rude, Mr Black – Roderick – Kay and I will watch from the bank,' Verity said.

There was no time for him to argue and, in any case, she could see that he was keen to have Edward to himself.

On the launch, Edward found Mary Black, the Bruce-Dicks and their daughter, Sybil. As he drove the launch towards the start, Black beckoned Edward to sit beside him.

'I wanted to thank you . . . congratulate you . . . on ridding us of that man Stille. I don't know how much he told you but I got too far in with Mosley's crowd – Jack Amery and his merry band. I was stupid, I realize that now. I thought Hitler had something to offer us. I still do, as a matter of fact, but it's all too late. I can see that now. We'll have to fight him this year or next. Stille blackmailed me into handing over some secret documents . . . nothing really sensitive, you understand.' He shot Edward a glance to see how he was taking his confession but Edward remained impassive.

'Anyway, Guy found out and made me go to Scotland Yard. They were going to use me to trap Stille . . . arrest him red-handed as he took the stuff I had left on Temple Island but you got there first. Damn glad you did. Much rather he was dead than merely deported. Scum like that always comes to the surface eventually. Do you blame me?' He glanced again at Edward. 'I blame myself. I was an arrogant fool. I hated Communism so much and still do. Not Miss Browne, of course, but the Party. It's a disease – more deadly than TB – and, if we catch it, it'll destroy England just as it

246

destroyed Russia. My idea was that Hitler would do the job for us. Go to war with the Soviets and they could fight each other until both sides were exhausted, but I see now that it was a pipe dream. As long as, when war comes, we don't have to fight alongside the Russkies. I couldn't stomach that.'

'I'm glad it's all over,' Edward responded non-committally. 'Hey! There's Guy.' Gratefully, he turned his attention to the race which was just about to start.

Black took the launch round the island so it was positioned behind the umpire's launch. Edward saw that, although there was a notice on the apron of grass which formed the island's 'prow', there was no sign of a police guard. There might, of course, be a constable dozing inside the temple but he would surely be outside on such a glorious day watching the activity on the river. There was, he supposed, nothing much to guard. Stille's body had been removed and the temple thoroughly examined. There was no doubt about what had happened and, although the Janus statue was still lying on its side, it was no longer blocking the stone steps to the roof.

The gun was fired and the race began. At first their sculls seemed almost relaxed as Burk and Guy used long, lazy strokes to propel their fragile craft over the tranquil water. Then, at the halfway point when they were level pegging, the American seemed to pull away. Just when Edward thought it was all over, Burk seemed to falter and, in less than a minute, Guy was once again alongside him. The last few hundred yards saw a battle of wills acted out on the most public of stages.

Perhaps it was because of an unspoken feeling among those watching that this would be the last regatta before war and these young men, striving on the river that ran through this quiet English town, might soon be fighting on a foreign front, but the struggle seemed, at least to

Edward, unbearably poignant. This was English decency on display, honest rivalry that men like Major Stille could never understand.

Still neck and neck, the two pairs of splashing sculls came down over the finishing line. The flag was waved and the race was over. But who had won? Could it even have been a dead heat? There was an agonizing wait while the officials deliberated. And then the announcement. Burk was declared the winner. A groan from Black was followed by a burst of applause which even he had to join in, knowing that it was for his son as much as the winner. The American had triumphed but the courage and sheer guts of the challenger had captured the hearts of the watching crowds.

Black hurriedly moored the launch and went to congratulate Guy. Edward and Bruce-Dick followed more slowly, not wishing to come between father and son.

'A very game lad,' Bruce-Dick opined.

'Indeed,' Edward said. It was not the English way to indulge in superlatives.

After Guy's race – it was announced that Burk had broken the record for the Diamonds by a full eight seconds, completing the course in eight minutes and ten seconds – Edward's interest in the regatta was all but over. Having shaken Guy by the hand, he went off in search of Verity. He had a strange premonition that he ought not to have let her out of his sight. He told himself that Stille was dead so there was nothing to fear, but why did his heart say otherwise?

He found Verity and Kay comforting Cathy Herold. 'Oh, Edward – there you are! Could you take Cathy home? She's had a rather unpleasant experience and she's very shaken,' Verity explained.

'Of course, but what's happened?'

'Harry sort of jumped on her,' Kay answered.

'In the launch?'

'Yes, they had moored behind the island, out of sight and were . . .'

'We were kissing,' Cathy sobbed, clutching a handkerchief to her face. 'Nothing more, I promise, and then he tried to . . .'

'He tried to rape her,' Verity finished her sentence, speaking with quiet anger.

'I told him to stop but he just wouldn't. I told him I liked him . . . I *did* like him but it was all going too fast . . . I screamed and then . . .'

'And then he hit her,' Kay said. 'Show Lord Edward your face.'

Unwillingly, Cathy raised her head and took away the handkerchief. Edward saw there was a nasty bruise on her cheek.

'Oh God! I'm so sorry, Cathy. I never thought he would be violent. How did you get away from him?'

'I told him I would scream the place down if he didn't take me straight back to the Stewards' Enclosure.' She managed a smile through her tears. 'He seemed to believe me, so here I am.'

'Let's go to the first-aid tent and have that bruise looked at,' Edward urged her. 'Do you want to make a formal complaint . . . to the police, I mean?'

'No . . . I'm all right, Lord Edward. You're all very kind but I'm not badly hurt. It was just the shock of it. If you can take me home, I'll be all right, honestly. It was partly my fault. I shouldn't have encouraged him.'

'I know what you mean,' Kay said. 'When Harry's being charming, one wants to give him anything. He did the same with me at the dance at Phyllis Court the other evening but I laughed him out of it. He said he wanted to take me to a secret place where we could be alone. I think he tries it on with every half-decent woman he meets.'

Edward looked angry and anxious. 'I'll take you home, Cathy. Fenton's around somewhere but in any case I think my knee is up to . . . Ah! There he is, just when we need him. Fenton, will you get the car? We're taking Mrs Herold home. She's not feeling very well. Will you two be all right?' he added, turning to Kay and Verity.

'Of course! Or would you like us to come with you?' Kay asked.

'Verity, you need to rest,' Edward said bossily. 'Perhaps it would be better if you came with me, Kay. A woman's touch and all that.'

14

All the time he was with Cathy, Edward felt nervous and angry. Even though this was the Harry he had known in Kenya, he had tried to convince himself that the man had changed – become something better, softer, more mature. But now he was forced to admit that the leopard had not changed his spots – nor could he. Harry was still the vain, heartless womanizer who had viewed all women – married or not – as fair game. He had the old hunter's belief in nature's innate savagery and the scars to prove it. You killed or you were killed.

As soon as he could, Edward left Cathy chatting away to Kay. They seemed to get along. Both were active, outdoor women with the same taste in men. It was not surprising, he thought, that their views on the world – which primarily meant men – were similar. Neither seemed to notice when he made his excuses, saying he had to get back to Verity. It was quite absurd, he knew, but he was convinced that some danger threatened her and that, in her condition, she would not be able to protect herself. He was not normally someone who set much store by hunches or premonitions but, this once, he was the victim of some terror – there was no other word for it – that had started as a vague fear and now had him by the throat.

Fenton drove him back to the regatta and Edward asked if he would help him look for Verity. 'With my knee,' he said, waving his stick, 'I can't move very fast. Let's meet back here in about an hour.'

He sent Fenton to walk along the river bank and gave him his binoculars so he could scan the hundreds of small boats still bobbing about on the water. Edward couldn't understand why he had failed to agree a definite meeting place with Verity even though he knew only too well that she never stayed in one place for more than five minutes.

He tried to think logically of all the places where she might have gone. As far as he could see, she was not in the stands on his side of the river. He limped over to the tea tent but there was no sign of her and everything had been cleared away. He thought the Booths might have seen her but they too had vanished. He looked in on George Bushell's photographic exhibition, wondering if she had wanted to look at her picture again, but she was not there and nor was George. An assistant told him that he had gone to photograph the finals of the Diamonds and had not yet returned.

Edward's knee was beginning to trouble him – perhaps because he had walked too much or possibly in sympathy with his anxious heart. It was ridiculous to think that Verity could have been abducted in the midst of the throng. If anyone had tried anything like that, all she had to do was cry out and someone would have come to her rescue. On the other hand, perhaps no one would have noticed anything unusual. He thought of Harry. Might he have tried something? But surely he would be licking his wounds after failing to seduce Cathy Herold. He turned on his heel and limped back towards the river.

There were fewer launches moored near the stands now the regatta was drawing to a close and he searched anxiously for Harry's. It was larger than most and to his relief he spotted it but whether Harry was there or not was another matter. Reaching it, he thought at first there was no one on board but then he heard voices coming from the cabin. Clumsily, he climbed aboard, almost falling over as he did so, and the voices stopped. The cabin door was closed and, feeling suddenly shy about barging in on his friend and perhaps interrupting some amorous encounter, he knocked.

'Who is it?' The voice was Harry's.

'It's me, Edward. Are you all right? I was looking for Verity. She seems to have disappeared.'

The door opened but it wasn't Harry's face Edward saw – it was Violet Booth's.

'Come in, Lord Edward – now that you're here.'

She held a black snub-nosed revolver in one hand but it wasn't pointed at him. In the confined space, she was no more than a few inches from Harry and the gun was pointed at his heart.

Edward was alarmed but not wholly surprised. He spoke as calmly as he could in the circumstances. 'Mrs Booth, is this really necessary? I know you think Harry murdered your sister but why don't I call Inspector Treacher and you can tell him all about it?'

She snorted. 'That was what Alfred wanted me to do but I told him the police were perfectly useless and, if anything was to be done, it had to be done by us.'

'You could have come to me.'

'That was what he suggested but I told him it wasn't good enough. I needed to confront Hermione's murderer myself.'

Edward looked at Harry. He was lying on a bunk, his hands behind his head, seemingly quite unworried by the gun or the accusation.

'Harry, you did kill Miss Totteridge, didn't you?'

'You believe this woman, do you, old man?' he answered lazily. 'Well, what if I did – and I'm not admitting anything, mind. She deserved to die and so did the others.'

'How did she deserve to die?' Mrs Booth was outraged.

'I'm not going to say anything more but I assure you she did. Ask Edward. He'll tell you.'

'It's all about Isabella, isn't it, Harry? She was the girl you told me about – the girl in Kenya you had an affair with – an affair she bitterly regretted. You said it didn't work out. You loved her but she didn't love you, did she? She loved her husband, Peter Lamming, so you killed him on a climbing expedition in the Drakensberg Mountains. But it didn't make any difference. She still didn't love you. She may even have suspected that you had killed the only man she ever loved.'

'Peter . . .? You killed Peter?' Mrs Booth's voice shook.

'Yes, my little Izzy's poor fool of a husband. We all went climbing in the Drakensberg – Lamming, Herold and I. I thought that, if Herold could get away with killing his wife in a climbing "accident", it should be possible to dispose of Lamming. We would never be suspected of murder. What possible motive could Herold or I have for getting rid of him?'

'Did Herold help you kill him?' Edward asked, aghast.

'No, I thought it was better he shouldn't know anything about it. I managed it rather well, though I say so myself. I think Herold blamed himself for the "accident". He never noticed that the rope had been cut.'

'You didn't have much luck with girls, did you, Harry?' Edward sneered. 'Perhaps it was because you always chose other men's wives. They all died in the end, didn't they?'

'You won't trick me into confessing anything more and, if I do, I'll deny it,' Harry answered sullenly.

'Answer him, damn you,' Mrs Booth broke in. 'I knew you had had an affair with Gwyneth Herold. It

254

was something Isabella told me before she died. I couldn't prove anything, of course, but – from what she said – I guessed you blamed James Herold for the accident. When I heard by chance that you were back in England, I thought – stupid me – that I might be able to warn him . . . to protect him.'

'Herold was an arrogant fool. Yes, I did blame him for Gwynnie's death and, even more, for making a fortune out of it – turning it into a sob story. The more I thought about it, the more I came to believe that he killed her – that it was no accident. She was an experienced climber but I was never going to get him to admit it. Even when I stood over him and watched him die, he wouldn't confess.'

'You're a heartless killer,' Mrs Booth said, raising the gun, 'and this death is too good for you.'

'I did him a favour, my dear lady,' Harry could not resist answering. 'Can't you see that? He welcomed me as his fate. I gave him freedom. I was merciful, which was more than he was. Yes, I loved Gwynnie. She was going to go away with me but her husband found out and killed her.'

'Wait, Mrs Booth!' Edward commanded as he saw her begin to squeeze the trigger. 'I still have some questions to ask him. Tell me, Harry, is that why you tried to seduce Cathy? Because she was Herold's wife? Because she *wasn't* Gwynnie?'

'That wasn't important, old chap,' Harry sneered. 'When I met Cathy with you, I knew I could have her if I wanted.' He spoke almost proudly as though unable to resist bragging about how irresistible he was to women.

'But she didn't want you, did she?' Edward jeered. 'So you hit her. That's cad's behaviour, isn't it, Harry? I knew you were a killer – you told me so yourself – but I didn't know you were a cad.'

This slur seemed to rile him, as Edward knew it would, and he abandoned his relaxed pose, removed his hands from behind his head and sat up.

'But Hermione . . . what do you accuse her of doing? Why kill my poor sister? What had she ever done to you?' Mrs Booth was breathing heavily.

'You really don't know? She poisoned Isabella's mind against me. She told her I was a common murderer and she ought to go to the police.'

'Isabella suspected that you had killed Peter – perhaps she *knew* you had. You probably bragged about it. That's why she hated you but she had no proof – no way of making you pay for what you had done. She convinced herself that *she* was to blame for his death. She never forgave herself for having let you seduce her, for loving you, if only for a few weeks or months.' Edward took a breath and added, 'And she never forgave *you*. She soon saw you for what you were. The immorality of Happy Valley – the easy sex, the drugs, the stupid, meaningless, hedonistic lifestyle – in the end she realized it wasn't for her. You had seduced her, Harry, but she never loved you – not when she knew what you really were. When she got back to England, she went to see her aunt and blurted it all out.'

'Silly old bat,' Harry said with a laugh. 'She poisoned my Izzy's mind so I put a little poison in her tea. She was showing me her albums. There was one of my Izzy on her wedding day I just had to have. I put it with the photograph of my other true love, Christobel.'

'Why do you keep on calling Isabella your "true love"?' Mrs Booth demanded. 'She was never yours. She was Peter's and she hated you for seducing her in a moment of weakness.'

'The old bitch told Izzy to tell the police what she suspected but Izzy couldn't bring herself to do that,' Harry said, almost dreamily. 'She wrote to tell me so.

That was when I decided I had to come to England to sort things out.'

'So you killed Isabella and then Hermione Totteridge!' Edward felt sick at the thought of such wicked, ruthless killing. He was face to face with a mass murderer, a psychopath. He thought he had known Harry so well but he hadn't known him at all! He had put him down as a rogue and a womanizer but not a maniac. And yet, if he had learnt anything over the years, it was that most murderers looked exactly like everyone else. They didn't have physical deformities or skulk around with their collars turned up. They were people like Harry – charming, attractive but somehow acting out their fantasies beyond the rules of normal behaviour. Harry's magnetism had drawn women to him and, under his spell, they had broken their most sacred vows and betrayed those who had loved them. And then, like a child tearing the wings off flies, he had thrown them aside or, if they struggled to free themselves from him, had casually killed them.

'I didn't kill Isabella,' Harry said, suddenly animated. 'I loved her. I wouldn't have hurt her. She died before I ever came to this godforsaken country. She died because of your husband's incompetence, Mrs Booth. If he had seen how ill she was, she would be alive today.'

'Don't you dare blame my husband. He loved her as if she were his own daughter. We both did. We did everything we could but she . . . she didn't want to live. You *did* kill her. You killed her because you burdened her with a terrible guilt . . .'

'We all kill the thing we love most. Isn't that what Oscar Wilde said?' Harry murmured, almost with regret. 'Even you, Edward – you killed . . . Did you really think I could forgive you for killing Christobel?'

'Are you suggesting that I killed Lady Redfern?'

'My darling Christobel, yes.' For a moment he

dropped his expression of amused disbelief and looked savagely at Edward. 'You killed the one woman I truly loved. I loved her more than Izzy. She gave me hope that this perfectly pointless world might have some meaning for me if she was by my side.'

'That's a lie and you know it, Harry. You have twisted the truth into fantasy. You've convinced yourself she was someone special but she was just another of your girls, wasn't she, Harry? Admit it. And if anyone killed her, it was you. Don't give me all that sentimental claptrap. I know you for what you are, Harry – a liar, a self-deceiver and a killer. You don't know the meaning of love. You can't even love yourself, can you? You despise yourself and we all despise you too.'

It wasn't often that Edward lost his temper but he had done so now and it made him feel better. He slapped his forehead. 'Oh, I see! That's why you no longer drive. I thought it was odd. You used to love your cars and your aeroplanes in Kenya but you lost your nerve, didn't you? After you broke her neck . . .' Another wave of anger overcame him. To be blamed for starting a trail of bloodshed . . . He simply would not have it. 'And General Lowther . . .' he continued. 'I suppose you are going to tell me you murdered him because he also killed with his car.' He turned to Mrs Booth. 'You told me Isabella's parents – your sister Daphne and her husband – were killed in a motor accident near Godalming. Did you know that was where General Lowther lived before he moved to Henley?

'Very good, Edward!' Harry sneered. 'Except I didn't murder him. I merely suggested that he do what he had wanted to do for so long – pay the price of his folly. I didn't need to kill him. He too was burdened by guilt. I discovered quite by chance that he regularly visited the church where Isabella's parents were buried. Every month he used to leave a flower on their grave. It was quite touching. I just "bumped into him" on one of these visits. I told him that Isabella – the daughter of the couple he had mown down in his car – had died of grief. I didn't mention that it was grief for her husband – not her parents – that killed her. I told him the time had come to make his peace with her and with himself and I gave him a little cyanide and a pithy quotation from the Bard. It seemed to do the trick. I even think he was grateful – as Herold was grateful. However, I have to admit that I was quite surprised when he did what I suggested.'

'Did he know who you were?'

'That was the strange thing. He wasn't in the least bit interested. I think he thought I was fate or nemesis. And of course I was.'

'When I read about the General's death in the paper, I suspected he was murdered by whoever killed Hermione,' Mrs Booth burst out. 'But what could I do?'

'You sent a wreath?'

'I did, and when you came to see me I tried to tell you that there was a connection with my sister Daphne's death in a road accident. I remembered that General Lowther had been driving the other car – not that the accident was his fault. Daphne wasn't used to driving on English roads.'

'Of course! You told me exactly where the accident happened – Godalming, where General Lowther used to live, but I was too stupid to pick up the clue.'

Harry hesitated and then curiosity got the better of him. 'So when did you first suspect me?'

'I never suspected you to be a madman. It's true that I was uneasy from the moment I came to Turton House and saw your reading matter. *The Revenger's Tragedy*, Shakespeare, *The Alchemist*. I flicked through it and saw you had underlined Subtle's words, "Art can beget bees, hornets, beetles, wasps out of the carcasses and dung of creatures" but I didn't allow myself to imagine you could do what you have done.'

'It was silly of me to leave that out for you to read but I couldn't resist giving you the clue and watching you congratulate yourself for being so clever. I'm particularly interested in the Revenge Tragedies and the sixteenth and seventeenth centuries' fixation with death and decay – with rotting flesh. You know they believed that the insides of a dead dog actually brought forth disgusting insects? A charming notion, I always thought.'

'Is that why you invited me to stay with you in the first place and why you left my family motto on Eric Silver's body? You were bored. It was all too easy. You wanted someone to challenge you. If the police refused to investigate, you thought I might be persuaded. It crossed my mind that you were taunting me but I did not know why. Then you said you blamed me for Lady Redfern's death in that car accident on the Naivasha road. That it was *you* who was to blame, not me, did not seem to concern you. Your only mistake was not to kill me when you had the chance.'

'I suppose I was being sentimental. Old school tie, that sort of thing.'

'You thought I was a fly caught in your spider's web! You thought to play with me just as you had with your other victims. How arrogant! That was always your undoing, Harry. You thought you were too clever to have to live by the rules. And to make sure I took the bait, you murdered poor Eric Silver and left my family motto on his body.'

'Rather clever, I thought. I had been following you, wondering how to attract your attention. I wrote inviting you to stay but you ignored my letter. Then I overheard your dentist. It was a wonderful stroke of luck getting in without anybody seeing me – no nurse, no receptionist. I had no idea he had been dentist to all three of them. And when I heard him spin that preposterous theory about bugs and insects . . . I was almost afraid you would hear me laughing. Fate does have a way of giving us what we want, doesn't it, old man?'

'So why didn't you kill me? It can't have been because we went to the same school. You had plenty of opportunities. I made things as easy as possible for you. Was it just too easy?'

'Too easy, yes. I couldn't quite bring myself to do it. And anyway, I enjoyed watching you work at the little puzzle I had set you. In the end, I thought it might be better . . . more fitting . . . more *amusing* . . . to deprive you of the woman you loved, as you had deprived me of the woman I loved.'

It hit Edward like a mallet. Harry had abducted Verity. For a few minutes, he had forgotten all about her. A cold dread made him feel faint and he leant heavily on his stick. Harry – the man he had once called a friend – was sneering at him and enjoying his final triumph. He had surveyed him like a lion watching his prey, deciding which was his weakest point, how best to hurt him.

'Verity! What have you done to her, you bastard? If you have harmed her, I'll kill you with my own hands.' Edward wanted to shout and scream but knew he must remain calm if he was to find out where she was.

' "How choleric you are, my friend! Must I budge? Must I observe you?"' Harry got up slowly. '"Must I stand and crouch under your testy humour," as the playwright has it? Well, I don't want to be ungenerous. After all, we were at school together. Mind you, I always thought you were a disgusting little prig. I'll give you a clue. Now, how does it go? "A little water clears us of this deed." *Macbeth*, a favourite play of mine.'

'Harry, I thought we were friends,' Edward found himself pleading. 'Tell me in plain English what you have done with her. I never hurt you. It wasn't my fault that Lady Redfern died.'

Harry looked at him and the loathing in his eyes chilled Edward to the core.

'I came back to this rotten little country to finish things off,' he said, for the first time showing some true feeling. 'I never thought I would be able to until that lucky inheritance made it possible.'

Edward was appalled and Violet Booth momentarily lowered her gun. Against such evil what was there to do? As the lion senses the moment to spring on his prey, Harry made a grab at the gun. He was much stronger than Mrs Booth and, even in her bitterness, she had never been sure she could pull the trigger. Now, as he tore the weapon from her hand, it went off. Whether she had squeezed the trigger as she tried to cling on to it or whether Harry had done so in his rage, it was impossible to tell but there was a loud report, amplified in the small cabin. Harry was flung back against the wall. A look of surprise and indignation crossed his face as he slid down on to the floor.

Edward took a step forward and knelt beside his body. He cursed himself for not having prevented this untimely death. Harry had cheated justice just as he had throughout his life. He had died an easy death and made no reparation for the damage he had done. More to the point, he had died without saying where he had imprisoned Verity.

A wave of nausea made his stomach heave. Verity might be in terrible pain or even dead and the man who knew where she was lay dead in front of him. His brain refused to work.

Fenton put his head round the cabin door and took in the situation. 'Is everything all right, my lord?'

'No, everything is not all right, Fenton,' Edward said, overcome with weariness.

Fenton knelt down beside Harry's body and felt for a pulse. As he looked up inquiringly at his master, Edward answered his unspoken question. 'He tried to grab Mrs Booth's gun and it went off. He's dead, isn't he?'

'Quite dead.' Fenton turned to Mrs Booth who had collapsed on a chair and was breathing stertorously. 'I don't like the look of her, my lord. Shall I call an ambulance?'

'Yes, and then call the police.'

As he went off to summon help, another face appeared at the door. It was Dr Booth. He took one look at his wife and hurried over to take her pulse. 'What's happened here?' he demanded. Edward explained and he groaned. 'I tried to stop her. I told her to leave it to the police but she gave me the slip. Did she kill him?' He nodded in the direction of the body on the floor.

'It was an accident. In the struggle . . . her gun went off.' Edward shrugged helplessly.

'I don't doubt it. She could never have killed anyone – even filth like him. Help me carry her up the steps, will you? I need to take her into the fresh air. Gently now!'

'Has she had a heart attack?'

'I'm not sure. I don't think so but I must get her to hospital.'

'My valet has gone to telephone for an ambulance.' Edward said, as they laid Mrs Booth on the deck of the launch.

Dr Booth put a cushion under her head and looked at his wife with undisguised love.

'Dr Booth, forgive me, it's Verity . . .'

'Miss Browne?'

'Yes, Harry has hidden her – God knows where – and, now he's dead, he can't be made to tell me. All he said was it was somewhere to do with water. Since we are on the river, that doesn't help much. It can't be far because he didn't have very much time. Assuming he took her somewhere in this launch, I doubt he could have gone further than Phyllis Court or . . .'

'Temple Island?' Dr Booth finished his sentence. 'But isn't it all sealed off?'

'I don't think so. When I was up there earlier, I couldn't see any police.' Edward was suddenly certain that Verity was hidden on the island. It would have been typical of Harry to play one last joke and hide her where Major Stille, had been killed by the man he blamed for ruining his life. To conceal her where the police would search last of all because they had so recently gone over it so thoroughly was just the way his mind worked. The terrible question remained – had Harry killed her before he imprisoned her or was she still alive?

He looked round. He could hardly take the launch with Harry's body down in the cabin and Mrs Booth so ill. The urgent bell of a police car broke the silence. He made a decision.

'Look, Dr Booth, will you hold the fort for me? I don't want to see Inspector Treacher yet. There will be so many questions and so much delay. For all we know, Verity may be in terrible danger even now.'

'Go,' Dr Booth told him, 'but go quickly. The police will be here in a few moments.'

'Tell Treacher . . . tell him I'll explain everything later.'

Edward ran as fast as his bad knee would allow towards where the umpires' launches were moored. He cursed himself for not being able to move at more than an awkward trot. Before he reached them, he was hailed by Roderick Black and Guy on board the *Hornet*. Her engine was idling and they appeared to be waiting for someone.

'Where are you off to in such a hurry,' Guy shouted, 'and why the police car?' He waved towards Harry's launch around which the police were gathering.

'It's Verity,' Edward panted. 'She's been kidnapped. I need to go to Temple Island. Can you take me? I think she's being held prisoner there.'

'Miss Browne? A prisoner?' Roderick Black demanded and then saw Edward's anxious face. 'Hop on board and you can tell us what has happened on the way.'

The powerful launch cut through the water leaving in its wake smaller boats bobbing up and down, their occupants shouting protests. Edward, standing at the prow, saw nothing. His whole being was concentrated on finding Verity.

15

After Edward had left with Kay to take Cathy Herold home, Verity walked slowly towards the stands. She was feeling tired and wanted to sit down. Her cough was worse and she had a horrid feeling that her illness was as bad as ever. The elation of surviving the Tiger Moth's death-defying dive had vanished. She wondered, even if she did recover, whether she would be left with unsightly scars, as she had been warned could happen. She tried to concentrate on pleasanter things – how much she loved Edward and had come to rely on him unquestioningly. She had become very fond of Kay too, even if she was slightly suspicious of her sexuality. She had the maudlin idea that, if she died, Kay and Edward would make a good match. She imagined herself lying, rather elegantly it had to be said, on her deathbed and giving them her blessing. She shook her head and laughed at herself. TB, the doctor had warned her, played games with the mind as well as attacking the body.

She reached the stands and sat on a rather uncomfortable seat, gazing out over the river. She didn't want to think about Cathy so thought instead of the race she had watched at Edward's side. She would never forget seeing Eton win and his innocent delight in his old school's victory. She turned over in her mind how fate had tossed her around like one of the pebbles in the water below her. Here she was in one of the most serene, most English of towns when she had expected to be in Prague – a city on the brink of destruction. How often in Spain, resting behind the front line, had her mind turned to England, green and pleasant land, and how she had longed to be back there. Now that she was, she felt only frustration.

She tried to be honest with herself. Did she feel well enough to take up her profession again? Would she ever feel well enough? She had no idea how depleted were her reserves of physical and mental strength. An all-important appointment with Dr Tomlinson at the Middlesex Hospital was scheduled for the week after next. How could she bear it if he said she was not getting better and sentenced her to months or even years in a Swiss sanatorium? She coughed experimentally and found her chest did not hurt. She longed for a cigarette but dared not light one. The doctor had made her swear to give them up. She closed her eyes in a moment of silent prayer to whichever god protected atheists for the strength to resist temptation and, when she opened them, found Harry Lestern bending over her.

'Are you all right, Miss Browne?' he asked with what sounded like genuine concern. She was touched and then remembered what he had done to Cathy.

'Quite all right, thank you. I was feeling a little tired, that's all,' she said coldly.

'Would you like me to take you back to the clinic?'

'No, thank you. Edward has just taken Mrs Herold home. He won't be long. She had a very nasty bruise on her cheek. In fact, she was very shaken up.' Harry made no reply and she was provoked into going further than she had intended. 'Is that the way you treat all your women – hit them if they won't do what you ask?'

'I don't know what she has been telling you. She hit her face on the corner of the cabin as she was climbing out of the launch.'

Verity looked disbelieving. 'I can't see how she could have done that. She said you hit her. We suggested she go to the police but she refused.'

'Of course she refused. She knew her story was a lie, if she really said I had hit her.'

Verity was almost admiring of his brass-necked impudence. 'Well, it's nothing to do with me but I thought she was telling the truth. I think, if you hit women, then you certainly aren't a gentleman.'

As soon as she had spoken the words, she regretted them. They were weak and silly. 'Not quite a gentleman'! The phrase sounded old-fashioned and priggish and, as a Communist, she didn't believe in the concept of 'gentlemen', a species expected to behave differently from other men. However, her words had certainly riled Harry. They looked at one another with mutual distaste. He was absurdly handsome, she was forced to admit. True, his complexion showed the wear and tear of living in a hot climate and, she knew from what Edward had told her, of drinking too much and taking too many drugs. And yet his eyes ... There was something commanding about his eyes and the deep lines around his mouth seemed to map an interesting and eventful life. But there was cruelty there too – or was she just imagining it?

'You are looking tired. Verity. You said I might call you Verity, did you not?'

'I did,' she agreed.

'And will you call me Harry?'

'If you like,' she replied carelessly.

'My launch is over there. Come and rest for a moment.'

'I had better wait here until Edward returns.'

'You'll be able to see him from the launch. Here, let me take your arm.'

Mesmerized, Verity allowed herself be led away from the stands. After all, Harry would hardly try anything on. He knew she had seen through him. When they reached the launch, she made one final protest but he took no notice and half-lifted her aboard. She made to sit on one of the chairs on deck but suddenly found herself propelled down the steps into the cabin.

'Harry! Please! What are you doing?' She began to panic. Surely this friend of Edward's wasn't planning to subject her to some kind of sexual attack? It wasn't as though he liked her and, anyway, he knew she had TB. 'Let me go. Why have you brought me down here? I shall shout for help if you don't take me back immediately.'

'You'll shout for your dear Edward, will you?' Harry mocked. 'You really think that man of yours will come to your rescue? I don't think so. Now keep quiet, you little vixen . . .' he snarled as Verity tried to bite the hand which he had placed over her mouth. It was dark in the little cabin but she was aware that her attacker was trying to open something and she struggled even more fiercely. 'Keep quiet, you bitch,' he said through gritted teeth, 'or I'll punch that pretty face of yours. I'd really like to do that, you know.'

Shocked, Verity momentarily stopped trying to free herself from his grasp. At that moment she felt the prick of a needle in her arm and was almost immediately unconscious. She collapsed on to the floor but Harry made no effort to break her fall. He stood there surveying her. She was pretty – he had to give her that.

'Better than a cosh, no question about it,' he muttered, bending over her. He then did something which, had she known of it, she would have found more hateful than any physical violence – he kissed her. Her lips were dry and he felt his damp upon hers. He held her face in his hands and kissed her again. It meant nothing, he told himself. He had always had more than enough women. He really didn't want this one. He merely wanted to take her from Edward and make him suffer. Expertly, he tied her up and gagged her. When she came to, he didn't want her calling out – not until it no longer mattered.

He went back on deck, started the engine and took the launch out into midstream. It had all taken just a few minutes and, as far as he could see, no one had observed him. It was all going according to plan.

Verity opened her eyes – and wondered if she had. The darkness was impenetrable. It was the most terrifying moment of her life. She was lying on her side, trussed up and gagged, on a damp, hard floor. She had never been happy in enclosed spaces. When she was in Spain, she minded the bullets far less than the fear of being trapped beneath a collapsed building after a bombing raid. It had never happened but now her nightmare seemed to have come to pass. In a state of literally blind panic, she struggled against the ropes that bound her but seemed only to make them tighten. She felt hardly able to breathe. With a great effort of will, she made herself cease her futile wriggling, and rubbed her cheek violently against the rough wall until the gag was pulled away from her mouth. She felt the pain from the scratches and tasted blood mixed with moisture from the wall. Oddly enough, the pain brought some relief from her claustrophobia. At least the pain was real and gave her a sense of her own actuality.

She lay quiet for a moment and tried to make sense of what had happened. The last thing she remembered was struggling with Harry Lestern in the cabin of the launch. He must be the murderer, but why had he not killed her there and then? Of course! He wanted to hurt Edward – hadn't he said as much? She had nothing to do with Edward's investigation, at least as far as Harry would be aware, so she was no threat to him. But Edward might have told him – or Harry could easily have discovered – that they loved one another and even that they were engaged to be married. He hadn't killed her because he wanted to use her against Edward. That idea gave her hope. For whatever reason, Harry needed her alive. But what if he forgot her, or abandoned her, or was killed by Edward before he discovered where she was? She tried not to terrify herself. She had to stay calm and work out a way – if not of escape, then to call attention to herself.

It was so dark and airless that she decided she must be in an underground room and the idea made her flesh creep. Again she told herself to stay calm. Panic was her chief enemy, after Harry of course. If there was a way into this dungeon, there must be a way out and – now that she had loosened the gag – she could scream. She tentatively tried a cry for help but it sounded so weak that she gave up. She must conserve her voice until she heard someone outside.

She strained to hear voices, anything at all, but there was nothing. Where had Harry taken her? She had no idea how long she had been unconscious but guessed it wasn't long, or she would have been even colder. She imagined Edward's consternation when he returned to the stands and could not find her. As soon as he missed her he would institute a search. The idea gave her comfort. It was odd how visualizing his face made her feel calmer and even warmer. She loved him and she trusted him to find her. If he did find her and if he still wanted to marry her, she would even if she had to do so from a wheelchair. She managed a fleeting smile. But

271

what if Harry did not tell anybody where she was? What if he left her to die? He was mad, quite mad, of that she was convinced. And she was buried alive. Would that drive her mad?

She shivered and, with a great effort of will, stopped herself weeping. Where was Basil when she needed him? He was a big dog. He wouldn't have allowed his mistress to be kidnapped by a madman. But he was miles away at Mersham Castle and had probably forgotten all about her. She closed her eyes and tried to listen. There must surely be some sound which would give her a clue as to where she was imprisoned. Why had her cry for help sounded so weak? There was no echo and the walls were thick and damp. Was she in a cellar? She had an idea. Moving her feet experimentally against the wall, she sensed that it was curved but she couldn't be sure of it. She lay still and listened intently. There was another reason why her voice had failed to carry – why had she not heard it before? – the cold, rippling sound of water. Of course! She was on the river!

This small victory over her panic made her feel less hopeless. Even here in this coffin, she was still part of that sunlit world outside. She told herself she must be quite close to where she had been kidnapped. She was now even more certain that she had not been unconscious for long. For one thing, she was not yet hungry although she was thirsty – perhaps the after-effects of whatever drug Harry had given her. And her bladder was not yet uncomfortable. She must be on the river quite near to Edward and that conviction gave her hope.

She relaxed and even slept for a moment or two. She was aroused by the wetness and the chill. Was it wetter than before? Suddenly, she shivered. Yes, it was cold but that was not why she had shivered. There was a definite pool of water beneath her which had not been there before. The river! Was it tidal? She did not know but there must be some sort of ebb and flow. What if . . .? She could hardly bear to think about it. What if her prison was flooded? She had heard of people drowning in just a few inches of water. What if she slowly drowned in this horrible dark hole? What if this dank dungeon was some sort of well? And what if . . .what if it were to be her tomb? She shuddered and despair gripped her.

Again, she rubbed her face against the wall and the pain, as she had hoped, made her stop frightening herself. She remembered how, in Spain, she had discovered that the reality of pain was not as bad as the fear of it. She must stay calm, she told herself for the twentieth time. She must use her intelligence. She must not panic. The sound of a small rodent scuttling across the floor broke in on her consciousness. She stiffened. She had a phobia about rats. She had seen too many disgusting rats feeding off corpses when she was in Spain and it had always been her particular fear to be in the same room with one and not be able to escape. She shuddered, imagining its damp nose on her flesh. Her two worst fears – to be trapped in an underground tomb with rats for company – it was almost too perfect a revenge. If only Major Stille had been alive to savour the joke.

She tried to control her fear by telling herself that an English water rat would be quite different from the disgustingly fat, fearless predators she had come across in the trenches. She made herself think of Ratty in *The Wind in the Willows* – 'messing about on the river'. Was that what she was doing? She stiffened. Oh God! She felt wet fur against her ear. She tried to shake her head but she could hardly move. She wanted desperately to stretch but the ropes that bound her would not give way – in fact, perhaps because of the wet, they seemed tighter than ever. Every joint, every bone in her body was telling her that her blood had stopped flowing. She remembered reading somewhere that, if one was tied up for a long time, the pain became excruciating and then, at last, the pain gave way to numbness and that was the time to worry.

It was only then that she started screaming.

She must have lost consciousness again. An age seemed to have passed but it might only have been a few minutes. She wished she could see her watch but there was absolutely no light even if she had been able to loosen her arms. She was so cold and the pain in her arms and legs was almost unbearable. She felt she must die soon. She must have slipped into unconsciousness once more because, when she came to, she noted – with a detached, almost scientific interest – that her fingers were quite numb and she could not move or feel them. A languor overcame her. Nothing seemed to hurt now – except the cold – and she knew this was dangerous. She struggled to keep awake. She had not known that cold could hurt so much. She tried to imagine blazing fires or Spain in high summer but it seemed only to make it worse.

She told herself she must hang on. She knew they would come looking for her and if she was unconscious . . . unable to call out, they might never find her. She tried to roll on to her other side but there did not seem to be room even to do this and she sank back in despair. She managed a smile. To think that she had been fearful of dying from tuberculosis! Anything would be preferable than to die this way. To see the light, to breathe fresh air, to be warm! She would give five years of her life – no, ten – to die in the open air. She wondered what the doctor would say about her predicament. She imagined Dr Tomlinson telling Edward in his rather pompous voice, as though she was not there, that the treatment for TB did not involve being frozen and half-drowned in a concrete dungeon.

She screamed again but, to her own ears, her cries seemed even weaker and she doubted they could penetrate the thick walls that entombed her. When she stopped screaming she lay still, ready to welcome death as the only practical escape from her suffering.

16

As Roderick Black moored the *Hornet* against the stone wall, Guy jumped out and helped Edward to scramble after him. It took only a few minutes to search the Temple. There was no one on the roof – just the Janus statue lying forlornly on its side waiting to be lifted back on to its pedestal. Edward was beginning to think that Verity was either imprisoned in the untamed part of the island or, more likely, somewhere else altogether when Mr Black remembered the cellar.

Guy bounded down the steps only to find the door locked.

'We'll have to break it down. No one uses the cellar. It floods from time to time so it can't even be used as a storeroom,' Roderick Black said. He saw Edward's look and added rather sheepishly that – when he and Stille had decided to make the island their poste restante – they had explored it thoroughly.

'Look at the keyhole,' Guy called excitedly. 'There's oil on it. Someone has opened the door very recently.'

They looked round for something to use as a battering ram and chose the bench on which Edward had first sat contemplating the beauty of the temple and its mysterious statue. They swung it several times against the door and, on the third attempt, the lock split open and Guy pushed his way through.

'Nothing here,' he called. 'Wait a minute, there seems to be another door at the back.'

'Verity, are you there?' Edward shouted, his voice cracking with anxiety. There was no answer so Guy rattled the door and shouted. Seizing the remains of the bench, he swung it against the door which opened but not very far. Something seemed to be wedged against it. As Guy pushed his way in, Edward held his breath. He had invested so much in his hunch that Harry had brought her here. What if he was wrong? Where would they look next?

With a cry of excitement, which quickly turned to dismay, Guy bent over something on the floor. 'She's here but she's hardly breathing. Quickly, out of the way, you two. I'll carry her into the open.'

Edward's stomach lurched as he saw Verity for the first time. She was wet, deathly pale, and the ropes which bound her were cruelly tight. 'Is there a knife on the *Hornet*?' he asked. 'We need to cut her free.'

'There may be,' Roderick Black called as he ran to the launch. He returned triumphantly with a penknife and a picnic rug and Guy started sawing at the ropes. It seemed to take an unconscionable time to cut through them but at last one and then the others fell away.

'We must massage her legs and arms and then wrap her in the rug,' Edward said.

'She's not looking good,' Guy said with some alarm. 'She's very cold – and look at her face. It seems to have been rubbed raw. What a swine that man must have been to leave her to rot in a place like this.'

Edward was unable to say anything as he rubbed the weals left by the ropes. As her blood began to flow, the pain was so acute that it roused Verity from her stupor. Her eyelids fluttered and then her eyes opened.

She saw Edward's anxious face leaning over her and smiled. 'I knew you'd come for me,' she whispered.

'I would have killed him without any hesitation, if that's what you mean.'

'But did you hate him?'

'We were friends once. He could have been the best of us but he lacked something . . .'

'Moral fibre?' Kay laughed. She and Edward were having a cigarette outside Verity's hospital room.

'Yes, that certainly,' he answered gravely. 'But it was more that he was reckless to the point of madness. It was almost as if he wanted to risk and die risking. He was a gambler forever raising the stakes and his bluff was never called. He told me once that he found it all too easy. He was terminally bored.'

'He had read a lot. Do you remember the night of the Phyllis Court dance? He kept quoting bits of Shakespeare in my ear. It was one of the things that put me off.'

Edward smiled. 'Yes, Verity doesn't like it when I quote Shakespeare at her.' He hesitated. 'Did you . . .? I mean – if you don't mind my asking – did you . . .?'

'Did I sleep with him?' Kay grinned at him. 'No, I didn't. He asked me to. He said he had a private place, a grotto . . . Oh! I wonder if he meant Temple Island? Anyway, he went a little too fast, even for me. Were the Happy Valley women rather . . . how shall I put it? – rather more willing . . .?'

'I think they were. Harry always had it too easy. His charm was legendary but perhaps it had worn a little thin lately. Maybe he wasn't quite the Lothario he had once been.'

They were silent for a minute or two as they dragged on their cigarettes. Edward was exhausted – 'done in' as he put it to Kay – but he absolutely refused to go back

278

to Turton House until Verity was given the all clear and then it would only be for a night. He hated the place now and would either return to London or stay in a hotel close to the hospital.

'So Helen Moody won Wimbledon,' he said in an effort to make conversation.

'Yes, for the eighth time! I think I may give up. She beat Helen Jacobs 6–4, 6–0. I ask you! What hope is there for ordinary mortals?'

'That was what Harry never had – something to aim for. He could have been good at so many things but he could never settle on any particular one. He wasn't a fool, not by any means, but . . .' Edward hesitated, trying to find a way of summing up what had gone so wrong for his friend. 'He liked Walt Whitman,' he said at last. 'If he were ever to have a gravestone, I think I would put on it that two-line poem of his.

'The untold want by life and land ne'er granted,
Now voyager sail forth to seek and find.'

'Only he never did find what he was looking for,' Kay said wryly.

'No, he never did,' Edward agreed.

The doctor came out of Verity's room and looked disapprovingly at their cigarettes which they hurriedly extinguished.

'How is she?' Edward demanded.

'As well as can be expected. She's asking for you.' Without a word, Edward pushed past him. 'Just five minutes,' the doctor called after him.

One morning, two months later, Edward went to pick Verity up from the clinic. While he waited for her to finish packing, he had a quick word with Leonard

Bladon. He wanted to find out whether she was better or whether he was going to have to console her as she faced long months in a Swiss sanatorium. To his dismay, the doctor was tight-lipped.

'She's better, Corinth, no doubt about it, but only the X-rays will show if the lesions have healed. I'm afraid you'll just have to wait and see. Her incarceration on Temple Island should have killed her but,' Dr Bladon rubbed his chin as though puzzled by the vagaries of nature, 'she doesn't seem to have suffered any long-term ill effects. No one would prescribe being almost killed in an aeroplane or drowned in the Thames for someone with TB but there we are . . .! Miss Browne is not a normal patient. She's rather tougher than she looks.'

'Her morale is good,' Edward responded rather defensively, as though it was his fault that Verity had so nearly been a murder victim.

'I'm not blaming you, Corinth,' Dr Bladon offered magnanimously. 'It's the nature of the beast, if you will excuse the expression. Miss Browne is a remarkable woman – courageous and determined. If disease is – as some doctors think – partly in the mind, then she will beat it. And your help is absolutely indispensable. I mean it,' he added gravely, seeing Edward's shrug of self-deprecation. 'You are her rock and her foundation. She loves you and she wants to marry you and get on with her job. Those are the two ambitions which drive her.' Edward was somewhat taken aback by his frankness. 'She told me so herself during one of our little chats,' he explained.

Verity was taking everything with her as, whatever happened, there was no going back to the clinic. She had rested for almost three months – it had been the most difficult thing she had ever undertaken – and, if that hadn't done the trick and her disease was still 'eating her up', as she envisaged it, she knew she would have to take another road.

It was good to be driving through the countryside. Although it was early autumn, summer lingered on and the leaves were still on the trees. Fenton had been left to bring the heavy baggage by train so they were un-encumbered. They decided not to hurry and about midday stopped at a village pub. Edward ordered a pint of the local brew while Verity had ginger beer. The landlord provided bread and cheese which they ate in the garden under apple trees laden with fruit and buzzing with wasps.

They avoided discussing Verity's medical prognosis and talked instead about their friends and, inevitably, about the growing international crisis.

'There's talk of the Prime Minister going to meet Hitler to try and sort things out once and for all,' Edward said.

'I hope he doesn't go,' Verity remarked. 'Hitler will bamboozle the old man. He's the sort of ordinary Englishman who can't understand that the lunatics have taken over and are running the world like an asylum.'

'It's the last hope for peace although I confess I'm very torn. On the one hand, any agreement Mr Chamberlain makes with Hitler will involve betraying the Czechs. On the other hand, if Hitler agrees to something now and then reneges – as he undoubtedly would – then I think people will at last understand what we are up against.'

'They ought to have understood that two years ago!' Verity protested.

'True – but we have to be realistic. The great majority of our countrymen are not interested in foreign affairs. They think foreigners are all as bad as each other and that we ought to stay out of any European quarrel. If they remember any history from their schooldays, it is Pitt paying other people to fight the French.'

'But in the end we had to create an army to fight Napoleon.'

'That's true but we – as a nation – didn't like it. The Royal Navy . . . that was what we liked to spend our money on. Our ships – "wooden walls" – that keep us free from Continental disease.'

'But now aeroplanes have made ships vulnerable.'

'Aeroplanes and submarines.'

'But do you think that, in the end, the proverbial man on the Clapham omnibus will understand that we have no alternative except to fight?'

'I'm sure of it, V. As a nation, we are slow to anger. We have to have it proved to us that there is no alternative. Any prime minister who goes to war without just cause and without taking the people with him would never be forgiven.'

'And will we win?'

'If the Americans come in on our side and the Russians keep out of it – then we might win.'

'And if the Americans don't come in on our side?'

'Then, I don't see how we can win.'

They sat in silence, thinking about the horror that was to come.

'And Harry . . .' Verity said at last. 'There are a few things I still don't understand.'

'I don't have all the answers but ask away.'

'Well, I can see he was a womanizer and totally unscrupulous but what made him a murderer?'

'Boredom . . . and perhaps an arrogance born of never having properly loved anyone and everything coming too easily. To be Victorian about it, he wasn't brought up properly. No one loved him enough as a child to show him the difference between right and wrong.'

'You think that's it – not having enough love as a child?' Verity said disbelievingly.

'I don't know, I'm not Sigmund Freud. Maybe something in his brain was missing. To put it scientifically, perhaps he had a screw loose.'

Verity giggled. 'Oh God! I'm sorry. It's not a laughing matter.'

'No, it isn't,' Edward said grimly. 'I shall never forget what he did to poor Eric Silver. He was never afraid – that was part of the problem. If you don't fear the consequences of what you do, then you think you can do anything.'

'I think I see what you mean. So he convinced himself that Christobel Redfern – another man's wife – was the love of his life?'

'Yes, and when he killed her in that car accident in Kenya, he transferred the blame to me. He was unable to take responsibility for his own actions.'

'But why kill Herold?'

'Because of Gwyneth's death on the Eiger which was either the result of Herold's incompetence or bad luck or because Herold had discovered about her affair with Harry. Harry convinced himself that she had loved him and was on the point of running away with him. Maybe she was. I don't know . . . nobody does.'

'You think Herold might have killed his wife if he had found out that she was about to run off with Harry?'

'It's possible but would he have written the book about her?'

'He might have, to tell the story he wanted the world to believe – that *he* wanted to believe. It was an act of homage to a loyal, loving wife – not to a woman who was about to leave him.'

'I told you, V, I don't have all the answers.'

'And then he fell for Isabella, Hermione Totteridge's

niece. Why did he always have to go after other men's wives?'

'Who can say? It must have been part of his character. He always wanted the toy that belonged to the other child and taking it made him feel powerful.'

'So you think he seduced Isabella and then killed her husband in the belief that she would be grateful.'

'Yes, but she was heartbroken and consumed with guilt. Once Peter Lamming was dead, she realized how much she had loved him. So she rejected Harry and returned to England to devote herself to her husband's memory.'

'It might explain the excessive mourning and her need for a gravestone even though there was no body beneath it.'

'I believe so, V. Harry followed her to England after she wrote to tell him that she had confessed to Hermione what had really happened to Lamming. Foolishly, she mentioned that her aunt had urged her to go to the police.'

'How do you know what she said to Hermione? Are you just guessing?'

'I can't be sure but Violet Booth told me that Isabella returned from a visit to Henley in much better spirits and said Hermione had been helpful. How did she put it? – That Isabella had seemed to have got "a lot off her chest".'

'But she soon relapsed?'

'Yes, I think because she couldn't bring herself to go to the police. After all, what could they have done? Unsubstantiated accusations about someone in Kenya who was alleged to have committed a crime on the other side of the world . . .? They would have put her down as a hysteric.'

'But Harry didn't kill her?'

'No, although I'm sure he thought she had betrayed him, but, before he arrived in England, she died, as the

Victorians say, of a broken heart. At least that's what Dr Booth believes and I agree with him. She lost the will to live and when she got appendicitis – something any normal person could have recovered from – she turned her face to the wall, as they say.'

'Why didn't she tell the Booths what had happened to Peter? After all, she was closer to them than Hermione. They had brought her up.'

'I don't know. Possibly because she didn't want to burden them. Perhaps she thought Hermione was tougher or something may have prompted her to talk about it even though she had meant to keep things to herself.'

'Do you think it might have been a photograph in Hermione's album?'

'Yes, V. It might have been the photograph of her and Peter on their wedding day.'

'How do you know?'

'Because before Harry killed Hermione they had been talking about Peter Lamming and she showed him the photograph. He ripped it out of her album and in a fury, I imagine, killed her using the poison she happened to be experimenting with. I found the photograph by chance at Turton House when I was looking at one of Harry and Christobel Redfern. I opened the frame and found the photograph of Lamming and his new bride.'

'Are you sure it was the one from Hermione's album?'

'Yes. I took it to Treacher. He got the album off Violet Booth and the experts confirmed it. There was no doubt that was where it had come from. I was almost certain then that Harry had killed the old lady but I couldn't prove it. I also sent Treacher a letter I had had from Harry and the graphologist decided that it was written by the same person who had penned those notes they found on the bodies of his victims – though of course he had tried to disguise his handwriting'

'Do you think Harry discovered you had taken the photograph?'

'It could account for what he did to you. If he knew I had discovered the link between him and Hermione Totteridge, he would have known that he had to act quickly.'

Verity thought about this. 'And he killed General Lowther because he had mowed down Isabella's parents in a motor accident? That sounds a bit far-fetched. Why should he do that?'

'Harry told me he had a thing about people who used cars as weapons – as he put it. First Christobel Redfern and then Isabella's parents died in motor accidents. I remember Jack Amery's driving was so bad that it sent him up the wall. He came to England to take revenge on everyone he thought had ruined his life. He convinced himself that he could have married Isabella but she ran away from him and then died of grief for her husband.'

'But I still don't understand how he could have been certain that General Lowther would drink the cyanide in a glass of Clos des Mouches.'

'He didn't. It was a coincidence.'

'A coincidence! You mean all that stuff about insects was wrong?'

'Yes, I'm afraid so. I did precisely what I always tell myself not to do. I selected a few "facts" and constructed a theory round them. To be fair to myself, Eric Silver suggested it first and initially I thought it sounded a bit fanciful. When he was murdered, I decided it must be correct. It didn't help that Harry had overheard Silver tell me his theory and was able to play up to it. He quoted the appropriate lines about rotting carcasses and, in a stroke of what he would no doubt have called genius, left my family motto on Silver's body.'

'And that motto happens to feature flies?'

'That's right, V.'

'So the theory led you to Harry even though it was wrong?'

'He led me by the nose. I kept telling myself he was too obvious a suspect.'

'He was taunting you?'

'Yes. He thought he would be able to kill me before I put the final piece in the jigsaw – but he left it too late, thank God. Mrs Booth worked it all out and got to him just before he got to me.'

'Golly!'

'Golly indeed. There's a French saying someone told me once: "*L'homme pense. Le dieu rit.*"'

'Though in this case *le diable rit*,' Verity said grimly. 'But the important thing is that he didn't kill you,' she added, putting her hand on Edward's knee.

'There was a time when I expected him to but then I was lulled into a false sense of security. You remember when our friend Major Stille appeared while Harry and I were searching Jack Amery's house? He would have killed me if Harry hadn't knocked him unconscious and saved my life.'

'Why didn't he let Stille kill you?'

'He wasn't ready for me to die. He wanted to play with me for a little longer. It amused him to confuse me. That photograph he found in Amery's house showing Amery with Peter Lamming in Kenya had no particular significance but he wanted me to think it had. But, in the end, he wanted me to work out who had murdered Miss Totteridge and James Herold and persuaded General Lowther to kill himself. Only then would he kill me. It was meant to be a sort of *coup de grâce*. He couldn't quite decide how to punish me and then it came to him. As I told you, he believed I had deprived him of the woman he loved – a complete fantasy, of course. He was just trying to transfer his guilt to me.'

'So he decided it would be poetic justice to take me away from you?'

'Yes, V, and he was right. I nearly went mad when I discovered that he had abducted you.'

Verity shivered as she remembered her ordeal. 'And when Violet Booth killed him – I mean, when her gun went off in the struggle – you had no idea where I was and realized you would never be able to force Harry to tell you?'

'It was the worst moment of my life. Fortunately, Dr Booth and I worked out where you might be. I blame myself for failing to notice that horrible dungeon when I went to Temple Island before but Roderick Black knew about it, thank God.'

'I still think Eric Silver's was the most horrible murder.'

'I can never forgive Harry for that. I think he must have been following me for some time while he tried to decide what would be the most painful way of killing me. Don't forget that he had already written to invite me to stay but I hadn't replied. He saw me go into the dentist and, on a whim, followed me. By coincidence – a coincidence he could never have foreseen – he got into the building and heard Silver tell me about his three dead patients. Then he had a brainwave. He would make it impossible for me not to investigate their murders by killing Silver and leaving my family motto on his body.'

'It worked.'

'It did, V,' Edward agreed. 'His only mistake was to "play" me for too long. He thought he could tease and confuse me indefinitely, as though I was a salmon on his line.'

'Instead of which,' Verity said, stroking his cheek, 'he had a shark. But, if Violet Booth hadn't confronted him on the launch, would you have been able to stop him?'

'I'd told the police what I suspected but they wanted proof. Perhaps I wouldn't have got to him before he finished me off but I think he was arrogant and I think he was becoming careless. He was also getting bored . . . that was always his problem. I don't think he would have killed me without giving himself the pleasure of telling me how stupid I had been, but who knows? Violet Booth saved my life as I have already told her. In the end, a woman Harry knew nothing about took her revenge for the death of her sister and the destruction of her niece's life.'

'And Stille's dead too. I can hardly believe it,' Verity said after a pause. 'I almost wish he had lived to see his precious Third Reich reduced to dust and ashes.'

'Assuming it is,' Edward said gloomily.

'In the meantime,' she said, cuddling up to him, 'we have a few more weeks of peace. What shall we do with them? What if I'm not better and the doctors insist I go to a sanatorium?'

'You *are* better. You certainly look better despite everything you've been through, but whatever happens, I think we should get married. I realized when I thought I had lost you – when I *had* lost you – that Harry was right in one respect at least – I couldn't live without you. It sounds melodramatic, I know, but it's the truth. I don't mean that, if you weren't here, I'd cut my throat. I suppose I'd be able to go on from day to day, but you give my life meaning. I think Harry sensed somehow that, because he didn't know what it meant to love, his life was meaningless.' He turned to look at her, almost spilling his drink as he did so. 'Will you marry me soon, V? We could do it secretly if you want, without any fuss, in a register office.'

'Yes please!' Verity said. 'I do love you, Edward. When I was in that horrid damp hole, I thought of you and it kept me going. I was sure you would find me so

I never quite gave up. I knew then that, if I did get out and you still wanted me, I would be very proud to marry you. You're the only man I trust absolutely – and I include my father in that. But I'm not much of a catch, you know. I'm ill and out of a job. I'm fractious and unreasonable and your relations think I'm not good enough for you. Shall we get married tomorrow?'

Historical Note

During the war, Jack Amery lectured and broadcast on behalf of the Germans, and attempted to recruit a 'Legion of St George' to fight the Russians from Britons who were interned in a camp at St Denis, outside Paris. He was unsuccessful. After the war he was arrested and tried as a traitor. He pleaded guilty and was hanged on 19 December 1945.

Ewald von Kleist-Schmenzin, the Pomeranian conservative politician who came to England in 1938 in a fruitless attempt to generate support for those who opposed Hitler within Germany, continued to work for Hitler's removal throughout the war. He and his son were involved in several plots to kill Hitler including Stauffenberg's briefcase bomb which just failed to kill him on 19 July 1944. Kleist-Schmenzin was arrested the following day and hanged at Plötzensee Prison in Berlin on 9 April 1945. His son was sent to the Eastern Front but survived the war.

Finally, apologies to Radley – they, not Eton, won the Ladies' Plate in 1938 when they beat an excellent Pembroke College eight in the remarkable time of six minutes and fifty-six seconds.